UNSPOKEN

Written by
A. K. Moss

2014

UNSPOKEN

UNSPOKEN

Book cover design by angelheartdesign.org
Book design by RedRaven - www.redravendp.blogspot.pt/

ISBN# 978-150 5637908

UNSPOKEN

This book is dedicated to my mom, Alice Saul, for her courage. To Papa, Roy Saul, and all the horses that have touched my life and helped shape my character. I also dedicate this book to those who look for a better way to work with horses. I commend you for your efforts. May you always keep an open mind and learn the unspoken language of horse to human.

This book is fictitious. The content is made up mainly by imagination. The author wants it understood that she does not promote kids training colts. Please enjoy the story but use caution when on or around horses.

Thank you,

A.K. Moss

May there be enough wisdom for us to share,
So all horses may trust in human care.

A.K. Moss

About the Author
A. K. Moss

Courtesy of Tanni Wenger Photography Studio

Unspoken is Kathy's first novel, but not her last and definitely not her first publication. Hope you enjoy the story and are looking forward to her next, *Finding Home*. Here is a little bit about her history.

With pen in one hand, camera in the other, and reins between her teeth, A. K. Moss has a passion for writing and western heritage that shows in everything she does. She has been published in *The Big Roundup*, *North American Hunter*, *Cowgirl Poetry*, and various other publications. She has been performing her own work since 1998 throughout the West Coast States. Living in remote Grant County, situated in Eastern Oregon, Kathy's writing comes straight from the heart and soul of the American West. She writes what she knows and believes in with pride in western history, heritage, and the people.

Through high school and beyond, Kathy enjoyed rodeos, working colts, calving heifers, day riding, and working on a cutting horse ranch which added finesse to her first passion, training horses. She teaches youth to ride and handle horses, along with teaching them the value of the western history and customs she has learned. She still starts a few colts and works with troubled horses. She can be found down on the desert working and sorting horses and taking photographs of the working western people while putting to rhyme their stories to preserve for the future. If not at any of those places, she can be found standing on stage performing at a poetry gathering.

Expanding her poetry to a new area of outdoor life, Kathy has a CD called *Of Elk and Men*, bringing to life the true values of the hunt and the thrill of elk up close. It brings the imagination alive with special effects to any who listen to the words.

She has written three limited edition poetry books, *Cowboy in the Making*, *Cowgirl in the Making* and *Cow Horse in the Making*, and her CD called *Dear Charlie* is a tribute to Charlie Russell and those who influenced her. Mixed with a little music and a lot of rhyme it is a CD to cherish in any audio library.

Her passion for Western history has brought her to study and write poems from the diaries of the Oregon Trail, which she performs at the Oregon Trail Interpretive Center in Baker City. The photographs she has taken preserve western lifestyles of today had found a spot in the Western Folklife Center Museum at Elko in 2001. Not one to sit idle for long, Kathy keeps busy doing what she loves—studying people, the habits of life and horses, and bringing pen to paper.

Like a good friend Billie Flick told her one day, "A spur is only a spur until the story is written."

So now that the writing is done, let the reading begin.

UNSPOKEN

UNSPOKEN

UNSPOKEN

by
A. K. Moss

It is our choices that show what we truly are, far more than our abilities.

J.K. Rowling

UNSPOKEN

1

It was still dark, just a glimmer of the new day's light beginning to sneak into the room, showing vague silhouettes contained within its walls. A light breeze teased the sheer curtain panel through the open window. Paige pulled the handmade quilt up closer under her chin. The warmth comforted her from the chilly morning air as she sighed and started to stretch herself awake. She rolled over on her side, opening her blue eyes to glance at the clock. She looked again—it was four forty-five. Paige thought for only an instant then jumped out of bed as if someone had catapulted her from sleep.

Her feet thumped to the cool bare floor. She grabbed her jeans and a t-shirt draped over her old oak rocking chair, where she had laid them the night before, and slipped them on. She glanced in her vanity mirror, raked a brush through her medium-length blonde hair, and grabbed her baseball cap, pulling her hair through the back of it to make a makeshift ponytail. After grabbing socks out of her top dresser drawer, she headed down the hallway. The old hardwood floor whined and groaned as her bare feet padded their way to the kitchen where the aroma of freshly made coffee lingered. A single bulb on the ceiling illuminated the entire room with a golden glow.

Her mother was at the sink washing potatoes for grating—fried potatoes, bacon, eggs, and toast for breakfast. Next to the stove sat three loaf pans with dough bellies peeking over the tops, waiting for the oven door to open and engulf them in its heat so the aroma of freshly baked bread could mingle with the smell of rich coffee and crisp bacon in the pan.

"Morning," Patricia said as she glanced up from her potato scouring to see her daughter. "You're up early."

"I have a lot to do this morning, Mom. Thought I would get an early start," Paige replied.

She grabbed her Levi jacket off the coat hook by the back door. Then walking onto the back porch, she sat in an old wicker chair, slipped on her socks, and pulled on her old worn-out boots. Out of habit, she stomped them to the floor with a hollow thud when they were on.

Normally Paige would have waited for her alarm to go off a couple of times before dragging herself out of bed. She was a typical teenage girl, not wanting to leave the comfort and warmth of her bed on a cool morning. But she had waited for this day for what seemed like her whole life. She stopped just off the porch and filled her lungs deeply with the brisk morning air. She stood still for a moment, bringing into her body the healthy fresh aroma of the morning dew and the unforgettable sweet smell of horses.

They lived in a remote area of Eastern Oregon outside a little town called Baker City. Beyond the reaches of the alfalfa fields and pastures, the sagebrush grew thickly and the grama grass sprang up in little clumps from the dry, silty alkali soil. The wind was forever teasing and playing with the sagebrush and tumbleweeds that danced to its tune across the rolling hills that were so barren a person could see for miles in either direction. Sparse juniper trees speckled the horizon, knotted and gnarled by age and harsh winters.

Magpies argued back and forth, their croaking voices repeating, "rat rat rat," in the old weeping willow. As Paige moved across the yard, she heard the hollow shuffling sound of hooves as the horses milled around, waiting to be fed in the corrals. They nickered softly as they heard the familiar screen door slam. The dew thick in the air gave the morning a hazy aura that carried an eerie, yet invigorating, feel of spring.

Patricia watched her daughter walk out the door. She thought of how time flies—her daughter was growing up. Ever since they moved here, Paige was her father's shadow. She would sit on the corral rails and watch her father work colts with his patient hands, reassuring attitude, and quiet tones. He earned their respect and trust, and in return, they could rely on him for his honesty and guidance.

When Paige was old enough, four or five, Abe would settle her on some of the colts' backs. He'd just set her there and let her feel them beneath her. They would flick their ears back and forth, lifting their heads slightly, curious at the weight on their back. But they would soon settle, seeming happy to learn something new.

Abe would give her instructions. "Talk to them, soothe them with your voice. Let them feel your confidence, Sis. Feel them breathe beneath you, their muscles, each footfall, become a part of them."

Patricia thought Paige looked like part of the horses when she sat there—part of their power, part of their movements. She rode them bareback as Abe led them around the corral, one hand on her thigh in case the unpredictable colt tried doing something silly. If that happened, he could pull her to safety. She would sit astride the horses as confidence seemed to grow within her as well as the colts. She became very comfortable adjusting to each as an individual.

In the isolation of this vast country living, neighbors were miles away. Patricia wanted to have another child, but considering Paige was a miracle child, with many complications during the pregnancy, one child, one gift, was enough. And Paige didn't seem to mind. She spent hours watching these animals play in the pasture and figuring out their personalities.

She thought it fun to pick out which one was boss, which had the short temper, and which ones just went along with what everyone else did. She would try to predict their movements before they made them and was becoming very accurate at knowing their moods, how they responded to one another, and what kind of discipline they would receive for silly things they might do.

She just loved to watch her father and the colts in

action. When she went to the corrals, it gave her a chance to see her father and to ride. There was no other feeling like doing something she loved and getting praised for it. At the dinner table at night, her father would talk of her accomplishments, which of course made her try even harder to better herself. As time passed, Paige analyzed her father's work, his actions, and his signals. He seemed to be speaking to the animals without saying a word. He never pressed her to come and watch, and since these weren't his horses, he wasn't allowed to have her work any.

This ranch her father was taking care of was owned by a doctor who lived in California. His name was Thomas Pitt, and he thought it was great to own a piece of property in Oregon. Although he didn't know a lot about animals in general, his accountant advised that it would be a good investment and a great tax write-off. So he found Abe Cason when Abe's family was having a hard time and employed him to work a few horses and build up the ranch. Build up meant putting in fences, putting in corrals, and building a few barns. It seemed simple enough for someone who was not familiar with how hard livestock was on fences. Thomas did forbid any animals on the place but his own, so Abe was not allowed to bring in any horses for himself or Paige.

"Employees are a huge expense, and this place doesn't need a bunch of cowboys yahooing around here, Abe."

With that kind of a comment from Thomas, Abe knew

there was no sense in arguing the fact. Paige would not have a horse or become an employee, no matter how good she was with horses. Thomas was not willing to add anyone else to the payroll for some time to come. Although Abe had mentioned it a couple of times, Thomas seemed to think Abe was getting things done and was not interested in the expense of an extra hand. Besides, Paige was willingly helping with the horses already and Thomas didn't have to pay her for it. Abe felt like Thomas had him right where he needed him. Paying a salary and supplying a house was enough to keep the wolves from the door for right now.

Paige would continue to watch her father with never-ending dedication and passion for the animals. Abe would instruct her with the knowledge he had to offer. "Confidence, timing, and release are everything, Paige. Without them you, as a teacher, have nothing."

She sat patiently, watching him teach a colt to lead without a halter or lead line, drape ropes around a young horse's legs and back without it moving a foot, or sack him out and saddle him without ever putting on a halter. With admiration, she knew one day she would be the same as her father. She not only felt it in her heart, but she felt it in her soul.

Paige easily remembered her fourteenth birthday, a little over two years ago. That morning was unusually quiet. Her father had apparently already gone to the barn and her mother must have still been sleeping. So Paige had quietly grabbed her jacket and headed out to do her morning mucking. As she walked out the back door, she heard a horse pawing and thumping in a stall. *Something is wrong*, she thought as she started to run to the barn. The horses always stood quietly, with only a soft nicker to greet her in the morning. Paige instantly thought of colic, abdominal pain a horse can get if they eat something they shouldn't have. It could kill if it was bad enough or wasn't tended to right away. Horses, she knew, couldn't tolerate stomach pain. They could withstand external pain such as cuts and bites, but the abdomen is the most sensitive part of the body. Her mind was racing as she entered the barn.

The barn was just as tidy as she had left it the evening before. All the halters hung by each stall. The thumping had stopped as she opened the large barn door. She couldn't tell which stall the sound had come from. In the dim light, she noticed the door to one of the empty stalls that was usually open had been closed, and something odd was hanging on the front of it. As she approached it, the thumping started again, and it startled her. Her heart was pounding in her throat as she approached. *This stall was empty last night*, she thought to herself. Maybe her father had brought in one of the mares from outside. She cautiously walked up and looked at the door—on it hung a large red bow, and in the middle was a sign reading "Happy Birthday, Sis."

Tears welled in her eyes as she peeked inside to see a yearling palomino filly standing in the corner of the stall pounding the dirt under the sawdust with her forefoot. She was a deep palomino gold with a wide blaze down her face and two neat white hind socks that came up to just below her hocks. Her mane and tail were a flaxen white that still had the baby curls, typical of a young colt. Her eyes were a bright soft liquid brown and were set widely apart, and her ears were little and alert as they twitched back and forth nervously. Seeing Paige approach, the filly lifted her head and snorted.

Abe and Patricia walked out of an empty stall behind Paige and stood next to her.

"Well, Sis, this is for all your hard work," Abe said as he put a hand on her shoulder, careful not to look down at her tear-streaked face. "I hope you like her." He walked away, hoping neither Paige nor Patricia would ever find out about the overtime he agreed to work in order to give his daughter such a gift and keep a personal horse on the place.

Paige wanted to run to him, give him a hug, tell him she loved him, and pour out all of her dreams of what she wanted to do with her new filly. But she knew now that she was fourteen years old, her father figured her grown up, and she would have to contain her excitement as adults always did. She watched him walk away.

She attentively reached her hand through the bars of the stall. The filly snorted and looked at her, then cautiously brought her soft pink nose to the waiting fingers. At first touch she jumped back. Tears streamed down Paige's face.

The horse standing in front of her with its golden hide and flaxen mane was hers. Reality was having a hard time sinking in, yet her heart was also torn because she had watched her father walk away without telling him how she felt.

Patricia put her arm around her daughter. "Happy Birthday, Sis," she said.

Paige gave her mom a hug. "Mom, this will be the best horse ever."

"I'm sure she will, Paige. I'm sure she will."

*****

When the day came to work the filly in the round corral, Paige wanted to do the work by herself. At first she was in awe of owning such a beautiful animal prancing around the pen. Then as she started to try getting close to her, the young horse would have nothing to do with her. Frustration and failure attacked her heart. For three painstaking days, she tried wholeheartedly to touch the filly she had named Liberty Bell. But each day, when her attempts came up empty, her heart sank. She knew she needed help, but she didn't want to ask. When she watched her father, he made it look so easy.

Defeated, she went to the house, her eyes burning as she fought her tears.

She grudgingly asked, "Papa, can you help me catch my filly? She is not doing what I want her to."

Abe looked at her silently for a moment. "What seems to be the problem, Sis?"

9

"I don't know. I am doing everything you taught me, but it isn't working."

"Well let's see what we have going on."

As Abe followed her to the round corral, he repeated the rules of horses with his quiet tone. "Remember—confidence, timing, and release, Sis. That's what this filly needs. Guidance for now, help her find what you're asking of her. And never lie to her, Paige, for she'll remember it later when it really counts."

Paige crawled through the fence and approached Liberty. The filly lifted her head and began to prance around, her golden hide shimmering in the sun, starting to play her now-regular game of tag.

Instantly Paige looked at her father, shrugged her shoulders, and pitifully said, "See, Papa, three days of this and I haven't gotten anywhere with her." Frustration was obvious in her voice.

Abe stood silently for a moment, then almost unconcerned stated, "Well, I 'spose I'll go back to the house if all you brought me out here to do is feel sorry for you." He watched the filly's smoothness as she arched her neck and continued prancing. "You either read that filly's movements, Sis, or go to the house, too."

Paige remembered those words as if it were yesterday, even though it was over two years ago. She smiled at the memory and in admiration of her father. She remembered looking back at that filly, determination filling her to the core of her being. *How dare he send me to the house*, she remembered thinking. *How could he think that I can't read this filly? I didn't do all that watching and studying of him for nothing.*

She straightened her young frame, threw back her shoulders, and in a stern, soft voice said, "We have a lot to learn, little lady."

With the help of her father, Paige worked with Liberty.

"Keep your eye on her hip, Sis. That's it, push her away from you."

Liberty raced around the corral, head high, and tail strutting straight away from her body like a flag floating in the wind. Her mind raced with her legs, looking to move away from the pressure that Paige was creating with her body language. Liberty was losing the power and intimidation she had impressed on the girl who was gaining confidence and definition in her actions. Liberty could understand and respond. Instead of trying to guess what the girl wanted, she could tell, and she responded willingly.

"Now watch her ears, Sis. Wait until you get her full attention. There, see how she has given you her full attention?"

Liberty had now fixed her ear on Paige and ever so slightly tipped her nose in toward the center of the round corral. Libby was wondering what Paige wanted from her. She lowered her head a little and continued around the corral, waiting on Paige's next instructions.

Abe spoke again, explaining what each movement meant and what actions Paige should take. "Now I want you to ask her to turn and go the other direction so you can work the other eye. That's it, Sis."

Paige abruptly stepped forward, and Libby shut off her forward motion. Paige's shoulders were square, her jaw set as she swung the rope. Liberty instantly put on her brakes. Her hind legs well underneath her, she dropped her tail toward the ground, arched her back, and swung her front legs in toward Paige. She pivoted around and took off in the other direction, easily and smoothly, spraying sand into the breeze.

Liberty loped off, her ear cocked toward Paige, wanting to please her. She awaited the next unspoken words to flow from Paige's body to her instinctive sight.

"That's it, Paige, now push her away again. There you go. Keep focused on her. Let your body do the talking." Paige did as her father instructed.

She had been surprised at the response, which she had seen for years and was now receiving. Liberty Bell was actually listening to her, and she was talking to Liberty in a way the horse understood. It was a challenge to quiet the mind and stay in the moment. But with determination and persistence, Paige continued reading her filly's movements. When her father told her to take the pressure off by looking at a post ten to twelve feet in front of the now trotting filly, Paige was shocked. Liberty suddenly stopped and faced her. She bobbed her head up and down looking at Paige. She looked like she was asking, "Is this what you want?" Then she started taking small uncertain steps toward Paige. She licked her lips and bobbed her head up and down asking to come into Paige's space.

"Take a slow deep breath. Let it all out, Sis, and relax," Abe whispered through the fence as Liberty approached Paige's shoulder. "Just stand there and look at the fence post. Want her to come to you. Breathe, Sis. Breathe and relax. Let the filly do the rest."

Instead of Liberty trying to run away from Paige, she now started to try to understand the connection of unspoken words between horse and human. Paige felt the soft prick of Liberty's whiskers and the hot, moist air of the filly's breath on her bare arm as Liberty inhaled Paige's scent. It sent shivers up Paige's spine. There was a sense of satisfaction and accomplishment. Every nerve and sense Paige had ever known was heightened one hundred times at that very instant—the breeze that blew, the smell of horse sweat, the beauty of the day. She wanted to reach out and touch that velvet soft nose, yet she remained stock still, waiting on her father's next words. Trying to keep her breathing relaxed.

"Okay, Sis, now I want you to walk away from her. Don't look, just take small steps to your right."

Paige did, and Libby followed.

"Keep breathing, Sis. You need to stay relaxed."

Paige hadn't realized that she started to hold her breath again. *How did he see that?* she wondered as she inhaled, feeling the air go completely into her belly then letting it out slowly. She didn't realize how hard this breathing thing was. She took in another deep breath and let it out. She felt her shoulders relax again and her body become soft, inviting Liberty into her space.

"Now stroke her on the neck, soft and gentle." Smoothly yet firmly, she turned her back to Libby's head, facing toward her hip. She brought her left hand up and for the first time touched Libby at the point of her shoulder and her neck. Her fingertips touched the golden, fuzzy, cotton ball hair. Libby cocked an ear back toward Paige and stood quietly. Paige rubbed Libby's shoulder, then up her neck, working her way toward her head and up to her jaw. Paige was talking in quiet tones as she rubbed and scratched. Libby accepted Paige without any hesitation, licking her lips and bobbing her head a few times, clearly feeling relaxed.

Abe said, "Let her think, Paige. Just rub and pet her for a while, just be with her." He was satisfied.

Paige had to control her excitement and remember to breathe. For the first time in her life, she had accomplished something she was only able to dream about, the trust of a horse. Her horse that no one had touched except her, Liberty had chosen to accept her as a friend.

2

Paige heard a barn door shut, snapping her out of the long-ago memory. She smiled and began walking through the hazy morning aura to the barn. As she entered, the now mature Libby put her head out of the empty stall of two years ago and nickered softly as Paige approached.

"Boy we have come a long way, little lady. We have waited two years, and today is the day," she said softly.

The filly nickered softly again in agreement as she bobbed her hooded head and neck up and down. She stepped back as Paige entered the stall. Libby was covered in a quilt pattern blanket that Patricia had made for Paige as a Christmas present. It was made out of canvas and denim material. The canvas was off an old tent that Abe had used elk hunting in November. He used it for years, packing in and out of the wilderness. Along with those years came rips from branches and worn creases, which weakened the fabric. When Abe figured it couldn't go another year and thought of throwing it away, Patricia stepped in with the idea of a horse blanket. With experienced hands Patricia had carefully measured and estimated the growth of Libby, and with Abe's help they cut out the strongest fabric of the tent.

Then with a few pairs of jeans, she added the breastplate, belly strap, and another piece over the tail. She took a couple pairs of well-worn jeans and made a neck cover as well. She even sewed in the pockets on the side so Paige could put in a comb and brush in them. On the hip of the horse blanket, in denim material, Patricia carefully sewed in PC on both sides for Paige's initials.

Paige filled Libby's water bucket, mucked the stall, put out hay, and carefully measured her grain into the manger. Then she went to grab the finishing brush to give Libby a quick grooming before she finished her chores.

Abe came around the corner just as Paige started to unbuckle the belly straps of Libby's blanket and said, "Come on, Sis, there are more horses to feed and chores to do."

"I know, Papa, I know," she said with a regrettable sigh. "I just want her to look extra special today." She re-buckled the straps, gave Libby a soft pat on her Wrangler neck, grabbed her pitchfork, and headed to the haystack. She had ten horses to feed and five stalls to clean, not including Libby's, and it took about an hour to do it all when she hurried.

On their way back to the house, Abe put his arm around his daughter's shoulder. "Well, Sis, are you ready for today?"

"I think so, Papa," she said, knowing he wouldn't go with them today and not really understanding why. She had waited two years to show her filly, and she wanted her father there to watch.

"Thomas Pitt wants those new corrals up. I also have the three colts I started that need to be ridden this evening."

He paused. "I have seen you ride, Paige, you don't have anything to prove by having a stranger watch and compare you to others. It don't make any sense."

"I wish Mr. Pitt would give you a day off, Papa," Paige said hopefully. "You could watch and maybe understand what a horse show is about."

"It don't put meat on the table if I do, Sis," he said as he opened the back door and allowed her to enter first. The smell of fresh-baked bread and breakfast wafted through the air.

Paige had to shrug it off and think to herself, *I am not a little girl anymore. I don't need him there to hold my hand, and today I am going to prove it.* She washed her hands and headed to the table.

Paige wasn't hungry. She sat picking at her eggs while her parents ate, talking of the planned events of the day. She usually loved this time of the morning when she got to hear of her father's plans—the talk of horses, water, and fences—and enjoy the morning rituals along with the clink of dishes, the smell of fresh-made coffee, the closeness of family, and good food. But this morning there was a heaviness in her heart. She really wished her father would come to the show with her and her mother.

Outside the gold hues of morning were becoming a golden glow of sunlight. Breakfast was over, and the dishes were done. A new day was the beginning of an untold adventure. Paige grabbed her old saddle that she had spent hours polishing two nights before from her room. *For its age and years of abuse, it cleaned up pretty nicely*, Paige thought as she grabbed it by the horn and slung it over her shoulder. It seemed to her this day looked brighter when it was far away. But now that the horse show had arrived, her father's words were echoing in her ears.

It don't make any sense having a stranger judge you on how you ride and compare you to others.

She put her saddle in the truck and went to get Libby to load her in the single horse trailer. Libby seemed excited to have a change in her routine. She looked at the ramp of the trailer, smelled it, then took her front hoof and pawed at it a few times. Her nostrils seemed to have rollers in them as she smelled it again. The funny noise she made when she was uncertain of things made Paige grin.

"Come on, little lady, you can do it," she coaxed as she waited for Libby to step up into the trailer.

Libby stepped around to the other side. Paige was getting anxious. "Come on, Libby, step up. You know how to do this." Paige made a kissing sound. Libby cocked an ear toward her, stepped on the ramp, and loaded. Paige put her hand on Libby's hip for a moment to stabilize her, hooked the butt chain, then reached down and grabbed the ramp. Then without a thought, she stepped up on the wheel well and tied her halter rope. They were ready.

She slid into the old Ford truck next to her saddle and mother. Abe had already gone to work on the lower corrals and hadn't said goodbye or good luck. He just got up from the table and left. Paige's heart sank. Taking a deep breath she told herself again, *I'm not a little girl anymore, I don't need him to hold my hand in everything I do.* Patricia put the old Ford in gear and headed down the familiar dirt road, kicking up dust as they traveled. Paige thought, *Thank God I left Liberty's blankets on. She would be a mess by the time we got there* .

She rubbed the seat of her saddle nervously.

Paige didn't see her father look up to watch them go, nor did she feel the best wishes and luck he sent her way. She just felt the dull ache inside her stomach and the pounding of her heart.

It was twenty-two miles to the small town of Baker City. It was a rare occasion for Paige to go into town, especially during the summer months, and it was always exciting to her. The nearest neighbors were ten miles away, so her best friends were the four-legged critters in the barn. They never judged her or talked back. They just accepted what was and coped with it the best they knew how. Although Paige had never been in a horse show before, she had seen a couple of them at the Baker City fair and thought she could ride just as well as any who competed. But now that the time had come, she wasn't so sure. Her mind was racing with thoughts of how Libby might act since this was the first time she had been in town. How was she going to handle the crowds, the music, the excitement? Oh how she wished her father had come. He would be able to walk her through everything and make it right. *Maybe he would come later*, she thought, trying to settle her nerves. *Okay Paige*, she told herself, *focus, confidence, timing, and release. Now just relax.* Taking a deep breath and letting it out slowly, she began to settle herself down.

Patricia interrupted Paige's thoughts. "Paige, you and Libby have worked very hard. Just don't forget that she is young. Handle her with care and confidence. Do your best, Paige, but try not to expect too much for your first time."

Paige gave no response. Her mind was working overtime as they pulled into the fairgrounds. The old green Ford pulled in, rattling and chugging as it always had. Paige, for the first time, was taken aback. The whole parking lot was full of new rigs, brand new campers, cars, and horse trailers—three and four horse slants with doors open and brand new tack hanging out of them. Saddles and bridles with silver glistened in the morning sun. Paige felt a surge of panic travel through her body. She was not prepared for this. She couldn't show against these people. She wanted to tell her mother to turn around and go back home. People's heads were turning and watching them drive by. Paige's face was hot and flushed. Now other people standing in a group next to a newer trailer were laughing and glancing her way. *Are they laughing at me?* Paige wondered. She had never looked at a horse show from this perspective before, nor did she care if she ever did again.

Watching the horse shows before, she had only watched

the riders and how they handled their horses and compared herself to the horsemanship that her father had taught her. But now behind the scenes it looked like a whole different world, and she didn't belong to it.

Sensing Paige's shock and panic, her mother said, "Paige, look at me." Then she added with a little more urgency, "Look at me!"

Paige broke out of her trance and looked at her mother for the first time since they had left the house. The confidence in her mother's face was sheer determination. "Paige, don't forget who you are and what you know. Focus, Paige, focus on Libby and yourself, not on what's around you. You know this, Paige, you know your horse and you know how to ride. The rest of this stuff is just stuff. Be in the moment, and just ride your horse." Her voice was calm and quiet.

Outside the cab of their pickup was alive with all the hustle and bustle of fair activities, but inside the cab, for a few precious moments, only Paige and her mother existed. And for the first time, Paige saw her mother with new eyes. She had always been a quiet woman and often overlooked in Paige's life, but today she was there for Paige and willing to help.

"Okay, Mom, I will do my best."

"Where are you going to focus?"

"On Libby and myself…with confidence" Paige added with a smile.

Even though not all of Paige's anxiety was gone, her

mother made her feel somewhat calmer. She felt a new determination well up inside her as she got out of the truck and walked back to the horse trailer.

Before parking Patricia had found a spot away from most of the excitement to give Liberty a chance to adjust to the crowd a little at a time. She then went to sign in. Paige knew her hands would be full because Libby was stamping and nickering in the plywood sided trailer. She untied her, let the tail ramp down, and Libby bounded out like a bullet fired from a rifle. She pawed the ground and nickered again, her hooded head high as her voice pierced the air. She pranced around Paige trying to take everything in at once. Paige talked to her but nothing worked. Liberty acted as if Paige didn't exist.

Oh God, this was a stupid idea bringing her here, Paige thought. *I wish Papa was here,* as she let Libby circle around her again and again, *I have got to get control somehow.* She was so deep in concentration that she was startled to hear a voice behind her. She turned to see a very pretty blonde girl about her age standing ten feet away, watching with a sarcastic grin on her face.

"I said, are you going to show that horse?" Samantha said with mockery in her voice.

Paige's face instantly turned red, and she felt suddenly hot. Samantha Greenly was standing there with her hip cocked to one side and her hand resting on it. Here Paige stood with a horse she couldn't control while the most popular girl in school was looking at her waiting for a reply. Paige said nothing. Samantha's long blonde hair was braided back and tied in a bun. Her brand new black jeans, forest green blouse with gold and green paisley vest, and black show chaps made Paige feel like a stable hand. Although Paige had never talked to her before, she was very familiar with Samantha's sarcastic attitude from school.

"What? Do I have to repeat myself a third time?"

"Yeah, I'm going to show her," Paige said, feeling defensive and needing to explain. "This is only her first time in town and she's a little nervous."

"I would say more than a little. You ought to have someone teach her some manners or buy a horse that already has some," Samantha continued, not wanting be interrupted. "See that red Dodge with the red and white slant trailer? It has living quarters in the front." Paige glanced in the direction Samantha pointed. Not pausing, Samantha said, "My father bought that so I could show my new horse this summer. His name is Piper, and Dad paid a lot of money for him this past spring. We buy expensive horses so we don't have any trouble with them. They're already broke and aren't spoiled, like some horses are." She paused for the effect.

Paige's head was swimming. No one could miss that pickup and horse trailer. The pickup was a brand new hot cherry red with chrome side panels and chrome wheels. The trailer hooked behind it was a twenty-two-foot three-horse slant with living quarters and awning. There were three lawn chairs set up along with a table underneath the awning. It had an air conditioning unit along with a satellite dish set up on top. The three-horse slant section had a white stripe down the side and chrome front down on the lower panel. There were four corral panels set up along the trailer. How was Paige going to compete with this kind of money? Paige drew her gaze back to her horse's neck, which was covered with a handmade blanket. Right in front of her was the hip pocket of a worn out pair of Wrangler jeans staring back at her. She felt herself flush red. All she had was an old saddle, blanket, and a single horse trailer with an old Ford truck to pull it.

"There, that's Piper right there with my dad brushing him. He's getting him ready for showmanship class."

Paige didn't want to look, but she couldn't help herself. She lifted her gaze from her excited filly and saw a well-built bay horse with a narrow blaze down his face and four white socks that stopped just before the hocks and knees. Piper was standing quietly looking almost bored as the tall, well-dressed man groomed him.

"Well," Samantha said, "I can see you have your hands full. See ya!" And she left.

The burning in Paige's eyes started a waterfall of tears as that girl walked away. She leaned against the trailer and let the tears run their course. She cried for stupidity and for coming here today. She cried for her own self-pity, for her father not coming, and for Liberty, who didn't understand what Paige was wanting from her. She sobbed for the embarrassment of what she owned and what her family couldn't give her. As these tears fell away, she started to feel a new inner strength building inside her. As the self-pity had erupted into tears, those tears washed away that self-pity and left her face clean as well as her soul. Opening her mind to strength she didn't know she possessed, the world fell away as Paige started to focus in the moment. Nothing else existed except Libby and herself.

Liberty tugged on the lead, pulling on Paige's hand and bringing her back to reality. Wiping her eyes and taking a deep breath, Paige had a different picture of what this day might bring. "Well, little lady, we have some work to do," she whispered to her horse. She reached into the horse trailer with a new determination, took out her lunge line, walked to a smooth grassy spot, and began lunging Libby. Liberty started out shaking her head, kicking up her heels, and sniffing the ground. Paige continued on, letting Libby feel her determination and her drive pass down the lead.

Paige asked for a lope and received it—short, choppy, and stiff-legged. Libby slowed back into a trot and Paige asked again, receiving the same. Paige continued, not altering her focus from her horse or the smooth collected lope she was looking for. She allowed Libby to find it on her own, knowing she would when she was ready to quit playing around and get down to business. Paige was waiting for any sign of acceptance—the dropping of her head, the smoothness of her gait, a softer expression in her eyes, or even her tail loosening that curious kink that sailed out behind her like a flag in the wind.

It took Libby about ten minutes of trot and lope transitions before her head dropped and she started accepting Paige's cues. At that point, Paige stopped her, led her to the trailer, and took off her hood and blanket, revealing for the first time the well-defined palomino filly hidden under the handmade blanket.

Her entire body was dampened with sweat and glistened like a dappled golden copper penny with deep gold highlights. Her well-conditioned muscles were easily seen in the brilliant sunlight. Libby's silky mane draped flawlessly on the right side of her neck. Paige took off the leg wraps, and her two white hind socks where immaculate. Paige grabbed the finishing brush, which was the softest of all of her brushes, and started with the filly's head, brushing tenderly around her eyes and down her forelock.

Libby dropped her head enjoying the familiar feel of Paige's brushing strokes and her smell. Paige worked down her sleek neck, the down her foreleg. She worked down Libby's back to her well-muscled quarter horse hips with long steady rhythmic strokes then finished that side by brushing down her hind leg. Paige walked to the other side and started again at the neck working her way back.

Libby was enjoying this familiar brushing routine. Her

expression softened, and she sighed and licked her lips. Paige knew this was a good sign. She finished her grooming, saddled Libby, and took her out to lunge again. Watching Libby move made her smile. Now that she looked at Libby from a distance and saw how she glistened, she wondered why she had doubted herself and Libby's capabilities.

"You are so beautiful, Libby," she said in awe of actually owning an animal this beautiful and graceful.

It might have been a mistake coming here today to show, but Paige decided they wouldn't go home like whipped pups. She had waited two years to show this filly, and a few sarcastic remarks weren't going to make her go home and cry to Daddy or feel ashamed at what she had.

"We are going to do this, Libby. We are really going out into this arena and show you off." Libby was in a canter lunging in a circle, her head in a perfect set. *She is ready*, Paige thought and stopped her.

Patricia had come back from registration and was sitting on the tailgate of the pickup watching. She thought about how her daughter was turning into a beautiful girl. Even though her tomboy ways gave her a boyish attitude, her features were well defined, and there was a feminine quality about her actions. Patricia noticed a different attitude in her daughter, the way she handled Libby, the confidence in her commands. Even her posture was more erect than it was this morning when they left. She wondered what had happened to make such a dramatic change but knew better than to ask. If Paige thought she should know, she would tell her in her own time. But for now, Patricia would just sit and admire her from a distance.

When Paige came back to the trailer, she listened as her mother laid out the show's schedule for the day. First was Showmanship, then English riding. After that was a half hour break for lunch, and Western Pleasure classes closed the day.

The morning went quickly. She worked Libby in the practice arena for about forty-five minutes, feeling that Libby had become accustomed to the loudspeaker, the crowds, and the other horses around her. Paige stepped off and headed for the gate. Just as she had gotten outside it and turned to close it, Samantha strode by.

"That isn't the same horse you had this morning, Paige. What did you do, trade her in on something you could handle or just dope her up?"

"This is the same filly," Paige said, grasping to control the few strands of manners that were swiftly dwindling down to pure fury. She was not the same girl she was this morning. Her confidence had shifted.

"I don't believe it," Samantha said. "That thing you had this morning was hardly broke to lead, let alone something someone could ride."

Paige's patience finally broke. "Look, Samantha, I really don't care what you think. You can have your daddy buy all you want. And if he wants to do all your work for you that's just fine with me. But I will tell you this, if you would worry about *your* horse as much as you do mine, your father wouldn't have to do all the work. I don't like you or your prissy little ways. I work hard for what I have and as far as this little mare goes, I raised her, I started her, and I didn't have to pay to have it done. So get the hell out of my way before I make you move."

She stood erect, her rich blue eyes blazing like fire as if they could burn a hole right through Samantha.

People walking by were looking at Paige, but she didn't care. She'd had enough of Samantha Greenly.

Samantha was silent for a moment, almost as if she was speechless, then turned on her heels and started to walk away. "Where did you get your show clothes from, the Sally Shop? Come on, Craig."

For the first time, Paige realized Samantha had someone with her. His name was Craig Curry, and he stood with his head down and one hip cocked, brushing his other foot along the dusty ground. He looked at Paige as if he wanted to say something but decided against it and followed his summoning party who wasn't waiting for him. His large lean frame looked to Paige like a long yearling thoroughbred colt that had yet to fill out. Paige heard Samantha say as he trotted up beside her, "Well, are you coming?"

Then they were gone. Paige looked down at her clothes—her white shirt, a black vest her mother had made, almost new Wrangler jeans, her black felt cowboy hat, and black boots that she had polished. *These are going to have to do*, she thought. Then she gathered her thoughts and started to focus again on her goal of participating in the show and what she wanted to accomplish today. She led Libby to the trailer for one last brushing.

Samantha never had anyone talk to her that way. She saw the fury in Paige's face and realized that maybe she had crossed the line. Why had she even said those words to Paige? Why should she even care about talking to her? Was it to impress Craig, this guy she had following her around like a puppy all morning?

It was odd. Paige wasn't intimidated by her money or her sarcasm. Nobody, not even her father, would speak to her in that tone of voice. She had an urge to know more about Paige Cason. She felt like she needed to talk to Paige or maybe even apologize.

She stopped in midstride and turned toward Craig. "Look, I forgot something, go ahead and go to bleachers. I'll see you later."

She turned and jogged toward where Paige was, saw them through the crowd walking back to Paige's old trailer, and jogged after them.

"Paige…Paige…" Samantha called, trying to get her attention.

Paige stopped, looked back at Samantha, then looked at the ground shaking her head. She had had enough insults from this girl. She wasn't going to listen to anymore. She whipped around.

"Look, Paige," Samantha started, "I just wanted to…"

Paige cut her off. "No, you look! You can take that fancy horse, your ritzy outfit, and your sarcasm, and go to hell! Now get out of my face! I will not let you belittle me, Samantha."

Shocked, Samantha said, "I'm sorry, Paige, that's what I wanted to say. I am very sorry. I shouldn't have said those things," she said as Paige straightened her posture and walked away. "Good luck!" Samantha said it loud enough for Paige to hear, but received no reply. The crowd walked by and soon swallowed Paige and Libby from Samantha's view. She stood and stared after them.

Samantha started walking to her horse trailer to see if Piper was ready for Western Pleasure class, which he was. He was standing pawing the ground, saddled and ready. He seemed to be a little nervous today she thought. Even in English class he spooked twice, which was unusual. But oh well, he would get over it, she figured, and her class was up next. She stepped on and started for the arena.

Paige brushed back her hair and pulled it into a bun. As she went to put the brush back into the pickup, she noticed a small black box sitting on the seat. A piece of paper with Paige's name was taped to the top of it. She grasped the black velvet box in both hands and stood looking at it. Then she lifted the lid. A silver-tooled barrette with a letter P in the middle of it stared back at her. The sun made it shimmer in the light. She brushed her thumb along the engraving, feeling the groove and indent of detail. Then she placed it in the middle of her bun.

She tried the best she could to see it in the pickup mirror shimmering in the light, then stepped into the saddle and turned Libby toward the arena.

The announcer spoke into the microphone, "Western Pleasure riders, please enter the arena at a walk." He called out the numbers signed up for the class.

When Samantha's number was called, she rode by Paige. "Good luck, Paige. I really mean it." Then she rode past.

Paige was surprised. Samantha sounded sincere, but she didn't have time to think about it now, her number was called and she entered. Her focus was totally on Liberty and herself.

"Breathe," she told herself. "Breathe, relax, and go with the flow."

Libby was in tune with her rider and responded nicely to every cue—the shifting of Paige's weight in the saddle to either speed her up or slow her down and picking up her leads gracefully and smoothly. The announcer asked for the class to line up. The judge walked up to each rider, asked a question about his or her horse, and then asked each to back up.

The judge approached Paige and kindly asked, "How old is your horse?"

Paige's heart was in her throat. "She's three." Paige's hands started to shake.

The judge said, "How long have you had her?"

"Papa gave her to me when she was a yearling." Paige's voice was starting to shake.

The judge saw Paige's nervousness and put her hand on Paige's leg. "You're doing a real fine job, keep up the good work."

Then she went to the next participant. Paige was filled with satisfaction and relief. The judge thought she was doing a good job. For an ice-breaking class, Libby had performed wonderfully. As for Paige herself, she had accomplished one of the biggest goals she ever set and felt very satisfied.

As she sat in line waiting, she realized that it didn't matter if she received a ribbon or not, it was just a great feeling to be here now.

The announcer came back on. "I think we ought to give this class a big round of applause. This is a tough class and personally, I would have hated to be the judge."

Everyone clapped and cheered which made Paige even more satisfied with her decision to stay and finish what she had started.

"Okay," the announcer said, "here are the standings. Fifth place goes to number 242 Lance Owens on Spike. Fourth place goes to number 268 Suzie Dixon riding Dandy Lady. Third place goes to number 221 Samantha Greenly riding Piper's Fair Day. Second place goes to number 255 Paige Cason riding Liberty Bell..."

Paige didn't hear who won first place. She was in shock. The hair on the back of her neck stood up, and her eyes began to fill with tears. She patted Libby's neck as she headed to the gate to collect her ribbon.

Her mother was enthusiastically waiting at the gate, her eyes brimming with tears she fought to keep from falling. "Paige, you did it! You two were absolutely beautiful!"

Paige wiped away her own tears streaming down her cheeks so she could get a clear vision of the rosette ribbon in her hand. It was absolutely beautiful, and it was going to look great on her bedroom wall next to the picture of Liberty Bell.

Paige's next classes came up fast, and Libby performed just as before, reading her rider with grace and softness. In addition to placing second in her Western Pleasure class, she received her first blue rosette ribbon in her next class of Green Horse. Libby was by now getting the hang of things and enjoyed the sights and smells that had overwhelmed her when she first unloaded that morning. Along with that first place ribbon came a silver platter. In the center was engraved *First Place, Green Horse, Baker City Horse Show*. The tears again flowed down her cheeks when she received this award.

Her second blue ribbon and platter came in her last class of Green Rider. Never before had she been so overwhelmed with pride and love for her horse and their accomplishments. After the last class, Paige took Libby to the trailer along with her awards. Her mother unhooked the horse trailer and said she would go do some grocery shopping while Paige rubbed Libby down and got her ready for the ride home. They would celebrate tonight. Paige put on Libby's halter and took the saddle off, setting it next to the tongue of the trailer. She hung the ribbons on the side of it so she could look at them floating in the breeze, and the two silver platters she set on the wheel well of the trailer. Then she grabbed her towel and started rubbing her filly down.

"You are the greatest, Libby. Did you know that? You were a born champion, and you are mine. No girl in the world is as lucky as I am to have a horse such as you." Libby stood quietly bobbing her head up and down, playing with the lead and enjoying her rub down. She was done for the day and seemed to have had fun with all the excitement, the sights, and the smells she encountered. Paige heard someone behind her and figured it was her mother back from the store. Paige was bubbling with excitement.

"Isn't she the greatest, Mom?" Her enthusiasm was overflowing.

"She is a dandy," came a deep voice in reply. "You both did a fantastic job out there today."

Paige froze and her heart skipped a beat. She looked behind her as she rose to her feet from where she had been down rubbing Libby's foreleg. There before her stood Samantha's father. His well-dressed figure and distinguished features towered over her small girlish frame. She just stood there unable to think of anything to say.

"Samantha said this was the first time this filly has been in town. You two make a pretty good team," he said, not taking his eyes off the filly and running his large hand down Libby's back.

"Thank you, sir," she said politely, then was quiet again.

After a pause he said, "I'm sorry, I should introduce myself. My name is John Greenly. You apparently go to school with my daughter, Samantha."

"Yes, sir, I do." She said it blankly not indicating like or dislike toward his daughter. "I am Paige Cason." She held her hand out in an adult fashion.

He shook it. "Pleased to meet you, Paige." John was a little surprised. He took his eye off the girl and looked back at the filly. He noticed the well-polished coat on Libby, which had taken hours to make shine as it did in the afternoon sun.

"Where is your father, Paige?"

"He is home building some new corrals," she answered questioningly. "Is there something I can do for you?"

"Well. I wanted to ask him who broke this filly for you and if she was for sale?" he stated, as if she wouldn't be able to answer those kind of questions.

She stiffened and her heart started to pound. "I trained this filly, Mr. Greenly, and no she is not for sale." It sounded to her as if someone else had spoken those words, but they had come from her mouth.

"Well I know you ride her now," he persisted, "but I wanted to know who did the ground work and started riding her." His tone was of a man talking to a child who didn't understand English.

She felt threatened. "Mr. Greenly," she said, her tone flat and serious. "I have had this filly since she was a yearling. And I am the only person besides my father who has ever touched her, until now," she added, looking at his hand sitting solidly on her withers. She continued, "I taught her to lead, sacked her out, and I was the first one to step in the saddle."

She was shaking, and she hoped it didn't show. "I have to finish rubbing her down, so if you will excuse me." She stepped past him and started on the other side of Libby, hoping the distance would give her a chance to think. She had never talked to a grown up like that, but an adult had never talked to her as a child either.

She started to rub Libby's other front leg with long steady strokes. She couldn't believe this was happening. Samantha wanted her filly and had sent her father over to buy her. No way was she going to sell Liberty, especially not to the Greenlys. Paige wished her mother would hurry and return from the store. She wished Mr. Greenly would leave. He was just standing there watching her. Paige had nothing else to say to him, and as for that daughter of his…

A loud pop from the arena made her jump and was followed by a scream. Although the show was over, there still were kids riding and playing tag games on their horses. Paige stood, turning to where the noise had come from. She had to take a second look before she realized what she was seeing.

A big bay horse was running frantically around the arena, trying in desperation to rid himself of the object he was dragging.

"He's dragging her! Somebody stop him! Oh God, He is going to kill her!" somebody screamed.

Without a thought, Paige untied Libby. She tied the end of the lead to the halter, threw it over Libby's head, and jumped astride. Libby surged forward sensing the urgency of her rider as Paige directed her toward the arena gate.

A man jumped the fence, flagging his arms at the frantic Piper and trying to stop him. "Whoa! Whoa!" he hollered.

Piper, with all the commotion, stopped abruptly and wheeled to the left stepping on Samantha's left arm. The bone snapped under his weight.

"Open the gate!" Paige hollered. "Open the gate!"

A blonde woman saw her coming in a full lope. She ran to the gate, flipped the latch, and swung it open as Paige approached.

When Paige entered, it took less than a second for her to get the full picture. Piper was in a complete panic, his eyes wild with fear and confusion. Samantha looked unreal, like a rag doll bouncing lifelessly. Paige could see the helmet still on her head. She was face down, her arms like rubber, appearing to have no bone structure left to them. Her left leg was caught in the stirrup and turned grossly upside down with the toe of her boot still sticking straight in the air.

In the seconds it took to see this, Paige didn't have time to think. She urged Libby forward running up beside the right side of Piper. She reached down to grab the right broken rein that was flying in the air. Piper's speed increased, and she missed the first time. Then she attempted again, leaning over Libby's neck as far as she dared. She felt the leather tickle her fingertips as she stretched a little more and was able to get a hold of the rein. Paige had no saddle on Libby, so there was no way to snub this frantic horse, no way to stop him in his panic and fear.

I have got to get her off of him, she thought in desperation. The saddle had to come off—that was the only thing she could think of. With all the strength and adrenaline she had in her, she grabbed the tug of the saddle, where the saddle and cinch connected, and gave a heave. The saddle gave way from around Piper's girth and fell in a heap on the ground with the lifeless body of Samantha Greenly still attached.

From the spectators' point of view, it looked like a pickup man undoing a flank cinch off a bronc in a rodeo.

Paige had her hands full, and now she had to figure out how to stop both animals. All she had on her now lively filly was the halter and lead she had made into reins. She nudged Libby with her left leg and started her into a circle with Piper on the inside. She pulled Piper's head as close to her knee as she could and got a hold of the headstall of his bridle. Paige circled the two horses again and again, in as small a circle as she could get them in.

As Piper realized the monster he had been dragging was gone and the comfort of another horse was so close, his eyes softened and his gait slowed as he began to settle down. Both horses by now were in a complete sweat. Libby had never done anything like this before, and her head was high with her ears twitching back and forth as she tried to read what her friend on her back was asking her to do. She slowed as Paige wanted, but having this big mature bay horse so close to her small three-year-old frame was a lot to ask. She put all of her heart into the task at hand as she pranced around Piper, trying to keep him inside the circle Paige was telling her to make. Libby felt Paige's legs grip around her sides. Paige was trying to maintain her balance, and Libby was trying to decide if the pressures were for cues or for balance.

For Paige, the comprehension of what just happened and what she had just done was beginning to sink in as she circled the horses into a slower and slower gait, finally coming down to a walk. The whole incident was more of a reaction than a thinking thing. When reality finally hit her and the danger was over, Paige's body began to shake and dizziness overcame her as she tried to look for Samantha.

She couldn't get her eyes to focus, and everything became a blur. Her mind started to spin as she thought, *I have to dismount. I have to walk these horses out. Oh God, Samantha is dead.*

Her body was becoming numb. She leaned forward on Libby's neck for stability, closing her eyes only for a second, trying to focus them, and then tumbled to the ground. She heard a horse trotting away, then felt warm breath and a soft muzzle on her cheek. Then all was black and silent.

3

Paige felt the soft pillow under her head and the blankets draped around her body. She curled up and pulled the blankets up closer under her chin, feeling the security they were giving her.

"Paige?" came a soothing voice. "Paige, are you awake?"

"Mom?" she replied, not yet fully awake. Flashes of the nightmare came back to her. "I had the most awful nightmare, Mom," she said, as she became more conscious and started to open her heavier-than-usual eyelids.

She now realized that they were in a strange, dark room, and she could hear people shuffling outside the door.

"Mom?" she said with more urgency.

"You're alright, Sis," her mother said reassuringly. "You are in the hospital, and you are okay."

Paige's head ached, and her eyes didn't want to open but she forced them. "Liberty? Piper? Oh God, Mom, Samantha is dead!" Everything came flooding back to Paige's memory.

"No, Sis, she isn't. They have her in surgery right now. We will know more in a while. Having that helmet on saved her life, but the rest of her body took a pretty bad beating. Her ankle was crushed, and both arms are broken, and so are a couple of ribs. The doctors are trying to save her ankle now, in hopes that she will walk again." She paused, her eyes filling up with tears as she blinked them back.

"You have done a very brave thing today. You scared me to death, but I am very proud of you." She paused again, taking a deep breath and said, "I have to go get the doctor. He wanted me to as soon as you woke up. He wants to give you a quick checkup to make sure you are ready to go home. I'll be back in a minute."

She left Paige's bedside, leaving the door ajar so a stream of light entered the room. Paige had closed her eyes, trying to comprehend all that had happened, when a young man came into the room.

"Paige?" came a soft male voice, "Paige?"

"Yes, come in," she said not knowing for sure who it was, but not wanting to be left alone.

Craig Curry stepped up beside the bed, his lanky form towering over her. "I just wanted to see for myself that you were okay," he said in a soft tone. His face was filled with anguish and despair. He began speaking nervously as if to explain the story to someone to get it off his chest.

"It all seemed to happen in slow motion, Paige. I was at a loss of what to do. Then you came in on your horse." He paused. "It was like you had practiced that move or something. Everyone gathered around Samantha after you had gotten the saddle off. I couldn't get next to her, and when I turned and saw you stopping the horses, all of the sudden you leaned over your horse's neck and fell off. Piper took off, but your horse just stood there with her head down next to you. I hollered and ran over to you.

Your horse didn't want to move, but I was afraid she would step on you, and as other people came, she started getting nervous, so I led her back to the trailer and tied her up. By the time I had gotten back, they were loading you in the ambulance." His soft eyes were looking directly at her and he paused. His gaze shifted to the floor. "I just had to see you and make sure you were okay."

"What made him panic?" Paige asked.

"That damn balloon. They were tossing it back and forth across the fence. Piper didn't like it squeaking and flying over his head. Samantha decided it was good for him and wanted to keep throwing it, but he started to throw a fit. She needed both hands to control him. She reached over the fence to hand it to someone else. She grabbed the balloon too tight and it popped, and she was half way out of the saddle when he jumped." Craig paused for a second, replaying the incident in his mind. "Samantha grabbed the fence, thinking that Piper could run off without her and she could sit on the fence to watch the fun, but her foot went through the stirrup. As Piper bolted, he jerked her off the fence, and she was flung onto his hips then she was thrown on to the ground. The rest is history."

"So that's what happened," Paige whispered in thought. "I didn't know for sure what was happening. All I saw after the balloon exploded was Piper running frantic with Samantha attached. Now it's making a little more sense." She closed her eyes for a moment.

"Thank you for taking care of Libby, Craig." She looked directly at him. "I sure appreciate it."

Craig's sandy blond hair was messed up. His cowboy hat in his hands, he was crumpling the rim nervously, "Sure, no problem."

After a silence, she asked, "Have you heard anything about Samantha?"

"No, only that she was pretty busted up, but she is going to live. That's about it. They were pretty vague." The doctor walked in and Craig glanced up, "I'll see you later, take care of yourself." He walked out the door then peeked back in and said, "Paige, I have your trophies, I'll bring them out to your place in a day or so."

"Thanks, Craig, I forgot all about them," she said with a smile.

That thought brought back the memory of all that happened, and she wanted to go home and show her father what they had won at the show. She was beginning to feel better until she realized that she couldn't show him because Craig had her awards. Well at least she could tell him. *Man, what a day*, she thought as the doctor approached her.

He thoroughly checked Paige over one last time before he released her to Patricia. He shined lights in her eyes, checked her pulse, and made sure her reflexes were active. He checked the bump on her head and looked inside her ears. "Yep, you are free to go home. Looks like everything tests out okay. Now, Paige, I want you to be aware of any dizziness or lightheaded feelings, okay. Take it easy for a day or two. If you get any headaches or feel like you're dizzy come back in here. Okay?"

All Paige wanted to do was go home, check on Libby, and see her father. "Okay, I will." She looked at her mother and then back at the doctor.

As they walked past the waiting room, Paige saw a distraught man sitting with his elbows on his knees, his hands cradling his head, and his fingers tangled into his uncombed hair. Paige took another look and recognized him as John Greenly.

"Mr. Greenly?" Paige said, unsure what else to say.

He looked up, his face streaked with tears, his eyes red and swollen. "Paige, thank God you are okay."

He rose and went to her. His distinguished look had disappeared, and an exhausted man with slumped shoulders and an untucked shirt came to her. He reached out and took her into his arms, drew her near him, and kissed her on the head.

"Thank you for saving my daughter's life. I don't know if I could have handled another death in my family." His voice started to break up. "She is the only thing I have left."

He looked at Patricia. "If there is anything I can do for Paige, would you please let me know? I feel I am indebted to her."

"No, Mr. Greenly." Patricia looked at him and knowing the grief he must have been feeling, said, "If ever there is anything we can do for you, please don't hesitate to call.

You have enough to deal with, and we won't hesitate to help out if we can."

Then she changed the subject back to his daughter. "Have they said anything about Samantha?"

He sat back down heavily and sighed. "They are trying to repair the shattered ankle, but they don't have any guarantees on how well she will walk. The X-rays looked so bad, I was surprised they could even attempt repairs."

Patricia sat next to him and they talked for a few minutes of the damage and of their daughters, and how they were both lucky to have not lost either of them.

"Samantha is a very stubborn child, and it will take some time for her to come to terms with this. It will be a very bumpy road ahead." He smiled. "She takes after her mother. She is a very independent young lady."

Paige smiled. *Boy, he hit that nail on the head about her being stubborn.*

"Paige," he looked directly at her, "I would like for you to come out any time. Maybe you and Samantha can ride or something, I mean after she heals and gets back on her feet."

"I would like that, Mr. Greenly." Not knowing if Samantha would appreciate her father's offer, but Paige also knew he was trying to keep his spirits up.

Patricia rose and draped her arm around her daughter's shoulder. "Well, Mr. Greenly, we had better be going. It has been a long day, and we still have chores to do."

"Please call me John. Mr. Greenly sounds so formal after

what we have just been through."

"Okay, John, just remember, please call if you need anything at all."

"I will do that. Thanks again for all your help," he replied as he watched them start down the hall.

Paige and Patricia left the hospital. It was after dark, and the old pickup felt like a comfort to Paige as her mother started the engine. They drove to the fairgrounds in silence. Libby was pacing back and forth in a stall. She stuck her head out of the stall door when she heard the familiar rumble of the old Ford. When the headlights hit her, she lifted her head and gave soft nickers of worry that Paige could see before she could actually hear them. Paige was out of the truck before it came to a complete stop.

"Hey, little lady, you're okay. We wouldn't leave you down here without any food and water." Paige comforted her, but Libby continued her complaints until Paige brought her halter. Libby dropped her nose into it willingly. She was excited to get out of that dingy hole they called a stall. Paige ran her hand down Libby's neck. Her once-soft coat was covered with dried, stiff sweat. She worked out of sheer habit in the dark, for there were no street lamps, as she put Libby's blanket on and prepared her for the trip home.

It felt soothing to have her familiar blanket put on and to have Paige's closeness. Paige's familiar scent and actions settled Libby's fear. She loaded in the single horse trailer in the dark with the complete trust of her handler.

They rode home in silence.

4

Craig Curry sat on his mother's white leather couch in the front room, his thoughts drifting back to the last couple of weeks and the trouble that was brewing in his family life. He knew his mother and father had been fighting quite a bit lately, but he hadn't figured on this. The morning sun filtered into the room with a bright glow that dampened his spirits even more. How could it be such a beautiful day when he didn't want it to be?

His mother was a successful author. She had three bestseller mystery novels published and was working on the fourth. The main character she created lived in New York, and she was struggling with the layout and flavor of the city. She knew she had to become more involved with her character and plot to make the story real. Her publicist wanted her to relocate and get the feel of New York, live the life, and become more of her character. She was all for it.

"Why waste away in the small town of Baker City when the real world is outside of it?" Craig had overheard her say when she was talking with his father. "Why can't you live a little bit and move out of your shell, Jim? You just lock yourself in your own little world of working this place, and it gives nothing back to you."

"I let you do what you want," Craig's father had replied. "Why do you want to travel clear across the United States to create a story? Why can't you just create it here? Everything you need is at your fingertips. If you need to go to New York, why don't you spend a month or so over there and then come back home?"

"You don't get it, do you? I am not at home here. I have never been at home here. I want lights, motion, action! I want something more than sagebrush and wind and a creek behind the house. I want out, Jim. I want Craig to experience more than open spaces and horse manure. I want him to know about the real world and sports and academics. He can't get that here." She paused. "That's why we are leaving. I'm taking Craig and we are leaving. There is so much more for him to see than this."

"You can't drag Craig into this, Alison. You can't. He is happy here, he only has a few more years of high school, and his friends are all here. How can you uproot him from a place he has known all his life?"

"That is what I am saying, Jim. This is all he has ever known and will ever know if I don't do something about it. I have tried for the last few years to stay here, and I can't do it any longer."

"So what you are doing is using him as an excuse? So you can escape this 'hell hole'? You want him to change his whole life so you can have an excuse to create your own and write a story? Think about it, Alison, who are you really doing this for—him or yourself?"

Craig looked through the railing of the balcony. He felt like a child being punished for something he didn't do.

Listening in on his parents stirred emotions deep within him. He had no control over his fate. He felt like a dog whose owners are deciding which animal shelter to take him to. Craig watched his father as his large frame strode into the front room. He had never seen his father so mad.

Jim squared his shoulders to face Alison, yet kept his distance.

"If you really want to go to New York," he said courageously, "go ahead, but don't take Craig. Leave him here and let him finish school. Then when he's out maybe he'll come and stay with you for a while. But don't do this Alison, please don't do this."

Craig's heart was beating in his throat at this point. He had never seen them argue this much, but what made his heart stop and feel sick was when his mother said the last words.

"There is nothing you can do about it, Jim. I already have the divorce papers being drawn up. When we are finished, Craig will be coming with me."

The house was silent. Craig thought he could hear a pin drop within the walls. *This house*, he thought, *is my home*. He heard the heavy footfalls of his father as he watched him walk out. He knew he would never forget the sound of the door closing behind him. The echo was deafening.

That was a couple of weeks ago. Now Craig put his feet on the glass coffee table. He hadn't seen his father since that day. He lay back on the couch and sighed deeply. His mother was serious. Since that day she had been busy on the phone making reservations and appointments with her publicist and attorney to get things together for their "new life," as she had put it to him. Craig tried to keep busy. He spent quite a bit of time with a few friends but never mentioned his life falling apart to anyone. He even went to the horse show with Samantha Greenly, but that didn't turn out like he wanted either. He liked Samantha but saw a side of her that day he had never seen before. With all that happened that day, all that was done, it didn't change the outcome. He was still moving to New York.

His mother walked into the room. Her makeup was as perfect as her hair, her high-heeled shoes echoing on the hardwood floor. Craig wondered why, with all that was perfect around him, his life was in disarray. He removed his feet from the coffee table and sat up.

"Well, if we are going out to the Cason's, we had better do it now," she said. "I have an appointment at 10:30 with the attorney and I have a lot of packing to do."

Craig didn't say a word. He had been trying to think of some place to go today and thought of Paige Cason. The girl he always saw but never really knew. He felt kind of awkward dropping in on her at the hospital, but he didn't know what else he could do. He had to tell her about her horse anyway. He had left her awards in the car and didn't have time to go get them when he was at the hospital.

His heart was in his throat when he thought of going out

there. He had never been to her house but knew where she lived. He grabbed his cowboy hat and strode out the front door.

His mother looked back at him. "You know, when you move to New York, you're going to have to leave that stupid hat here with those horses! I don't think they are going to like seeing you play cowboy in the city."

"This hat is part of who I am, Mom, and I think they have horses. And anyways I'm not in New York yet."

He got in the Chevy and his mother started the engine. "You will have a better life in the city, Craig, you will see. There are things for you to do there, better colleges for you to look into, and great sports programs. You just wait, you'll see." She put the car into drive and pulled onto the road.

What if I don't want to go to college? He thought to himself. *And sports…are sports so important that I have to move clear across the United States to play? Crap, I'm not that good, and I don't want to be that good. I just want to stay where I'm at, ride a few colts, and work on the ranch.* He thought all of this in silence. He didn't want to fight, and he didn't want to argue. He wanted family, he wanted security, he wanted things back the way there were.

5

A reporter from the *Baker City Harold* came out to interview Paige. It seemed that Paige was the talk of the town and folks wanted to know a little more about her. She answered questions enthusiastically. She talked of how Libby was nervous at the beginning of the show and how she settled down as the day wore on. She talked of the accident, that there was no time to think, just react. She talked of how, after she had gotten the saddle off Piper and had slowed him down with Libby, she had felt really dizzy just before she passed out. She then talked of waking up at the hospital, about Samantha's injuries, and how Samantha was going to walk again.

The reporter spent an hour or so taking pictures and jotting notes down. She then took her note pad and camera, thanked Paige for her time, and left.

Paige's spirits were high. It had been an exciting two days for her. She had never had so much attention before in her life.

"I can't wait till the story comes out, Mom," she said before she went to bed that night. "I am going to hang it on the wall when we get it."

Patricia smiled at her daughter, thinking this the biggest thing to happen in Paige's life.

A shiny silver pickup truck pulled up in front of the Cason house the following morning. Patricia looked out the kitchen window and saw Craig Curry get out of the passenger side. He had something wrapped in a large yellow towel in his hands. He talked for a moment to the driver then shut the truck door. The driver kept the truck idling.

"Hey, Craig, it's good to see you," Patricia said as she opened the screen door to let him in.

"I told Paige I would bring these out." He handed over the awards wrapped carefully in the large soft towel.

"They are beautiful," Patricia said as she looked at the platters shimmering in the light. "Paige is going to be pleased. She is in her room. I'll show you." Patricia looked out the screen door and waved at Mrs. Curry. She waved back.

"I can only stay for a few minutes, Mom needs to get to town," he said almost in a depressed tone.

Patricia knocked on Paige's door and cracked it open. "Paige, you have a visitor." She opened the door wider so Craig could enter.

"Hey, you!" Paige said in a chipper voice. "Hey, you brought my awards! This is great."

Patricia left as the two started to talk and headed to where Mrs. Curry was waiting.

Mrs. Curry touched a button to lower her window half way down as Patricia approached. "If you don't mind, Mrs. Curry, I can bring Craig home a little later this afternoon. I have to go the store anyways, so it wouldn't be any trouble."

"Are you sure? I have several appointments today and

he really didn't want to come with me until I told him we could bring the awards out here. Paige sure did a fantastic job at the show. She has been the talk of the town these last few days."

"We are pretty proud of her too. She worked hard to have Libby ready."

"If you are sure it won't be an issue, I will head back into town."

"No, no problem at all, they seem to have a lot to talk about," Patricia answered.

"Well, I had better be going, I have an appointment in thirty minutes. These dirt roads are awful to drive on." She sighed, "If you have any problems call me at my attorney's. Craig knows the number, but here it is, just in case." She handed Patricia a card and started to pull away.

Patricia watched her leave down the dirt road. She looked down at her hands then over at the old Ford truck. She heard laughter in the background through Paige's open window. She smiled and walked back to the house.

She walked down the hallway. Paige and Craig were trying to figure out where to put her silver platters. They were laughing and having a time of it.

"Oh shoot…Mom…I have got to go," Craig said when he heard the screen door slam, as if he had lost all sense of time.

"No, Craig, I talked to your mom and she said it would be fine if you stayed here. I will take you home when you are ready."

"Really? That's great! I really didn't want to spend another day in town. It gets old after awhile."

"Why don't we hang these awards on the wall and then go out and watch my father work a colt in the round pen? He's starting a new one today."

"Sure," Craig said. "I would like to see that."

They hung the platters next to Libby's picture on the wall, then stood back and admired their work.

"That looks pretty good." Paige sighed. The little photograph looked small with the two platters next to it, but it framed in nicely with the ribbons hanging below. The breeze coming through her window made them ripple against the wall.

Craig straightened one of the platters. "Perfect," he said.

"Let's go out and watch my father. I'll introduce you to him when he has a minute," Paige said with enthusiasm.

"Sure!" Craig said as they headed out the door and started down the hall.

"Do you want some iced tea?" Patricia asked as they walked into the kitchen.

"Yes, please," Craig said. Paige grabbed the glasses, and Patricia grabbed the ice out of the top compartment of the freezer.

"We'll take some down to Papa too," Paige said as she grabbed a third glass.

Craig felt at home as he stood and watched mother and daughter get the drinks ready. What a change from what he felt not more than two hours earlier. He smiled as Paige turned to him with a glass.

"Are you ready?" she smiled.

"Yep," he said, his eyes sparkling with the excitement of what this day might bring. He thought for a moment of what he could be doing today, and sadness filled his heart. *No, no thoughts beyond right now. No moving, no New York…just today,* he thought again.

"I'm so ready," he said with a grin.

"Back in awhile, Mom." With both hands full, Paige bumped her shoulder into the screen to push it open.

Craig reached out with his empty hand to steady the door as she walked through. They headed to the horse barn.

Abe was already scratching the colt on the neck that not ten minutes earlier had never had a hand on it. Paige walked quietly up to the corral and waited for Abe to acknowledge her before speaking.

Abe leaned a hand on the colt's withers and looked at her. "Hey, Sis, what is going on?"

"Not a lot, Papa, just thought I would bring Craig down here so you could meet him. He brought me my awards from the other day and took care of Libby at the fairgrounds."

Abe stroked the horse's neck one more time and walked to the fence to meet Craig. The colt followed. Abe reached through the fence. "Abe Cason," he said without hesitation.

"Craig Curry. Good to meet you, sir," Craig said in a firm tone as they shook hands.

"Are you Jim Curry's boy?"

"Yes, sir, I am."

"Good man," Abe replied.

Craig smiled. *Yes, he is,* he thought, and a pang of pride and remorse filled his heart.

"Here, Papa, we brought you some iced tea." Paige stepped in and handed him the glass.

"So what's your dad doing these days? I haven't been around town lately."

Craig thought for a moment then swallowed his heart. "He has been working on a new hay barn, he wants to get it built before the first cutting."

"Don't blame him there," Abe said.

Craig continued, switching the conversation from his family. "This horse barn is a dandy. I really like how it's set up."

Abe stroked the colt's head standing beside him, then reached to open the gate. "Yeah, not every man gets to design his own barn. I was fortunate enough to have Patricia help me design this one. She is a master at drawing what I described. You want to take a look?"

"Sure."

They all three walked into the coolness of the barn. They talked of walls, boards, and construction, as well as the floor plan, easy access, and stalls. Craig knew the language of construction from working with his uncle, and the conversation flowed easily.

Abe finished his iced tea and handed the glass back to Paige. "Thanks, Sis. I have got to finish up with this little guy and get down to the corrals. Craig, it was good to meet you. Sure appreciate you taking care of Paige's mare the other day." He reached out his hand one more time.

"You too, Mr. Cason." He took Abe's powerful hand in his and shook it firmly.

"Call me Abe."

"Yes, sir." Craig's face turned red.

Paige grabbed the glasses and started back to the house. "See you later, Papa."

"See you, Sis," Abe said as he returned to the corral where the colt stood waiting by the gate.

6

They ate lunch with Patricia and Abe on the back porch under the weeping willow. They spent the afternoon in the shade and talked like they were best of friends for a lifetime.

"So what do you do out here all summer?" Craig asked, as he sprawled out on the grass under the weeping willow tree.

Paige was lying on her stomach facing toward him. "I ride a lot, but when I'm not around the horses, I like to draw things."

"Really?" Craig now rolled on his side propping his head up with his hand. "What do you like to draw?"

"Anything, really," She felt her face get a little red. Paige had never talked to anyone about her drawings. "I guess the one I like to draw the most is of course…"

"Let me guess," Craig cut in, "horses."

Paige smiled, her face hot as she stumbled to change the subject, "So what about you, what are your hobbies?"

Craig was quiet for a moment, "Well, I always wanted to build things, so I don't know, maybe construction or something. But Mom wants me to play basketball. So I guess my hobby is basketball. I do have a pretty good advantage with my height and all, but I don't think it's what I want to do the rest of my life." Then in the same breath he said, "Show me some of your drawings."

Paige could see he was just as uncomfortable talking about what he wanted to do as she was, "Only if you don't laugh."

They got up from the shade tree and headed inside the house and down the hall to her room. She crawled under her bed on the far side and pulled out a large tablet. He watched her.

"Boy, you must be proud of them to have them that well hidden."

"Mom gave me this tablet about two Christmases ago and I've been kind of sketching in it since. But I've never shown anyone, not even my parents. They're only silly sketches anyway."

He flipped the cover open and saw the head of a colt. It was pretty good, better than he could do. Paige instantly felt self-conscious and took the book from him.

"Those were my first drawings." She hesitated, seeing the shocked look on his face having taken the book so abruptly from him. She flipped through the pages to find something a little bit better to show him. She was about three-quarters of the way through the book when she finally stopped at one she had drawn of Libby with her saddle and snaffle bit on. Her mane was blowing in the wind and her head was facing toward Paige.

He was speechless as he looked at the detail of the shadings and markings. "Are you kidding? You drew that?"

"Do you like it? I have a bunch of different ones. Here

are some coyotes tucked in the sagebrush." She turned the page and he was looking at a badger, peeping its head out of its hole.

"Not so fast, Paige, let me look at these." He took the book from her and flipped back to the coyotes tucked up under the sagebrush. It was as if it was looking directly at Craig. Its eyes looked so real, and so did the sagebrush. "Man, this is fantastic," he whispered, looking at the detail from each hair and whisker of the coyote to every leaf and shape and form of the barked branches on the sagebrush. Turning to the badger, he caught a glimpse of life in the eye, as if he was actually staring directly at him, maybe even challenging him. He slowly turned another page to see the snowcapped Elkhorn Mountains. "Man, Paige," he sighed, "These are incredible. How do you do it? I mean…"

Paige blushed, "I don't know. I kind of lose myself in the motion I guess, or in the moment maybe." She paused. "I really don't know, Craig, I just turn my pencil loose and let it go." She stopped again and looked at him for a moment. "I just don't think about it, I just let it be what it is." Paige shrugged her shoulders, running out of explanations, and focused her attention back on the paper before her. "Honestly," she blushed, "I don't know how to explain what comes from my pencil. I just know sometimes I'm surprised at myself and what I draw." She flipped another page. "My favorites are the horses and their different expressions."

"Horses have different expressions?" Craig was intrigued as he flipped through more pictures.

"Sure, but you have to know what to look for. Like if they're curious or excited or mad, they have different facial expressions." She said this as if everyone knew they did. She took back her book and flipped through some more of her pictures to show him the different expressions she tried to create.

The day was going fast for both of them, and all too soon it would be chore time. They set the book down. He didn't feel like he ever wanted to go home.

"Paige, do you think I can help with chores? I don't have anything to do at home."

Paige looked at him. "Well sure, but you should ask my father."

He jogged out to the corrals where Abe was working. "Mr. Cason, uh, Abe, do you need any help doing chores tonight?" Craig stumbled over the words clumsily as if he was just learning how to speak.

Abe looked at him. He had just finished digging a hole and was getting ready to drop a nine-foot post into it. Abe grabbed one end of the foot wide post and started to drag it around to the hole.

"Here, let me help you with that," Craig said, not giving it a second thought. He got on one side and Abe was on the other.

Abe felt the weight being lifted from his arms. Craig

64

walked backwards, stepped around the hole, and at the count of three they dropped the post over the hole. Then they both walked to the other end and lifted together. As the post rose higher, they walked down the underside of it to fit it in the hole. It slid in and sat leaning to one side.

"Man, did you do all these by yourself?" Craig looked at the corrals that were standing. Then he looked at what was still to do. "You still have these to go?" He looked at the string along the ground framing out four other corrals, each about eighty by one hundred twenty feet in length and width.

"Well I got this far, no sense in stopping now," Abe said. "Sure, if you want to stay and help with chores then you'll probably have to stay for dinner."

"Well if you need help tamping down this post, I'll help you," Craig said enthusiastically.

"No, you go ahead and visit. I will be inside in about fifteen minutes," Abe replied as he grabbed his shovel and started putting gravel around the base of the post, then started sifting the dirt back into the hole.

Craig never said a word. He watched for a second then grabbed the tamping post. Abe began to fill the four-foot hole, and Craig began to stand the post up and tamp the dirt around it.

Abe paused, looked at him for just a moment, and then continued shoveling not saying a word. When he got ahead of Craig, he would grab the post and set it straight so Craig could tamp more dirt on one side or the other, making the post stand straight.

Sweat was running down both of them before they headed to the barn for chores.

"Well, Craig, you make a heck of a fence builder," Abe said with appreciation. "Sure appreciate the help."

"Not a problem, Abe. I spent two summers out on my Uncle's ranch over in Durkee, and he had lots of fence to build after the elk got done tearing it down during the winter. He had plenty things for me to fix, along with working his working cows."

"Sounds like he keeps you pretty busy," Abe analyzed.

"Between him and Dad I don't have a lot of free time to be wasting around town."

"I guess that's not a bad thing," Abe said with a smile.

Craig grinned back.

Paige was already at the barn feeding horses when the two walked in. Abe grabbed the wheelbarrow and headed with the pitchfork to muck out the stalls while Craig caught the horses.

When they got to the house, it smelled of fresh-baked bread and roast beef in the oven. Craig called his mom to let her know he would be a little late and got the answering machine, so he left a message. He felt his stomach start to growl as he hung up the phone.

They took turns washing up, then sat at the dinner table. Craig's mouth watered as he looked at the food—green beans, green salad, fresh tomatoes, mashed potatoes, and that roast beef, just the smell of it…

Abe sat silently for a moment. "Let's say grace."

The three of them bowed their heads. Craig did a quick glance then bowed his, closing his eyes as he listened to Abe's words.

"Lord, if there is a better day than this, please let it be lived and appreciated. As for now, thank you for this day and the food we share. Now let us privately say our peace."

There was a silence in the room. Craig opened his eyes and realized this was a moment of silence, a moment of truth between each person and God. He closed them again, letting the quiet melt into his heart.

Then he heard Abe say, "Amen."

And the room came alive again.

"Are you going to load up your plate or just look at the food?" Abe asked with a grin.

"Well, I just hope there is enough for all of us because I haven't seen a dinner this good in a long time."

Patricia smiled. "There is plenty, and if you can eat all that I've made, I'll have to have you come to dinner more often. I have an apple pie in the oven."

"Mrs. Cason, I will come to dinner anytime you offer," Craig laughed.

Patricia smiled a warm smile. "You are welcome here anytime, Craig, anytime at all."

Conversation was easy and Craig found himself wrapped

up in the warmth of this family. For the first time in a long time, he felt the outside world fade completely away. He looked across the table at the blonde girl, and his heart began to pound.

He thought of Abe's prayer and repeated it to himself. *Lord if there is a better day than this, let it be lived and appreciated. As for now, thank you for this day and the food we share.*

It would be etched in his mind for the rest of his life, a quiet man with a quiet life and a simple prayer.

After dinner and the dishes were done, Craig and Paige sat on the porch alone. He said, "Your parents are super people, Paige." He paused. "I wish my family was like yours." He paused again, reality creeping back like a rock tossed into a pond, the ripples sending out distress. He searched for words that he had not yet uttered out loud. "But I guess that will never happen," he finished his thought.

"What do you mean?" Paige looked at him solemnly. She could see that he was searching for the words of something she was probably not going to like and that he liked even less.

She really liked this boy. He had never judged her on what her family had or didn't have. It felt so good to talk to someone her own age, and for the first time she didn't feel like she had to defend herself or her family.

"Paige," he stumbled over the words, "my parents are getting a divorce, and my mom and I are moving to New York." He blurted it out. *There, I said it out loud*, he thought to himself. *Does that make it real?* His heart was hollow. "She's writing another book," he continued, almost numb, "and her publicist wants her to relocate so she can get in with the right crowd." He paused. "I don't want to go. I love this town."

He could hear the tears build up in his voice. He swallowed hard fighting them back. "We're leaving next week."

Silence and tension filled the air.

Paige heard the words that felt like a rock hitting her heart. She felt a warm tear run down her cheek. She didn't know if it was for him or for herself, and she brushed it away. They got up, and he turned to face her. "I have to tell you something, Paige, and if I don't tell you now, I might never get the chance." He paused for a second, took a deep breath, and said, "I have never met a girl quite like you before. I have always wanted to talk to you but never had the guts. Now that I am leaving…" He bent down, gave her a kiss, and felt something warm run down his cheek. He turned and went in the house to tell Patricia that he was ready to go.

Paige just stood there for a moment dumbstruck then walked to the house.

7

When the story came out, Patricia bought two papers. She took some money out of her Christmas stash she had been saving, went to a frame shop, and found a nice oak frame with a pretty, antique gold matting. With the help of the clerk, the story fit very nicely inside. The clerk had read the article and sold the frame to her for fifty percent off. It was a special he was running for that day, he added. When Patricia read the story in the truck, she felt a little odd about the way it read. It had a really nice picture of Libby and Paige standing side by side with Libby's head over Paige's shoulder. But the headlines read:

POOR GIRL SAVES WEALTHY MAN'S DAUGHTER

Patricia read on. *A poor girl named Paige Cason saved Samantha Greenly, daughter of John Greenly, from death at the Baker City Horse Show last weekend. Though the Casons don't have money, they do have spirit, as Paige risked her own life to save Samantha from a stampeding horse. Samantha is now in the Baker City hospital with two broken arms and a shattered ankle. Paige stated that John Greenly did offer her anything she wished for saving his daughter's life, but at this time Paige stated she didn't know what she wanted.*

That doesn't sound right! Patricia thought as she looked at the article. Paige didn't know what she wanted John Greenly to give her? She stated that John was very appreciative.

"Wow." But maybe she was reading more into it than what it said. She knew it didn't matter to Paige what it said, it was the idea of her picture in the paper that made her happy. She drove home deep in thought. It seemed that the paper had labeled Paige as an underprivileged child. She knew that Paige had a lot of ambition and enthusiasm and wasn't afraid to speak her mind. "POOR GIRL" kept ringing in Patricia's mind. Is that how the world saw her? What about her talents, her humor, and her shy little ways? Did anyone see Paige as she did? Or did they see her for what she didn't have?

She pulled the old Ford up next to the house and turned off the engine. She sat there looking at the two-bedroom board and bat shack that was before her. The owner of the little ranch, Thomas Pitt, said he was going to buy some paint for the place some day. That was four or five years ago. Patricia never brought it up when he came around, for he never had any time to stop and talk to her. He would go to the barn with Abe, look at the horses, and tell Abe what he expected to be done. Not once did he come in to have coffee or sit and visit. She didn't even think he knew Abe had a family.

He was a psychiatrist in Los Angeles. He had bought the little rundown place about a month before he hired Abe. The corrals and barn needed to be ripped out and totally rebuilt. Thomas had the barn built to what Abe thought would be a good working barn, and Abe was supposed to do the corrals which he had done to perfection. Now Thomas was talking of adding more corrals and getting a couple hundred head of cattle. He just bought the property adjoining his three-hundred-acre place. Now he owned another five hundred. Abe needed to get a couple of hired hands if Thomas wanted to actually make this place into a real working ranch. Patricia knew that Thomas' knowledge of cattle and horses was almost nil. His dream of having a ranch and being a "cowboy" was secondary to having a tax write-off.

It took more than money to run a ranch. It took understanding of the animals, persistence, common sense, and the understanding of nature. Patricia thought that Thomas had persistence and money but was lacking in the rest. That is where Abe came in, and Thomas depended on him for making this place work.

Abe was raised on a ranch. It wasn't big, but his family worked colts, calved cows, and put up hay. His father was a perfectionist, a jack-of-all-trades, and taught Abe to be the same. Both parents were killed in a car accident a week after his nineteenth birthday. He lost the little ranch in probate. Abe then struck out on his own. He met Patricia when he was only twenty, they fell madly in love, and married six months later. A year later, just before Paige was born, Abe was working for a construction company. He was employed with them for five months when he fell off an overpass. He broke his back in two places, and it took every bit of three years to recover. The construction company went belly up in that time. Although he was released to go back to work, nobody wanted to hire him for fear he would injure himself again.

The insurance quit paying as soon as he was released to go back to work. The family savings kept them afloat for a while as Abe continued to look for work, any work, just as long as he could feed his family. They were two months behind on their rent when the landlord said he could work it off or move out. He started to work for his rent—patch that roof, build a deck, fix that drain. Patricia did other peoples' laundry and little odds and ends to try to help out, but with a child only two years old, she had limited capabilities. Things were getting very desperate, and then Thomas Pitt came one day to offer Abe a job working colts. The pay wasn't great, but it would put a roof over his family's head. He accepted, for he always had a love of horses and learned how to understand animals from his father's guiding words. The rest he learned from experience.

Patricia remembered Abe telling her, "Horses are so much like people. Two are never the same. They have their own point of view on life, and sometimes it's a challenge for them to change that point of view and understand a new one."

So here we are, thought Patricia, still sitting in the truck. "Well at least we have a roof over our heads," she said sarcastically. "If nothing else, we do have that. We should put ol' Thomas Pitt in the round corral and run him around a little, maybe change his point of view."

She got out of the old green truck, grabbed her present for Paige, and headed for the house. It was supposed to be a night of laughter and cheer, but that night Patricia had a hard time keeping a sincere smile on her face.

8

Anne Rhymes pulled into Baker City late. *The damn van is making that clanking sound again*, she thought. They really needed it looked at. She wasn't going any farther until something was done. She was a reporter for the five o'clock news out of Portland. Her TV crew and she had just been to Vale doing a story on an eight-hundred-pound pig. They stopped at a Texaco to fuel up and to see if they could find out what was making the clanking sound.

She thought, *There has got to be more to report about than a pig*. She milled around the station, poured herself a cup of coffee, and out of habit glanced at the local newspaper. On the cover was a cute girl with her horse.

"First pigs, now horses. Animals, the wave of the future, a reporter's dream. God, I have got to get something big, and soon," she said to herself. Talking to herself had become a habit she was unaware of and it caught quite a few people off guard.

"I need to find a good story, one that will make some money." She knew there was a market out there for good gossip. "With my news salary," she said with a sigh to herself, "I could be selling day-old donuts on the sidewalk and making just as much."

Jack, one of her cameramen, was standing at the counter, trying to ignore her comments.

A man walked by her, looked at her talking to the candy

bars, paused to make sure he saw correctly, then shuffled off.

She walked back over to the paper rack and picked up the thin copy. "This can't be more than six pages. Boy, there's a lot of news around this place." She read the headline,

POOR GIRL SAVES WEALTHY MAN'S DAUGHTER

This captured her attention and she read on.

"How could a girl save another girl on horseback?" She reached up and pushed her blonde hair behind her ear. "What is this place the wild, wild west?" She snorted as she looked and read on.

The young store attendant interrupted her searching. "Well yeah, don't you know you're in Eastern Oregon?" he said with a smile. "Around here one minute a person can be an enemy and the next can save your life."

Anne looked up, surprised that anyone answered her. A young man who barely looked eighteen was standing behind the counter. Anne was confused. "What do you mean?"

"Oh, ya know, around here ya pretty much know everyone. If not, ya know someone who knows the ones ya don't." He chuckled.

Anne returned his smile but she didn't get it.

"I graduated last year and know both of those girls," he continued, "not so much about Paige, she never was one to be in the crowd, if ya know what I mean." He paused. "She is kind of cute though," he said with a grin.

"But now Samantha," he said a little more seriously, "now

she's a pistol. Has the money and looks, no one usually messes around with her. No one wants to cross her path and make her mad. She has a pretty big temper on her, especially since her mother's death."

"Really?" Anne interrupted, pleased to have this kid tell all he knew in a few short minutes.

"Yeah, it is pretty funny," he continued. "I was at the horse show that day, and Paige, the girl who saved Samantha, had argued with her. It was pretty intense. I heard her tell Samantha to get out of her face and that she could go to hell! For no apparent reason that I saw. Then not two hours later, she saved her from a stampeding horse. Sounds kind of funny, huh?" He paused then said, "Kind of like putting a burr under your saddle then saving you after you get bucked off."

"Yeah," Anne replied. "It does kind of sound weird."

She was quiet for a minute as she began creating a story in her mind. She walked out of the station with paper in hand. "Jack!" she hollered to one of the two-camera crew. "Pay the bill and call a motel, we're staying here for a day or two. And get that van looked at while we're here."

Anne was twenty-five with a slender build and blonde shoulder-length hair. She had high cheekbones and a bright, white smile. Her eyes glittered a mischievous blue. She had an hourglass figure, and she made sure her clothes fit to turn heads as she walked in a room. Her determination to become someone big in the news world had been a dream from childhood. She thought it was amazing how reporters could make something out of nothing. Anne prided herself in doing the same. She knew she was going to make it big one day, and with the way this story sounded, it just might be a good beginning.

She read the article again. Words started to jump out at her: "wealthy man, poor girl, money."

"This could be a scandal." Anne kept her imagination running. "Sure, it could be a scandal. A small town in Eastern Oregon, looking so innocent no one would know what really happened. I bet she goes for a hundred grand if not more. I wonder if her parents put her up to it. This might be something to dig into. We have to call these folks first thing in the morning and see if we can set up an interview, Jack."

Jack looked at her questioningly. "Whatever, Anne, I'll call first thing in the morning."

"We need to find some eyewitnesses and some participants at the horse show. Maybe we can even get Mr. Greenly and that other girl, his daughter, what's her face… do some research on Greenly, see how much he's worth and dig into his family history. And this gas attendant, get his name and phone number and we'll get him on camera."

9

The next morning the phone rang at the Cason's home. *Who could be calling at this time in the morning?* Patricia thought. *The chores aren't even done.* She looked at the clock it read five minutes until six. She picked up the receiver.

"Hello," Patricia said.

"Is this Mrs. Cason?" a soft female voice asked.

"Yes it is."

"This is Anne Rhymes, I am with the five o'clock news out of Portland. I'm sorry to be calling you so early. Did I wake you?"

"No, Anne, you didn't. You have to get up pretty early to beat this household up." Patricia couldn't believe she was talking to a TV reporter.

Anne continued, "We were just going through town when I read the story in your local newspaper. I thought it would make one heck of a TV story and would like to interview your brave daughter and her wonder horse. We'll be in town just today, I could probably meet with you folks a little later this afternoon, if that's okay with you."

Her voice was very sweet and sincere, but just a little rushed as if she were a very busy lady. Patricia, not wanting to keep this professional waiting, was having a hard time believing the TV news wanted to do a story on Paige. She was flattered and shocked.

"My boss is very excited about this story too. He really

likes to air stories about kids."

Patricia couldn't think. Her heart was pounding in her throat. She knew she shouldn't agree without checking with Abe. They didn't watch much TV—everything on the news always seemed so depressing.

"How about two o'clock, Mrs. Cason?" Anne ventured as more of a statement than a question.

Patricia gave directions to their house and hung up the phone. *Boy howdy, is Paige going to be excited about this.*

Anne hung up the phone. Then she called her boss and said she might have another story there in Baker City, about a girl and her horse. Then she told him the van had broken down and they were stuck in Baker City for a day or so anyway. "These damn small towns," she told him, "don't keep parts in stock, they have to order them."

Mr. Greenly was still at the hospital with his daughter so she would just show up there and maybe get a few pictures of a distressed father and his poor crippled daughter.

"If we could capture his sorrow, get sympathy from the viewers, and maybe create a little doubt in this naive little town, then the story will create itself," Anne said to no one in particular.

They spent all morning talking to the townspeople. Most didn't have anything bad to say about Paige or the Cason family. But what they did say was that they were distant from the townspeople and kept to themselves most of the time.

"Were the two girls friends?" Anne asked several.

Not that anyone knew of. They didn't see Paige around town that often.

One boy on camera, liking the idea of being on TV, said, "Well, I saw them arguing several times throughout the day."

Another man stepped forward, seeing the attention the boy was getting, and thought he would get his two cents in. "Paige threatened to hit Samantha, I remember that. Samantha was calling to her and Paige just started hollering at her and threatened to hit her," he repeated.

As the crowd grew larger around the TV crew, the doubts grew and became more suggestive about Samantha getting set up.

"What about John Greenly offering Paige Cason money for saving his daughter?" Anne asked innocently. "Do you think Paige's family had any plan of this? Did they know that John Greenly's wife had died a few years ago in a car accident? Doesn't it seem odd that a teen would do such a thing without a motive?" Anne's questions had now set the stage and as she predicted, and the story started to create itself.

Damn, this is going to be good, Anne thought. *Of course, there will be a lot cut and edited but that's the news business.*

After an hour Anne and Jack headed for the hospital. They found Samantha's room and peeked inside. She was asleep. Both arms were casted, so was her ankle, and her face was badly bruised. "Get a shot of this, Jack," Anne whispered.

Jack felt a little odd but did as he was told. They never entered the room, but with the zoom lens, Jack got a fantastic shot of Samantha's battered face and casts. They were setting the scene of a poor little girl all alone in a huge hospital bed. Jack cut the camera and they both propped themselves up against the wall, just outside Greenly's room, waiting maybe to get Mr. John Greenly on camera.

A few minutes later, his big frame ambled down the hall. He was in a t-shirt and jeans and his solid frame moved beneath the shirt with a confident air. Although he looked tired and stressed, he was in great shape. Anne instantly was attracted to him, even though there was about a twenty-year difference in their age.

"Mr. Greenly?" Anne said with her most professional attitude.

"Yes." His voice was deep and quiet.

"I'm Anne Rhymes with the five o'clock news and I would like to offer my deepest sympathy for your daughter, Samantha."

"Thank you, I appreciate that," he replied again with that deep, husky tone.

Anne felt her face flush. "I was wondering if we could interview you and your daughter and let the people now what kind of tragedy has happened in this nice little community."

"My daughter doesn't want to be seen for now, and I intend to respect her wishes. All I can say is it is a miracle that she is here today. I owe Paige Cason and her family so much for what they have done."

"Are you planning on giving her money?" Anne asked. "I hear they are quite poor."

"I haven't decided how I will pay them back, but I will when the time is right."

Jack had the camera rolling as they talked, and Anne was doing her best to create doubt about Paige doing this out of kindness.

"Did you know the Casons before the accident?"

"No. Not really. I knew who they were, but that's about it. They seem to be very nice people. They've come to visit Samantha, but she refuses to be seen by anyone."

Well this is a dead end road, Anne thought. *Paige has this guy thinking she is an angel. But when he sees the news and finds out what other people are saying about her, he should change his mind.*

"Well, Mr. Greenly, if you ever want to talk to me, or if Samantha feels up for an interview, give me a call." Anne reached in her purse and pulled out a card. "Thank you for your time." She wrote the motel and number on the back and handed it to him.

10

Paige was happy to do another interview for TV. She hadn't realized what she did was such a big deal, and it made her feel special that people were interested in her. But also, she was getting tired of telling the story. Friends and neighbors came and talked to her about it, and it was getting old. So she thought this was the last interview she was going to do.

At ten to two, Anne with her crew pulled up in front of a little rundown shack. It had no paint on it, and the curtains were towels.

"My God, look at this place," Anne gasped under her breath.

Although the place was very clean and uncluttered, it was old and rickety. The house not only could use some paint, but a new roof as well. The old wood shingles were warped and bone dry from the hot dry summers and the harsh winters. They did have a small well-kept yard and a rather large garden. The big weeping willow was next to the back porch which had a little awning and deck. There was a little breakfast table and three chairs with a small bouquet of wild flowers sitting on it.

Patricia came out of the house with a pitcher of lemonade and glasses. She saw the big TV van pull up, and her heart jumped. "Well, here we go," she sighed, grabbed the tray and headed out the door. She couldn't have timed this better, for she had just finished with lunch and the cleanup.

Abe had left for the weekend to pick up some horses Thomas Pitt had purchased and wouldn't be back for a day or so. So Patricia and Paige were looking after things until he returned.

Anne stepped out of the passenger side of the van. She had an impressive and expensive cream leather jacket with fringe hanging down to her narrow waist. Her hair was parted at the side and combed straight down with curls at the bottom. She had no bangs so she tucked the excess hair behind her ear. She wore jeans and high-heeled suede cowboy boots to give herself a western look.

Patricia looked at her. Anne was a beautiful girl, a little overdressed, but everything about her said she was a professional and took her job seriously. Her makeup was perfect, her hair was perfect, her clothes, her walk. Suddenly Patricia felt underdressed in her nearly new jeans and her freshly pressed simple white blouse that she only wore on special occasions. Her blonde hair was French braided back and the wind had already blown strands out that swept silently across her face.

Anne looked at Patricia and thought, *She's plain.* But with an impressed voice she said, "Boy now, this is a cozy little place you have here. Are you Mrs. Cason?"

"Yes, I am. You can call me Patricia, that's what everyone does. So you are Anne? I am very glad to meet you." Patricia held out her calloused hand for Anne to shake with her soft well-groomed one.

Paige came running up from the barn as Jack and his co-worker, Scotty, started to set up. She had waited all day to see how the news was made.

"So, are you the girl with the wonder horse that does miraculous things?" Jack asked as they got acquainted.

"I 'spose I am," Paige answered questioningly. "I have the best horse ever born in these parts, if that is what you're asking."

"That is exactly what I asked," Jack replied, taking a sudden liking to this girl in a baseball cap and blue jeans.

"What's a girl like you doing out here in the desert? You should be in the movies or something. Don't you think so, Scotty?"

"Yes, I think she should, with those pretty blue eyes and everything." Scotty answered, only half interested.

"Tell you what," Jack leaned toward Paige, "we'll give you a debut, and if the public likes you and you make a million dollars in movies, you have to split it with us."

Paige looked at him questioningly. "But I don't want to be a movie star."

Jack was surprised. "Well what do you want to be?"

Paige's eyes lit up as she thought about it. "I want to go to college and become a horse specialist."

Jack was shocked. He had expected something extravagant, something a person could make lots of money at. "Not a movie star or lawyer?"

"Heck no. I want to always work with horses. So a horse veterinarian is what I'll be."

Jack looked at her and saw she was serious. "Well I suppose if you are going to dream, a person better dream big."

They talked and joked with her as they set everything up, and with her curiosity and inquisitive nature, she bubbled over with questions. They answered them and asked her some of their own. Like what she did for fun around here. They were fun and easygoing guys. Especially Jack—he had a disarming way about him that made her feel at ease right off the bat.

She thought Scotty was far more distant, but he smiled when she asked about what that thing-a-majigger or gadget was for. Paige enjoyed talking with them as her mom and the news lady got acquainted. Paige couldn't wait to take them down to the barn and show them the horses, especially Liberty. It was going to be great to see Libby on TV. She said goodbye to the guys and headed to the house.

Paige thought Anne was a nice lady, although she didn't seem to like dirt, and she was constantly trying to fix her hair because of the breeze that blew. Paige guessed she wanted to look good for the camera because she seemed to wear a lot of makeup, and her fingernails were longer than any Paige had ever seen.

11

After they took a tour of the little house and the camera crew saw the very basic lifestyle this family led, they sat on the porch to do part of the interview. Paige couldn't resist it any longer, so while the cameras were rolling she said, "I just can't help it, I have to know how you work with those fingernails so long?"

Anne was silent for a moment, hoping Jack would cut the camera, but he just panned a close-up to Anne and waited for a reply.

"Well what do you mean, Paige?" She stammered, trying to stall for a little time to think of a good professional reply.

"Well I've been watching you and you have to hold your pencil kind of awkward to write, and you can't pick up anything small. I don't think you could even weed the garden or saddle a horse with them that long. I was just curious, I've never seen fingernails that long before and I wondered what good they were."

Patricia looked at her daughter and stifled a smile as her face turned red. She glanced down at her own calloused hands, her fingernails trimmed short, and back at Anne's beautifully groomed ones. Then she slid hers under the table.

Anne was silent for a minute. That was too long because Paige had something else that was bothering her and it had a very simple solution. And now that Paige was on a roll, she couldn't be stopped.

"I also know how you can fix your hair problem, too."

"Excuse me." Anne was floored at this child's boldness and it was really irritating her.

"Well," Paige said innocently, "I know that your hair is very important to you, and with this wind it's hard to keep out of your eyes. What I do is wear a baseball cap. I could go get you one if you like."

Jack couldn't hold back a snicker as it escaped his mouth. This didn't happen to Anne, the Goddess, very often and especially not by a teen. Boy, Anne had this coming to her for a long time. He could tell that she didn't think this was funny though, and he didn't want her to lose her temper. He knew Anne's looks were everything to her, and she hated to be made fun of in any way. He learned a long time ago never to cross her because it seemed she was always out for revenge. She either had it her way or no way.

Patricia could sense the tension, although she couldn't see it in Anne's face, and said, "Why don't we go down to the barn and see Liberty and maybe watch Paige ride?"

Jack replied for the now-furious Anne as he cut the camera. "I think that would be a great idea. I heard earlier today that someone couldn't wait to show me her horse." He winked at Paige. "I have to see this fantastic animal."

They got up from the table and started off the porch. Jack thought of his own daughter at home—how much she wanted a horse and how little time he was able to spend with her since he was traveling so much lately. He almost felt homesick.

He watched Paige jump off the porch and say as she raced down the well-worn path, "I'll go get her saddled."

Jack turned toward Patricia. "It would be great to turn back the clock and have that much spunk again."

Patricia smiled back. "Yep it would."

"I could think of a million things I would change if I could," Jack sighed.

"You know, Jack, sometimes I think the same thing," Patricia said earnestly. "But then I wouldn't have what I do now, if I did."

Jack was puzzled for a second thinking, *What do you have?* Then he understood.

Anne was walking behind them on the gravel path, watching carefully where to put her high-heeled boots. She didn't want to scuff the suede or step in anything that came from any animal.

They approached the barn, and Paige came out leading Libby. The filly almost reflected the sun, her mane shimmering a flaxen white and her coat a deep rich gold. Her white blaze ran down her flawless face down to the soft pink skin of her nose. Paige had a grin on her face from ear to ear.

Paige walked up to Jack. She seemed to like him best out of everyone who came for the interview. "This is the best friend I ever had," she said with pride as she stroked Libby's neck. "Libby, this is Jack and he's going to take pictures of you today so you can be on TV."

Jack reached out his hand slowly. Libby smelled him and dropped her head to be petted. Meanwhile Jack was racking his brain, trying to remember what he was taught to do while being around a horse. When he was a child, he had only been around them twice that he remembered and once they were in a circus. *This horse is huge for a child to handle,* he thought. He couldn't imagine this girl training it.

Anne finally caught up with them after she had taken such care in walking up the path. Feeling as if Jack had taken over her job, she stepped in between Jack and the filly and threw her hand into the air to pet the horse's face. Libby pulled back, throwing her head up. Paige settled her, talking in soft tones.

Anne was startled, yet remembered what she read somewhere—to show the horse who was boss and show no fear. She approached her again as if she knew how to handle horses. Just as she was about to touch her, Libby raised her head and snorted, blowing horse mucus, stall dust, and hay into Anne's face and onto her cream leather fringe jacket. She snorted again and shook her head before Anne had a chance to retreat. Anne jumped back, looked down at her coat in shock, and felt the wetness of horse mucus on her face. She thought she was going to vomit.

Jack was quiet, looking off over the hills with his face away from Anne. He couldn't contain himself any longer and said, as soberly as he could, "I'll be back in a minute."

He started to walk away and laugh at the same time. He

made it about five feet before he couldn't take it any longer. He doubled over and burst into laughter like he had never laughed before. Paige and Patricia smiled as they watched him, then with laughter being contagious, they both started to laugh simultaneously. The three of them laughed until tears ran down their faces.

In between laughter and gulps of air Jack said, "Did you see her face?"

Patricia chimed in, "Fire when ready, Captain."

Paige replied, between gulps of laughter, "She was loaded and right on target. Ready, aim, fire! Now that's what I call an eye opener."

They all laughed until their sides hurt.

The laughter echoed in Anne's head as she stood there dumbstruck about what just happened. She had to think of a professional way to act. Her job came first, revenge would come later.

She forced a smile across her lips and said, "Well maybe I need to change my brand of perfume."

Jack heard the sarcasm in her voice, and his laugh quieted down. The fun was over and she was all business. He straightened, took a deep breath, sighed, wiped the tears from his eyes, and looked at Anne. He could tell she was furious, but only because he had seen that look before. On the outside she looked happy, but behind those eyes of hers, Jack knew from experience she was conjuring up a devious plan to get back at this family. But he didn't know how to stop it.

"I am sorry, Ms. Rhymes, I'll go get a towel and see if we can clean you up a bit," Patricia said with a half-grin on her face, yet realizing that Anne's jacket was probably worth more than her whole wardrobe. "I'll be back in a minute." She left for the house.

Paige stepped onto Libby. Their movements were flawless as they loped and jogged around the barnyard. Paige's hair flowed in time with Libby's mane as they became one with each other. Anne was ready to go back to the house and finish the interview.

Jack was mesmerized by the beauty and flow of human and animal—how each could read the other's mind and work so gracefully together. He saw how Libby always had an ear cocked back toward Paige, waiting to feel what she wanted next. Jack had never been so moved watching horse and rider, never before had he thought of them as a team. He was told it was a control thing—people like to control the horse and tell it were to go. But seeing Paige and Libby, they were a team, part of one another, neither taking advantage of the other.

Patricia returned with a damp towel and a dry one, not knowing for sure which one Anne would want but hoping it might help clean up a little of the mess.

Paige stopped Libby next to the small audience, and Jack asked, "Is that how you rode when you saved Samantha?"

"No." Paige stopped Libby with a subtle hand movement. "I was getting her ready for the trailer ride home." She thought back at Mr. Greenly wanting to buy Libby. A twinge of anger crossed her mind then vanished as the sequence of events played out in her memory. "Here, I will show you though. I was brushing her when I heard the balloon pop." She jumped off Libby, pulled off the saddle and bridle, and slipped on Libby's halter and lead. She tied the end of the lead to the halter under Libby's jaw, just as she had done the day of the accident, and swung up on Libby's back again as she walked Jack through her memory.

Anne looked at Patricia. "How can you let her do that? Do you realize how many kids each year get killed doing dangerous stunts like that?"

"What do you mean stunts?" Patricia looked confused.

Jack nodded in agreement. "Don't you get a little nervous letting her ride without a helmet and without a saddle? What about safety?"

"Paige does this every day. It's just like you stepping behind the wheel of a rig or a car. You never know if you'll get in an accident or not. I don't think it's something you really think about, but it could happen. It's a chance you'll take to get where you're going. I wouldn't make her stop just because it could happen, just like you won't stop driving a car." She paused for a moment. "This is the only time I can say that Paige is equal to this world, and where she is the happiest, too. We might not be able to buy many fancy things, but this girl has what few will ever have—freedom, common sense, and choice. Not necessarily with material things, but with morals and instinct. She knows what she's capable of and if not, then she'll figure it out."

"Look, Jack," Paige said, "we can go right." Paige slightly pressed her leg against Libby's side. Libby willingly moved to the right. "Or we can go left." Paige shifted a little to the right and Libby moved sideways to the left. "We can back up," she said. Again with a subtle movement and almost like magic, Libby began shuffling her feet backward. "We can go fast." With a flicker of an ear, Libby lifted herself into a nice canter. "Or we can go slow," she said, with an undetected signal. As if Libby understood the words, Libby slowed to a walk and then stopped right beside Jack. "Libby is my legs as my legs are hers, we can open gates, go up stairs, or cross the creek. We are one and the same, Libby and me."

"You can open a gate?" Jack was a little confused.

"Sure." Paige was surprised at the curiosity but walked Libby to the corral gate, leaned over, flipped the latch. Libby stepped sideways to push the gate open, stepped though, then helped push the gate closed and Paige latched it.

"I'll be darned," Jack sighed.

The cameras were still rolling as Paige rode, and Jack was deeply moved by how this family could live in this day and age. Didn't they know those things didn't mean diddley-squat in the real world?

Paige rode up and slipped off Libby's back, then untied the lead line from the halter. "What do you think, Jack?

Isn't she the neatest thing you ever saw?"

"Paige," he said, "I have never seen anything as beautiful as you and Liberty Bell." He said it with complete honesty.

Libby stepped up to the fence and poked her nose toward Anne. Anne stepped back, a little weary of what might happen, then cautiously reached out and with her fore and middle fingertips touched the velvet soft nose.

"I think she likes you, Ms. Rhymes," Paige said, hoping the little incident earlier was forgotten.

"I hope so," Anne said without any passion in her voice.

Paige took Libby to the barn, put her in her stall, and locked the stall door, giving her a soft stroke down her face. "See ya, little lady, be back in a while."

They started back to the house to finish the interview. This time Anne decided to be first as they walked. They weren't going to leave her out of the spotlight again. *This is my story and I want it done my way*, she thought to herself.

As she walked, she could only devote her attention to where to put her feet so she wouldn't scuff her boots or step in anything green. Scotty was close on her heels, then Paige, then Patricia and Jack following in suit, waiting patiently for her to pick her way through. She was so busy with herself she didn't notice the beautiful scenery all around.

Paige saw Jack looking toward the Blue Mountains and she said, "If you look at the highest peak over there, Jack, you can see an Indian brave laying face up. That high peak is his nose. See his forehead and his headdress?"

Jack stopped and looked, trying to visualize what she was saying. "You're pulling my leg, Paige, I don't see an Indian."

"Look," Paige said as she brought her hand up, as if to outline the sculpture entrenched in the rugged mountain walls.

Jack squatted next to the girl's small frame. As she traced the Indian's face in the air, he focused on where she was pointing until he saw it.

"Oh my God, it *is* an Indian's head, isn't it? Look at the detail!" He was shocked.

There, etched in the top of the mountain was an Indian in full headdress—his forehead, sunken eyes, nose, and chin, facing the sky in a sleeping manner. It made the hair on the back of his neck stand up.

"How did you find him, Paige?"

"Papa showed me one evening, just as the sun was going down behind his head. I wish you could meet him, Jack, I think he would like you."

"It sounds like he is quite a man, Paige, quite a man." Jack repeated.

12

Anne stood on the porch under the old weeping willow tree and looked back down the trail from which she just came. She saw Jack squatted down next to Paige as Paige was tracing something in the air. Patricia was standing behind them looking in the same direction. She sat down at the table and watched as Paige moved her hands and talked of something and Jack listened intently to her story. Anne listened to the silence, and the aloneness. All she heard was the wind blowing through the tree above her head. She could hear no cars, no screaming children, no hustle or push around her. She felt as if she might get swallowed up in this nothingness. What if she broke a leg out here or needed an ambulance, how would they know she needed help? What could people do out here in this isolated hole that has nothing to offer except dirt and wind?

"Can you believe these people, Scotty?" Anne said in disgust. "A black and white TV and a rotary phone. These people live in the ice age."

"I am here just to film, I really don't care how they live," Scotty replied.

"For your first job, I think you and I are going to get along great. Keep up the good work."

Then she turned back and looked at Patricia. She knew now that Patricia had to have put on a fabricated smile to seem happy to live here, only because she knew that John

Greenly was going to give them something big for saving the life of his daughter. Now all she had to do was figure how to get the story she was wanting. She could feel the dirt attacking her face and the wind grinding it in, making it dry and gritty. If she didn't hurry and get this story over with, all the beauty cream and soap in the world would never be able to touch the grime she was feeling. She would look like she was thirty by the time she turned twenty-six if she stayed in this sun much longer. She looked back at Jack and the two females standing in the elements. *They are so stupid,* she thought, *don't they know sun causes skin cancer? Don't they read any health magazines or keep up on the health news?* Thinking of health, she felt as if she needed to wash her hands and face. She did pet that stupid horse, and it blew snot on her too. She had read somewhere that animals carried germs and diseases in areas such as petting zoos and similar places. The thought made her skin crawl and her stomach turn again. She needed to get some handy wipes or something.

Anne looked down the path again and she couldn't figure it out. Jack always seemed to be the center of attention with this family. "Jack, come on, we have a lot to cover yet," she called down to him. Her patience was wearing thin, and it was becoming obvious in her voice.

Jack turned and looked at Anne sitting on the porch. She looked so out of place in this setting. Her fair skin looked pale and sickly compared to the two ladies standing next to him. Their skin glowed with health and vibrancy, their faces tanned and eyes shining with natural life.

"The Queen has spoken," Jack said. "After you, my ladies," he bowed toward Paige, extending his right arm out and his left across his abdomen so Paige and Patricia could pass by like royalty.

Paige giggled, "Thank you, kind sir." She passed and headed undeterred to the house.

They positioned themselves on the porch and the cameras started rolling again as Anne asked more questions about Paige's life.

"So, Paige, do you want to go to college?"

"Yes I do, I would really like to be a horse specialist, or I would like to teach kids how to ride. I don't know if I have to go to college to do that or not, but it's something I'd like to do."

"Well, where do you plan to get the money to go to college? Do you realize what kind of money it takes and how long you will have to be in school to get a degree in animal science?" Anne asked in a quiet tone.

"Well," Paige started, "I don't know for sure how much it will cost, but Mom and Papa said they could help me out, and I have already started saving for it. Anyways I have a few more years before I can go, so I'm sure I can save enough if I work hard."

Patricia started in, a little concerned where this was leading. "As Paige becomes certain on what she wants to do, whether it be going to college or teaching students, Abe and I will support and back her with everything we have. And if we don't have it we will find a way to get it."

Anne in a nonchalant tone said, "What exactly is, 'it,' Patricia? Money?"

Patricia's face turned flush with embarrassment, "Well yes I guess, I mean we will go to great lengths to see our daughter get the education she needs to be successful at her own dreams."

Anne cut in, "Paige, I heard that you and Samantha were never friends and that you had threatened to hit her the day of the show. Is that correct?"

Paige now felt her face go red as her temperature rose. What? She didn't say that. How did Anne know they had words? She hadn't even said anything to her mom. Being caught off guard, she tried explaining to defend her actions, "She wouldn't leave me alone. She kept insulting my filly and the way Libby was acting. She made me feel so small and worthless, I had to say something, I was tired of being treated like I didn't belong. I told her that I would make her move if she didn't get out of my way, but nothing more."

Patricia was shocked, "Paige, why didn't you tell me?"

Paige looked at her mother, "Well after I told her that, she left me alone, then later came back and apologized."

Anne had to hide a smile, "So, Patricia, you didn't know the two girls were rivals? And you also didn't know that Paige wanted to get back at Samantha that same day? We have an eyewitness on camera who said he heard Paige say, that she planned on getting Samantha back for insulting her horse. Tell me," Anne continued, "do you know anything about your daughter?"

"That ain't true!" Paige blurted out.

Anne continued without any hesitation. She was getting the response she wanted, and the cameras rolled on.

"We also have other people stating that when Samantha went to apologize to you, you threatened her."

Paige was silent. Patricia looked at her daughter, having a hard time comprehending everything being said.

"Are you saying, Patricia, that you don't know what your daughter is doing behind your back? And you know nothing of the little scam she is pulling." Anne paused just long enough to let the doubt start to creep into Patricia's mind.

Patricia looked at Anne silently. "What are you getting at, Ms. Rhymes? I thought you were here to interview the bravery of our daughter. Instead you sit here and insult us."

"All I'm getting at, Patricia, is that your family is sitting here at your little isolated ranch, all happy and bubbling over, inviting reporters over to cover your daughter and wonder horse, while there is a little girl in the hospital, badly beaten and bruised who will probably never be the same, and you're getting all the glory. Then," Anne continued, "you sit here and tell me that you would do anything to get your daughter through college. It sounds like a setup to me."

"Get off our ranch! All of you! Get off our ranch!" Patricia hollered. "Get off now!"

Jack was so dumb struck he didn't know what to do. He had never seen Anne hit with such venom. He had no idea what was in her mind at this interview, and now it was all on tape. He stumbled off the porch with his camera in hand, and Anne followed. He put the camera in the van and got in the driver seat. Anne and Scotty stepped in the passenger side, and they headed down the dusty road. Jack looked straight ahead, not knowing for sure what to say to this mad woman beside him.

Anne started laughing, "Did you see their faces? Now who has the last laugh, you little witch. That'll teach you for letting your horse blow snot all over me. Tell me what I can do with my long fingernails or my hair. You pissed off the wrong girl." She paused for a second, then said, "Now let's just put the icing on the cake. Jack, I want to go back to the motel and get this horse stench off of me. Then you can take me to where John Greenly lives. We need to get some footage."

Jack looked straight ahead not acknowledging her commands. He had a decision to make and it was going to be a tough one. His whole career depended on it. By the time he had made it into town, his mind was made up. He pulled up to the motel, parked, turned off the ignition, and tossed the keys to Anne.

"What are you doing, Jack?" Anne was surprised. "You

going to meet me here in a half hour? I need some footage of John Greenly's place."

"Not from me you don't. Anne, I quit! I will not destroy this family."

"Jack, you know you can't look at it that way. You can't go soft on me now, we have been together for almost a year. Remember, Jack, it's nothing personal." Anne was searching for some idea to hold Jack to his job.

"Nothing personal, do you hear yourself, Anne?" Jack stumbled, "Nothing personal, to you maybe, but it's very personal to this family. And you're making it personal for yourself too." His emotions started to get the best of him. "I can't do that to this family, they haven't done anything wrong." Jack's voice started to waver. "After this story is aired, you continue to look for another and forget that there will be a family who is left to pick up the pieces of their life from family, neighbors, and friends. Bringing in speculation and doubt on their integrity in front of the whole town, hell the whole state where they live. Who the hell do you think you are, Anne?"

"That is not up to us to decide, Jack. We run the story as we see it and let the public be the jurors."

"You don't get it do you, Anne? All you're seeing is the recognition you'll get. You don't care if the story is true or not. What about the lives you'll be affecting?"

"Don't give me a sob story, Jack, it's not like you've never done this before. And anyway, you know as well as I do that they're going to take John Greenly for a lot of money he doesn't need to lose. And John is going to feel sorry enough to give it to them."

Jack got out of the van and slammed the door, "Greed has you around the throat, Anne, and one day it'll choke you." He walked to his room.

She thought for a moment, "Well, Scotty, looks like you just got a promotion. Meet me here in a half hour, then we'll go to Greenly's place and get some footage."

Scotty crawled in the driver seat and started the engine.

13

After the day was finished for Anne and all the footage she needed was taken, she soaked in a hot bath for a half hour trying to get the farm smell off of her, put fresh makeup on, did her hair to perfection, and headed to the hospital to see John Greenly.

He was sitting in Samantha's room, holding her hand as she slept.

Anne tapped at the door.

"John?" she said.

He looked up at the beautiful young woman standing just outside the door. Her blonde hair hung down perfectly, settling just at her shoulders. The pearl necklace draped loosely around her neck and the black dress she decided to wear curved around her body, coming down just above her knees which complemented her already long legs and enhanced her feminine quality.

"Well, Ms. Rhymes. What are you doing here this evening?" John said in his natural deep tones.

"Well, I was going out to get something to eat, and I was concerned about your daughter, so I thought I would stop by to see how she was on my way through."

He walked up to her and quietly said, "She is doing much better. She should be out in a couple of days, although she is going to need constant attention for a while with both of her arms in casts." He stepped into the hall and closed the door behind them.

She stepped out of the doorway as he approached and leaned up against the wall. "That's so good to hear. I've thought of her all day and of how this accident is going to affect her whole life."

She could smell the cologne he was wearing as he passed by. His t-shirt was snug against his build, and his tanned face and square jaw tantalized her.

"Well I guess I had better be going." She knew that if she acted like she was going to leave, he would ask her to stay.

But John didn't. Anne stalled expecting him to call her back, like every other man she met.

When it didn't happen, she turned back, "John, do you know where there is a good place to eat, some place quiet, where a lady could have a glass of wine?"

John looked at her and felt an urge he hadn't felt in a long time. Then he shook it off. *She's a girl, for God's sake,* he told himself. He put his hand on the doorknob.

"The Geiser is a pretty nice place, on Main Street, second light on your left, corner building," he said, as he started back into the room where his daughter lay peacefully sleeping.

Anne came back to the doorway, "Would you like to have dinner with me? I really don't want to eat alone and you could probably use some fresh air."

John looked at her. She had leaned against the doorframe with her shoulder and head touching it and her long legs crossed at the ankles. *Well,* he thought, *it's nine thirty, and*

Samantha will sleep the rest of the night. He also hadn't eaten since that morning. It also would be nice to have company for dinner, and it was better than sitting in the empty house eating alone.

"Ms. Rhymes, it would be nice to have dinner with a lady such as you."

He escorted Anne out of the hospital. The night air sent a chilly little breeze up John's spine. He walked silently down the walkway, touching the metal handrail. It was cold on his fingertips. The night air was cool and brisk. Breathing deeply he filled his lungs with it, trying to get rid of the hospital smell that seemed stuck on his clothes. The unforgettable odor seemed to cling to his skin, like a haunting nightmare. He breathed in again, lifting his head to the sky. The stars were dimly lit and clear. He looked to the moon, full and bright.

They walked to his Cadillac, and John opened the passenger side door for Anne to enter. She glided in, and he carefully shut the door. The interior smelled of leather mixed with a new car smell. Anne breathed in deeply, appreciating John's taste of quality.

John slid in the driver side, put the key in the ignition, and turned it on. The dash lights came on along with a soft ding that repeated a few times as a reminder to buckle the seatbelts. John reached over and pulled his seat belt on out of habit. He looked over at Anne for a moment, and she smiled at him. He put the car in reverse and pulled out of the parking space.

14

They entered the Geiser Grande and a waiter walked up, "Well, Mr. Greenly, nice to see you."

"Thank you."

The waiter escorted them to a table lit with a candle and seated Anne.

John said, "The lady would like some wine, please. Could you get your best Chardonnay?"

The waiter left the menus and disappeared behind the double swinging doors. He returned a few minutes later with a full bottle. "This is the best Oak aged Chardonnay in the house," the waiter said as he pulled the cork and poured some in John's glass so he could approve the choice.

John tasted it, held it for a moment, and enjoyed the well-roundedness of it, tasting the complexity and buttery smoothness of it with a hint of vanilla. He closed his eyes. "This is very good, thank you."

The waiter nodded and poured some in Anne's wine glass. She nodded and smiled but said nothing.

Dinner went smoothly for John. He thought of how nice it was to have a woman across from him as he ate and how easy it was to make idle chit chat with her.

"So, John," Anne said as she sipped from her second glass of wine, "how long have you lived here in Baker City?"

"All of my life," he answered. "My parents and grandparents were all raised here. Eastern Oregon is where

I belong, I suppose. I have no inkling to move anywhere else."

"Oh really? Being a reporter and everything it entails, I find I'm never really home for any length of time. I think I enjoy moving around, always going on another story and always finding new areas to see. But none of them were ever better than Portland." Anne changed the subject, "How old is Samantha?"

His face changed as he looked at Anne, "She will be sixteen in July. She is quite an independent kid for her age. She has so many things she wants to do, and with her mother gone, I have a heck of a time getting things right most of the time. Now with this accident, I kind of feel like I should have done more, but I don't know for sure what that might be. How does a father raise a little girl through her teenage years? How does he know what to say and do at certain times?"

He looked at Anne, then apologized. "I'm sorry, Anne, I just got caught up for a minute."

"Oh that's fine, sometimes you just need someone to talk to," she replied.

The candlelight caressed her features, her beautiful smile when he said something silly, and her serious visage when he discussed his daughter. This was so very nice.

Dinner came and went, and the bottle of wine was gone. John had two glasses, and he felt warm and comfortable.

As he escorted her back to his car, she had draped her arm into his, "This has been a very lovely evening, John. I am ever so glad you decided to have dinner with me. I didn't mean for you to pay, though. I will have to figure out some way to repay you."

"My pleasure, Anne, no need, I really enjoyed this evening. It was a real treat to accompany you."

He stopped at the passenger side of his car, opened the door, and stepped aside to let her enter. Anne stepped in front of him. She put her hand on his shoulder, then slowly brushed it along his chest.

"I mean it, John. I would really like to pay you back." She turned her head up and tipped it to one side and gently pulled him down to her awaiting lips.

John hadn't felt a woman's touch in a very long time and his body responded to her willingness. He bent down and touched her lips with his, lightly at first, then as a rush overtook him and he no longer contained himself, he wrapped his arms around her narrow waist and brought her fully to his body. She pulled away from him, breathless, slid into the car, and moved toward the center of the seat. John climbed in the driver side and pulled from the curb.

"Take me to your place," Anne said, her breath was hot and close to his ear. She ran her hand up to his thigh.

John was having a hard time keeping his mind in the road. How long had it been since he felt like this? His heart thumping in his chest, he felt a warm sensation go through his body. He closed his eyes a moment enjoying the feeling for a brief second. He turned and looked at her young face gazing back at him. Then he suddenly turned to ice. He pulled off to the side of the road, turned off the ignition, pulled the keys out, and got out of the car.

"Where are you going, John?" Anne asked, surprised at his sudden change of mood. Anne quickly looked in the mirror and checked her lipstick and hair before she got out of the car and went after him.

Oh Jesus, what was I thinking? This is just a young girl, only half my age, he thought to himself. *I will not let this happen.* He looked back at the car and the girl getting out and walked back to her.

"Anne, you are a very beautiful young woman, but I can't do this, not with you. Get in the car, Anne. I am taking you back to the hospital to get your rig. It's been a lovely evening, and I enjoyed it immensely, but it won't end like this."

He got in and started the car, Anne sat next to the door, looking insulted. Not a word was said all the way back to the hospital

When he pulled up next to her van, she didn't wait for him to get the door for her. She stepped out. He leaned against the steering wheel for a second and took a deep breath then got out.

Anne looked across the hood of his car and said, almost amused, "You know. I have never been turned down by a man before, John. I don't know if I should be insulted or flattered."

"You are a beautiful young woman, Anne. Don't waste yourself."

He left her standing there, pulled around to the main entrance of the hospital, and parked the car. He went in to say goodnight to Samantha who lay sleeping peacefully in the large hospital bed. He squatted down next to her, grabbed her small childlike hand in his, and gave it a kiss. "God, please make sense of this. Give Samantha a chance to walk again."

Anne drove back to the motel. She sat in the driver seat, contemplating what happened this evening. She had never met a man such as John Greenly, with his gentle manner and striking looks. She thought of her story. She would make sure that family wouldn't receive a dime from him. By the time she was done with them, Samantha would look like she was the victim of more than a horse accident.

She went to her room, changed into sweats and a t-shirt, and rang Scotty's room. It was midnight, but she didn't care. They would have the story done by dawn.

"Scotty, get up. We have a lot of work to do."

They cut and edited all night until she had the story flawless. In three hours, they had taken four hours of taping and cut it down into a five-minute story.

"It is perfect, Scotty. Now let's run the whole thing one more time and see what it looks like as a whole story."

First, they showed the Casons' house, how it stood all alone out in the middle of the hills, and then Paige riding her Libby around the corral. A close-up of her smiling face and her mother, Patricia, smiling at her as she rode. Then you heard Anne's voice,

"This happy family should be happy, for their daughter isn't the one lying in a hospital bed. This young girl is supposed to be the one who saved Samantha Greenly's life at a horse show here in Baker City. But is there a side of the story that is not being told? We went out to the Cason place to find out, and this is what we heard."

Then Anne cut to the part where Paige said she threatened to hit Samantha and cussed at her when Samantha tried to apologize.

Scotty zoomed in on Patricia as she looked shocked at what her daughter had done. Then Anne put in where Patricia said they would do anything to get their daughter through college followed by the footage of Patricia kicking them off of their place. Anne then cut to the part of the gas attendant's comment about how funny it was that first Paige cussed out Samantha then two hours later saved her. Then Anne added in a few more people with their points of view that would create the perfect picture of Paige scheming this whole thing up and Samantha a helpless victim. She ended the story with a quick scene of Samantha in the hospital bed alone, badly bruised and beaten with her arms and leg in casts. She divided the screen, one side with the Cason shack and the other side with the Greenly mansion, her voiceover, "So, did this poor girl really save Samantha Greenly? I guess this is one way to go from rags to riches, in a matter of speaking."

"That's it, Scotty. We got it." Anne said, as she stretched and yawned. "Why don't you get this mess cleaned up and we'll call it a day." She looked at her watch, it was a quarter to four. "We'll get a couple hours of sleep before we start making phone calls." She stepped out of the van.

"What do you want me to do with the extra tapes that we took the footage from?" Scotty asked, a little irritated that he had to do the clean-up himself.

Anne turned to face him. "Put them in a box, and I'll discard it when I get back home. I have all the footage I want right here." She patted her oversized purse that hung from her shoulder. Then she left the van with Scotty inside to continue cleaning.

Scotty grabbed the four tapes he and Jack shot the previous two days, threw them in a box, and set it beside the van's sliding door. He then filled a paper sack with Styrofoam cups, candy wrappers, and other garbage that lay strewn around the van and set it next to the box of tapes. He double-checked all the equipment making sure everything was off and turned out the lights before he left. As he stepped out of the van, he accidentally kicked the box and sack of garbage over, and they tumbled into the parking lot.

"Well hell." Scotty mumbled to himself as he started picking up the garbage and tapes once again. As he picked up the last of the tapes, he saw a dumpster to his left, behind a restaurant about fifty yards away. He thought to himself, *Why wait until we get back home to throw the tapes away?* He grabbed the box and the sack of garbage and walked to the dumpster. He lifted the lid and a pungent stench slapped him in the face. He threw the box and the sack of garbage in, closing the lid quickly. The smell of garbage and rotten food almost made him gag. *Someone must have thrown something dead in there,* he thought. He shook his head then started to his motel room. He couldn't wait to feel the pillow under his head.

15

Jack had been waiting patiently all night. When he left Anne earlier that day, he requested another room next to the parking lot and hung a do not disturb sign on his door. He then went out, rented a car, grabbed some fried chicken and potato salad, and made himself at home in his newly assigned room.

When Anne returned from dinner, he waited until the coast was clear and quietly made it down to the van and unlocked it with his spare key. He rummaged through everything looking for the tapes but couldn't find them anywhere.

"Damn, Anne, sometimes you are almost too good," he said to himself. He figured it would be a long shot to find the tapes just carelessly left in the van, but he knew he at least had to look. Knowing Anne as he did, though, he knew they were in the bag she always carried with her.

He heard someone coming. *Great,* he thought sarcastically, it was Anne and Scotty. *Don't they ever sleep?* He left quietly, closing the door with a slight click, stepping into the bushes in front of the van. His heart was pounding. *I would never make it as a thief. I would die of a heart attack or hyperventilate*, he thought as he struggled to control his breathing and get his heart rate back to normal.

"You know, Scotty," he heard Anne say as they approached the van. "I've been giving this a lot of thought, and I really think this story will be worth something if we play our cards right. I mean I won't burn my bridges with my job now, but I think I found my niche in life. Really," she rambled on, "to actually create something out of nothing gives me an adrenaline rush, you know?"

Scotty was quiet as he attempted to unlock the van, still trying to get his eyes to focus after being dragged out of bed.

Jack sat in the bushes until he knew the coast was clear, then silently headed to his room. He knew this was going to be a long night, and he made himself as comfortable as possible sitting in the chair by the window in his room. He sat for hours, waiting and watching. His mind drifted to his family and how they would always whine when he had to travel, sometimes for weeks at a time. They just didn't understand, this was how he paid their bills and mortgage. He tried to explain it to them, but now he understood what they were trying to tell him.

He started nodding off, so he went to the bathroom and splashed water in his face trying to fight it off. *Keep awake*, he told himself as his eyelids got heavier and heavier. Then he nodded off into a dream of his daughter riding Liberty Bell, loping past him, waving and smiling as she rode effortlessly just as Paige had done the previous day with her long hair blowing in the wind, the color on her face and the look of youth and vibrancy radiating from her. All of a sudden, the ground ended and they loped off the edge of the earth without a care in the world. They just floated off and disappeared into space or somewhere beyond. He couldn't believe it. He ran after them screaming. They had just passed through his life and were gone. He jolted himself awake breathing hard, feeling empty and alone. He looked at the clock and it was a quarter to four. He picked up the phone and started to dial his home number. He just needed to hear his wife's voice. He glanced out the window as he was dialing the last digits and saw Anne leaving the van.

He hung up the phone and saw the bag swinging from her shoulder. She patted it as she talked to Scotty. Now he knew the tapes were inside her bag and Scotty must still be inside the van because she continued talking in that direction and the lights inside were still on. He sat racking his brain, trying to figure a way to get his hands on those tapes.

He looked up at the ceiling, "God, if you are up there, give me a sign." He prayed, "How do I get those tapes?" He felt pretty stupid trying to make amends with someone or something he hadn't talked to since he was a kid. "I've always been a fairly honest man, God, but right now I'm feeling really desperate. I need to get those tapes!"

Jack looked down as he saw Scotty leave the van and kick something out. Then Scotty bent down and started to pick up something black and shiny. Jack jumped out of his chair and did a jig!

"Yes! Yes! Yes!" He said with a burst of air coming out triumphantly. "The tapes, the bitch doesn't have them!" Then suddenly he looked at the ceiling and said, "Sorry," then corrected himself. He started to dance and sang a song of triumph, "Anne doesn't have them, Anne doesn't have them!" He sang and danced around his room for a moment then peeked out the window and watched Scotty throw them in the dumpster and walk to his room, shaking his head.

Jack waited five minutes before he went to the dumpster to retrieve the tapes. He lifted the lid and the stench overtook him in an instant. He let the lid drop with a crash as he gulped for air. *Man, someone should clean this thing out.* He opened it again, trying to hold his breath. The sides were caked with rotten food and grease, which combined with the smell of fermented dough. He saw the box in the middle of the dumpster. He closed the lid and took a few gulps of fresh air. Then he lifted the lid again holding his breath and leaned in as far as he could. He grabbed the box, took out the tapes, and threw the box back in. It fell upside down back in the middle of the dumpster.

He then headed to his room and glanced through each tape to make sure they were the right ones. His next move was to call his boss, Steve, at home. The phone rang seven times before the groggy voice of a man answered.

"Hello?" the male voice said, not yet awake.

"Steve, this is Jack, over here in Baker City. I'm sorry for calling so early, but I think we have a problem."

"What is so important it couldn't wait until I got into the office this morning, Jack? Do you have any idea what time it is?"

"Yes, sir, I do. That's why I'm calling so early. I think Anne has gone off her rocker. I have a story here I think you need to see."

After sketching out the situation, he hung up the phone. Then he dialed his home number to talk to his wife.

She answered in three rings. "Hello," she said, her voice was worried. She wondered who would be calling at this time in the morning.

He was so happy to hear her voice. It calmed him and made him realize he was doing the right thing. He asked a couple of favors of her after he briefly explained the situation.

Before hanging up the phone he said, "Honey, I love you."

Clair was silent a minute, stunned, then said, "Well, I love you too. Be careful coming home today, alright?"

"I promise," he said, then hung up the phone.

He jumped into the shower to revive himself, shaved, put on some clean clothes, and grabbed his suitcase. On his way out, he left the motel key in the room and shut the door. He jumped in his rental car and headed for Portland. He pulled onto the freeway at four fifty-five in the morning.

16

Anne woke up at twenty to nine. She had a lot of work cut out for herself, so she dragged her tired body out of bed and headed in for a cold shower. As the cold water hit her, she thought of the previous night—of John Greenly and the kind of life she could have with his kind of money. Maybe she was a little too forceful last night. Maybe she would call him when she got home. She knew with a little persuasion he would fall for her. Every man did. He was such a gentleman, and she liked his morals—a small town man she knew she could trust when she was out of town doing other stories. She would have John Greenly wrapped around her finger, and he would be so blind, he wouldn't know what hit him. She felt a surge of confidence run through her as she thought through the little scheme in her head.

She called Scotty and they made a list of the people they would call. First was Jack. She would deal with him herself. First, she needed to apologize and ask him if there were any hard feelings. She knew he left yesterday and would be home by now. She had to make sure he wouldn't let her boss know about the story they were doing. She thought all Steve knew was they were broken down, which only took fifteen minutes to fix. There was a kid and horse story, and he didn't have to know any more than that. She could start creating the story, maybe she could find a couple of news producers that might be interested, then she could dump ole Steve on his butt. He would really kick himself for not treating her with respect and giving her the big jobs she deserved.

She was thinking all of this as Jack's phone was ringing. Jack's wife answered, "Hello?"

"Hi. This is Anne. Is Jack home?" Anne asked as if this woman was always in the way of Jack's work.

"No he isn't, Anne, I thought he was with you. He called the other day and said that you were on another story and he would be a few days late."

"Oh, well yeah, we were. But he left yesterday, and I figured he went home." Anne was stumbling through her words.

"You don't know where his is?" Clair commanded. "Why didn't he call? When did he leave? I wish he would call and let me in on what's going on," she lied.

Anne was shocked yet satisfied that Jack was going to get an earful when he did get home. *Teach him for leaving me,* she thought as she answered Clair's questions.

"He left about three yesterday afternoon," she said hoping to stir a few emotions.

Clair was playing her role well. It was kind of fun deceiving that little witch. She never liked her in the first place, especially since she ran around the country working with her husband.

Anne had a funny feeling running up her spine. "Scotty,

grab your bags and get ready to go. I have one more call to make, and we'll do the rest of the business at home."

She dialed Steve's office, and the secretary put her through instantly.

"Hey, Steve, this is Anne, how are things going in my home town?" She asked in a chipper voice. "We got the part for the van and the boys have us up and running, so we'll be home today."

"That's really good to hear, Anne. I have another job I want you to do when you get here, so the sooner the better. This is going to make a real change in your career. I hope you are ready for it." Steve's voice was eager, and it surprised her.

"Well I have been ready ever since you hired me, Steve. It's about time you let me do something big." The sarcasm was obvious, even though she laughed through the phone, "I would be thrilled. I have big plans for the future."

"I am glad you have a lot of drive because that's what we need on this next job. I'm assigning you as lead, if you would like to accept."

"You bet I would. God, this is great!" Anne said with the excitement running through her body and coming out in her voice. Then she thought of something and without hesitation said, "Steve, while we were broken down here, I was able to do a story on a girl and her horse. I think it's one that you'll be very interested in. She saves another girl from being trampled to death. It's very heartwarming to see what this family has done and how they live. It'll be a tearjerker to the public."

"Is it edited and ready to go?" Steve asked. "I have an opening for a spot this evening."

"Yes, it is." Anne lied, trying to make Steve see that she was going to be reliable for her promotion.

"Bring it in as soon as you get here. We need to get the prelims done on it so it can be aired. I'm counting on you, Anne."

After Anne hung up the phone, she hollered at Scotty, "We have another tape to edit, Scotty. So hurry up."

She knew that from the four spare tapes Scotty boxed last night, the ones she was going to discard when she got to Portland, she could put together a very heartwarming story about Paige and Samantha Greenly. Then later on, she could come back and air the tape that she and Scotty spent all night on. That way she could get paid for two stories for the effort of one. And the public loves a follow-up on a story that has been aired before, especially when the viewers have a chance to be the jurors of a saga, such as the one she was creating.

17

After Patricia kicked the TV crew off of the place, Paige ran to the barn, seeking comfort from the only friend she would ever be able to trust. What did the TV crew want from her family? And Jack, he seemed so nice and yet they sat there and tormented the whole family as if they were criminals or had done something wrong for helping Samantha. But Anne did bring out something Paige did not want to face—the fact that she would never make it to college. There was no way, she knew now. She had been kidding herself into thinking that they could afford it, but it wasn't going to happen and she had to face that.

Paige cried on Libby's shoulder, and the horse stood patiently, waiting for her usually cheerful friend to rid herself of all her sorrows so they could play as they always had. Libby turned her head around toward Paige's back and nibbled on her shirt. Paige turned her tear-streaked face toward Libby's playful advances. She looked at Libby's soft loving eyes and the mystery behind them.

"I wish you could understand me, Libby, there is so much I want to tell you," she sniffed. "I don't understand people. I don't understand why my parents have to be poor, or why people have to judge other people on things they have or don't have. Oh, Libby," Paige said, tears starting to flow down her cheeks again, "I have embarrassed Mom and Papa. I don't think Mom will ever want to talk to me again."

Libby listened silently to all of Paige's problems as if she understood every word. Then, when Paige was finally quiet, Libby gave her a nudge toward the stall door.

Maybe Libby's nudge was for Paige to speak to her mother and tell her how she felt, or maybe it was a nudge to jump astride Libby's back and run from all the feelings that were locked in her mind and heart. Paige took it as the latter.

"I think that's a great idea," she sniffed again wiping her eyes on her sleeve.

She went to the tack room, grabbed Libby's bridle, put it on her, jumped astride her shiny back, and headed across the field at a high lope. Eager to feel the power underneath her and the wind on her face, Paige urged Libby to go faster to race all the pain and sorrow and leave it behind for someone else to deal with.

Patricia watched through the kitchen window as her daughter loped past the house. She wished she could escape the same way, wanting to run across the green treeless pasture and up into the horizon, run free to wherever the horse wanted to take her. She could almost feel the wind in her face.

18

Abe returned that afternoon with four fillies and a scrawny looking stud colt. He pulled up to the corrals and backed the six-horse fifth wheel trailer up to the gate. Abe unloaded the stud horse first. He looked at the ground, smelled the edge of the trailer, squatted down, and then effortlessly hopped out of the back of the trailer.

Abe pushed him into an adjoining corral and shut the gate. Then he went to the trailer and opened the dividing gate for the fillies.

The fillies had never been handled before, and when he opened up the trailer door, they were a little apprehensive to leave the safety of it. Abe left them to figure it out themselves and went to fill the trough with fresh water and give them clean hay. Patricia approached Abe as he stood watching the horses try to figure out how to get out of the trailer. They snorted at the edge of the door, looking down at the ground trying to figure out how far they would have to jump to get to the safety of the corral in front of them. It was only about six inches, but to them it looked like miles. Then quietly and easily, the fillies each tested the edge of the trailer and skipped out of it without incident or mishap.

Abe slipped his arm around his wife's shoulders and propped a foot on the bottom of the rail. "Looks like I have my work cut out for me, babe. I'll get an extra four hundred dollar bonus if I put thirty days on these guys. The guy threw in that little stud horse for taking all four mares. I'm thinking that extra money will buy the tires we've been needing for the pickup. What do you think?" He sounded excited and happy at the thought. Patricia just stood looking through the rails of the corral and hardly heard a word. He looked down at her when she didn't reply.

"Pat, what's wrong? Where is Paige?" His heart started thumping in his throat.

"Abe, I think I really messed up this time. Paige left on horseback. I haven't seen her for hours."

Abe wrapped his arms around his wife and just held her. She pulled herself together and began to explain the whole story of the day's events—Anne, Jack, the interview, the accusations, and the rivalry between Paige and Samantha at the show. Then she said, "I kicked them off the place, and I hope I never see another TV reporter again. All I wanted to do was give our daughter a chance to be in the spotlight and give her a day she would never forget."

"Well," Abe smiled. "I think you did a pretty good job of that. Sounds like she won't forget this for a long time."

Patricia smiled, looked at her husband, and wrapped her arms around him.

"I'm so glad you're home, I thought you wouldn't be back until tomorrow," she said as she laid her head on his shoulder and looked through the corral rails at his future prospects while they explored every inch of the corral.

He looked down at his wife and kissed her on the head, "Nope, it wasn't as far as I thought. You are beautiful, Patricia Cason." He stood a moment longer, looking at the colts. "I think I need to take that sorrel colt for a ride. I haven't been on him in a couple of days," he said as he rubbed Patricia's back. He bent down gave her another kiss and headed for the barn.

19

Patricia watched her husband as the red colt walked up to greet him. She watched as the horse dropped his nose into the halter and followed trustingly to be brushed and saddled by the man's honest hands.

Abe stepped into the saddle and they walked past Patricia. "I'll be back in a while. Keep dinner warm, and set the table for three."

He smiled and winked at her. Abe nudged the red colt into a trot and headed across the pasture in the direction he figured his daughter had gone. It felt good to be in the saddle again, away from the hustle and crowds of the world down the road. As he rode, his body swayed to the rocking rhythm of the colt's jog. He felt the openness of the rolling hills, sagebrush, the meadow grass, and his horse. He had the feeling of being whole and complete out here. *This is how life should be,* he thought. Where a man has to deal with his own self, his own responsibilities, and not worry about what the man down the road is spreading around. He had a lot to think about, but mainly he set out to find Paige.

He had a pretty good idea where she was. He set out for a spring about five miles away, next to the tree line. He had found her there twice before this summer, and she had quite a little fort set up there. Paige didn't realize he'd found her, for he never stopped to talk to her while she was playing there. He just rode past making sure she was okay.

He asked the colt to slow to a walk about two miles out, letting him catch his wind. The little red horse responded, not because he wanted to, but because he was asked.

"Boy, you're turning out to be quite a little horse, aren't you Red?" Abe said in his quiet tones. "Yep, I think you're going to make someone very happy."

The colt cocked back an ear listening to the man sitting astride him. His lowered head and the loose reins swung with the rhythm of his fast-paced walk, as if he was trying to cover as much ground as he could with each stride. Suddenly the colt stiffened and raised his head to the breeze that was blowing. Abe followed his gaze as he asked Red to stop. There under a juniper tree was a mule deer doe and two fawns. The babies still had spots on their backs but were old enough to retreat with their mother this late in the year. They bounded off together, stiff-legged and heads high, making as much noise as they could to alarm other deer around them of the intrusion. They stopped when they were another forty feet away and behind another small bunch of junipers. The mother was leery of this man on horseback and wanted to give her babies a lesson in survival. The doe was stone still behind the safety of the trees. The babies mimicked their mother, waiting for her to give the next signal so they could follow her lead. The doe was an older one and wise to the ways of life. She taught her babies well, for they wouldn't even flicker an ear or move a foot until the mother moved first. Abe admired the doe's instincts and the ability to communicate with unspoken words. They were camouflaged so well Abe wouldn't have seen them there if he hadn't watched were they had gone. Then silently they disappeared, no trace of them ever being there or ever existing.

"They sure look good, Red, this wet summer has made feed plentiful this year."

Red had watched the animals that stared back at them. He was tense, but sensing no panic or tension from his rider, he stood quietly and alertly waiting for Abe to give the next commands.

"You are a real dandy, Red." Abe said with admiration as he nudged the red colt into a lope and galloped the next two miles to where he figured Paige to be.

As he topped the hill he looked down. There sat Paige with a notebook, writing in it with total concentration, oblivious to her surroundings. He sat there on top of the hill looking at the tidy camp she had built. The little lean-to, the stump she had for a table, the log for her chair, and even the little corral for Libby she had put up where there was a clump of trees. Libby was next to the spring, dragging her lead line on the ground eating the tender shoots of grass.

Watching from up there, Abe felt like he was looking at a stranger down on that log. She seemed taller than he remembered, or maybe it was her hair, braided back out of her eyes. She was working so hard on her writing. He felt odd, not being able to pinpoint what was so different about his daughter.

I didn't know she liked to write, he thought to himself. Then he smiled, *I didn't know she could build either, but this is a well set-up camp.* He noticed that she had dug a hole and placed rocks around the fire pit that was never used. It was wisely placed far enough away from her lean-to and the trees so it wouldn't catch anything on fire if ever lit.

What else did he not know about his daughter? He felt kind of silly asking himself that kind of question. She was beginning to look like an adult instead of the child he had always viewed her to be. Where had the time gone?

Libby looked up and nickered a hello to the rider looking down on them. Paige jumped at the sudden noise and followed Libby's gaze. There on the skyline sat a man on a horse. She recognized the shape of him instantly. It was a perfect silhouette of man and horse as one, and it held the beauty and harmony that all would love to see. She etched it in her mind so she would never forget that pose. Red's head was down, his reins hung slack and his ears alert, but not nervous. The man on his back was leaning a little forward in the saddle, one arm on the horn. Abe's frame was square and solid in the saddle but not threatening, more like completely at ease with himself and his life. This man had nothing to prove. His face, shadowed by the evening hue and the dark cowboy hat, made Paige think of a mysterious man, nameless and forever unknown.

"Hello in camp," Abe called down. "Can a man rest his weary horse at your camp?"

"Papa, how did you find me?" Paige asked then quickly put her pad and pencil away.

"I had to track you, and that ain't all too easy, you leave a pretty tough trail to follow," he teased.

She smiled at him. It was good to see his leather-like face and old Stetson hat that should have been thrown away a year or so ago. He stepped off Red and walked the horse into his daughter's camp.

"Your place looks pretty nice, Sis," he said as he looked around.

"Thanks, Papa. I hadn't expected company." Her face turned red to have her father here at her silly little corner of the world. "I kind of like coming here to get my life back together when it all falls apart."

Abe led Red to the spring, loosened the saddle, took off his bridle, and put his hobbles on so he could eat with Libby. Then he took off his leather gloves and put them in his hip pocket as Paige began speaking to him. He turned toward his daughter.

Before she could even think, Paige fell into her father's arms and began to sob. She thought she had her emotions under control, but as soon as she felt her father's strong arms engulf her, tears started to flow. He didn't say anything. He just let her cry it out.

"I'm so sorry, Papa. I think I've gotten you and Mom in trouble. I embarrassed Mom in front of the TV crew with all this talk of college. I know now though that I'll never be able to go."

Abe's heart went out to his daughter. He knew that college was one thing she always talked about doing, and he and Patricia didn't know for sure how they were going to make it happen.

Paige continued, wanting to get everything out into the open. "I know I shouldn't have said those things to Samantha, Papa, but she made me so mad. I wanted her to know it wasn't how much money a person had that makes a winner. It's the dedication you put into something. Am I right?"

"Sis, yes you are. But it's a material world out past these pastures and hills, and people will judge you for what you have. So all I can say for now is you have to be strong and be proud of who you are and what you know." Abe paused to let her think. "I know it won't buy your way into college, Sis, and there is a better life than the one we're living. But it'll do for now until it is time to change."

Paige poured her heart out to her father, and he listened patiently. The evening was beginning as the sun started to set its bright face behind the Indian head that Abe showed Paige so long ago sleeping silently in the mountain folds. The crickets and grasshoppers started their evening songs, and pretty soon the frogs that were hidden next to the spring joined in. Paige and Abe were silent for a while just listening to Mother Nature as she started playing her evening lullaby to put some to sleep and beckon others out of their sleeping places.

Paige broke the silence, "Papa," she hesitated, "do you believe in reincarnation and that kind of stuff?" It seemed to be an odd question, but it had crossed her mind several times. She felt her face redden as she looked over at her father. "Well, you know…" she paused again, "Like God and stuff like that."

She felt a little sheepish now for just blurting out the question without thinking about it first. "Well I have been kind of wondering about it and thought I would ask."

Abe looked at her for a moment, his eyes looking directly at hers. He hadn't thought about religion or life after death stuff for quite some time, and now his daughter was asking what he thought about it.

She looked directly at his sun-aged face to get an honest answer.

"Well, Sis, I don't know. I 'spose a person has the right to believe in whatever they want to."

"But we pray at dinner every night, Papa," Paige seemed confused about his answer.

"Sure we do. We say a prayer to the creator and give thanks for all that is good. But I could only venture to guess what he has in store for us once we're not here anymore."

Paige looked over at Libby and Red standing side by side, content to be where they were at that time. "If there is," she said thinking nonchalantly, "I think I would like to come back as a horse, just like Libby. I would be free-spirited and be able to race the wind with beauty and grace and yet be strong and athletic." She had a dreamy voice and a longing in her eye as if she could actually picture herself running in the wind with no cares or worries about her—just freedom to be who she was.

"You are already that, Paige, you just don't see it."

She looked at him, curiously silent.

Abe closed his eyes and thought for a minute, "Well now if I were to come back, I think I would come back as an eagle."

Paige looked at him in surprise, "Why, Papa? You love horses so much I figured that's what you'd want to be, too."

"No, Sis, a horse has no say in life. They are what a person would call herd bound. They like to follow and have a leader. That's why they are so trainable. They adapt to whatever life hands them. Also they have to depend on man for food and water and can be sold to someone who don't care if they get either."

"Now an eagle," he said after a pause. "Can hunt, fish, and fend for himself and live as God intended. His life is his own responsibility. He can view the world in many different ways." Abe smiled, "Also he can crap on anyone who was mean to him in his previous life."

Paige laughed, "Papa, I already have a list started."

They were laughing together as they got up and caught the horses. Twilight was setting in, and the shadows were long.

"Come on, Sis, we'd better get back, your mom is worried sick about you." He draped an arm around his daughter's shoulder.

Paige looked at him, "Do you think Mom will ever forgive me? I really didn't mean for all of this to happen, Papa. It just got blown out of proportion."

Abe tightened his saddle. "Sis," he said, "it doesn't matter what happens as long as you know what you done was right."

Paige looked at the ground. Abe stepped in the saddle.

"Do you feel that way, Sis?"

"I don't know what I feel, Papa." Paige slipped Libby's bridle on over her halter as she ran the reins through her hands.

"Paige," he said. She looked at him, surprised to hear him say her name. "Would you do anything differently if the accident happened again?"

She looked up at him. "No," she said without hesitation.

"Then you know you've done right. Be proud of it. It don't matter what anyone writes, says, or even puts on TV, as long as you're proud of what you've done."

Libby brought her head around to be rubbed as Abe talked, and Paige stroked her, listening intently at her father's words.

"I am proud of what I did, Papa."

"Then let's go home and tell your mom because right now she's feeling the same way you did. It doesn't do any good to run away from your problems, Sis. You have to face them head on."

"I never thought Mom would think I was mad at her. I

was just so frustrated with myself I didn't know what to say to her," Paige said as she swung on Libby's bare back.

The full moon was casting shadows in its blue light. It was so bright and full it dimmed the stars and Milky Way that cast themselves across the sky. Paige nudged Libby up next to her father. Abe looked at his daughter with a grin. "Let's go home." They rode side by side, the horses easily picking their way back to the ranch. Paige talked of Libby blowing snot on Anne and of how Jack had laughed until he cried.

"I have never seen a man cry before, until this week. Mr. Greenly cried at the hospital and Jack..."

"We all do it, Sis. We all do it," Abe replied with a sigh.

Paige smiled. She couldn't imagine her father crying.

Abe changed the subject, "I brought home some fillies and a stud colt."

There was an ease about the conversation and mood. The world seemed to have fallen away and time stood still for a moment. So with the rocking rhythm of the horses, they talked of horses and life the rest of the way home. With the moon overhead to light the way and a chill in the night air, it would be a night that Paige would never forget.

20

Anne hung up the phone. Something about Jack was making her uneasy. She packed her things and hollered at Scotty. They had no time to check out, so they would just leave the keys in the rooms. Anne had her overnight bag slung on one arm and her large purse draped in the crook of her elbow when she reached the van. Scotty was straggling behind dragging her two suitcases and his one suitcase in his hand with his overnight bag slung over his shoulder. He said nothing, just tried to keep up and get things loaded while she seemed to be mumbling to herself of all the things that should've been done. Anne fumbled with the keys. She wanted to get home. There was something odd in Steve's voice. She had also promised to have that story done and ready to air by the time they reached Portland. It shouldn't take her too long now that she had reviewed the tapes several times. It was just a matter of finding the right scenes to put together a heartwarming story for Steve. She could be doing that as Scotty drove.

"Come on, Scotty," she said as she opened the sliding van door.

Everything was neat and tidy inside, and she thought Scotty was a good guy to have around. He always kept everything he worked with in immaculate condition and very clean. She set her bags on the ground in front of the van door and stepped in. She started looking for the four tapes.

"Okay, Scotty," Anne stated flatly as she rummaged through the neat van. "Where are the tapes? I told you to put them in a box."

"They're in the dumpster," he said.

"They're where?" She looked at him anger and panic all at once.

"The dumpster," he repeated. "They fell out last night when I left the van." He tried to explain.

"Oh just shut up! Let me think," she spat at him, her eyes were staring right through him as she stepped out of the van.

She stepped directly on her bag and something crunched under her weight. *That damn make up kit*, she thought when she looked down to see what it was. She kicked the bag to one side and devoted her attention to the dumpster.

"I'll be damned if I'm going to get them out of there," she said and whipped around to Scotty. "You put them in there, you get them out!" she ordered.

"Not a chance, Ms. Rhymes," Scotty stated defiantly. She turned abruptly back to the dumpster, walked over to it, and lifted the lid. The stench of rotten food and rancid grease from the restaurant overtook her and she dropped the lid. Suddenly it seemed as though a light had turned on or a switch had been flipped.

Anne regained her composure. She looked back at Scotty and seductively walked up to him. Her entire focus was on him. She was oblivious to the cars driving by that had stopped at the stop light. She didn't see John Greenly's Cadillac pull up, waiting for the light to turn green. She didn't know he watched her drape her arms around Scotty's neck and tilt her head the same way she had done to him the night before.

But John Greenly watched from the stoplight, not surprised. When the light turned green, John smiled, shook his head, and drove on to the hospital.

"Scotty, you really don't want me to crawl in there to get those tapes, now do you?" Anne said in a smooth low tone that made Scotty get goose bumps on his skin. "I mean, you're the one who put them in there. Don't you think you ought to be the one to get them out?"

She knew he wasn't man enough to turn her down. He didn't have the heart. He always did everything she said, and with a little sweet-talking, she knew he would crawl in the dumpster.

He looked deeply into her eyes, those beautiful blue eyes, and leaned toward her.

Anne had to think. She really didn't want to kiss this guy, but if that would get the tapes out of the dumpster, then it would be worth it. But only a kiss.

Scotty ran his arms gently up Anne's that were caressing his neck. He leaned in past her face, his hot breath breathing in her perfume.

Anne felt shivers run up her spine as she thought, *Well maybe if he asked it probably could be more than a kiss.*

He leaned closer, his lips almost touching her ear, running his hands up and down her arms and gently caressing her. He took another breath and quietly whispered, low and seductively, "Ms. Rhymes, I wouldn't crawl in that dumpster for you if my life depended on it." He pulled her arms from around his neck.

She was surprised, and in desperation her temper flew. She whipped away from him. "How come when I need something done, I have to do it myself? I ask one simple task and not one person can follow my instructions. Tell me why, Scotty, just tell me why."

"Do you really want to know, or do you want me to lie, like you have been doing to everyone who comes in contact with you? You treat us like dogs. You call and expect us to come and sit where you tell us to, then when you're finished with us we have to go lay in the corner until you need us again. You've had me at your beck and call for forty-eight hours straight. You call when you feel like it. Edit this, Scotty. Go get that. I need this, Scotty. Hurry up, Scotty." He mimicked her voice the best he could. "I'm sick of it! If I wanted to be treated this way I would've joined the military or gotten married."

He looked at her directly, "I'll be damned if I'll crawl in the garbage just for you to fix one of your lies, Anne." Scotty paused. "How many have you told in the last two days? I bet you couldn't count them all, even if you took off your shoes." He walked away. He knew now he was unemployed and would have to take the bus home.

Anne watched him start to walk away. *That is just fine, he can go ahead and leave*, she thought. Then reality hit her and her temper cooled just as quickly as it had flared.

"Wait, Scotty, I'm sorry." She thought for a second. "If I crawl in the dumpster and get the tapes, will you drive me home so that I can edit the story for Steve?"

Scotty looked back at her for a long moment as if he was contemplating. *She is so pretty*, he thought. "No, I don't think I will. I need to take a few days off." And he continued walking.

"Come on, Scotty, you can't leave. How will you get home?" she whined.

Anne stomped her foot like a child as she watched him continue walking, not looking back. She looked at the garbage bin and bit her lower lip. She then walked up to it, took a deep breath, and lifted the lid. The box was upside down. *Well at least they are in there*, she thought. Flies flew in her face and she winced at the smell. She threw back the lid all the way and took another gulp of fresh air. She looked around the dumpster for a box to step on so she could reach into it without having to crawl in. The closest thing she could find was a large rock that blocked one of the dumpster wheels. She pulled it out and stepped on it. She reached for the box that held the tapes. She stretched farther, standing on her tiptoes and reaching with everything she had, and the dumpster started to roll. She jumped off the rock, grabbed the handle, and brought it to a standstill again. She stepped on the rock again, turned her head, took another big gulp of fresh air, and did the inevitable. She crawled into the dumpster. The garbage squashed under her weight. Old, used deep-fryer grease soaked in her socks. She reached down and grabbed the box. It was empty. Panic hit her as she started to thrash around, looking for any sign of the tapes.

"Scotty!" Anne hollered as she rummaged around, not caring she was covering herself in the filth.

A flash of light caught her eye and then another. She looked up to see a police car with its lights on and a uniformed officer walking her direction. Behind him, a couple of camera flashes were going off. The press followed.

"Excuse me," the officer said as he approached. "Did you know it is against the law to go through someone's garbage?"

"This isn't what it looks like, Officer. I am a reporter with…"

"That doesn't give you the right to go through other people's garbage. I am going to have to ask you to step out of the dumpster."

21

Paige was straightening her room, singing with the radio. Garth Brooks was singing *The Dance*, clear and true. Although Paige was singing with him word for word, she sadly distorted the song. A cool summer morning breeze was blowing her curtains through her open bedroom window.

She had creatively decorated her walls with her show ribbons and pictures of Libby. She also had her picture and story of Libby that came out in the newspaper. Beside that was another picture of Anne in the dumpster with a caption that read, *Digging in Garbage for News?* Paige dusted that one with a smile. It was a little over a month since the whole incident, and it seemed as if things were falling back into a normal kind of life.

Patricia was out in their garden picking beans. She and Paige were going to can them later that evening after the sun went down so it wouldn't make the house so unbearable through the heat of the day. Patricia and Paige were working well together, and this canning season Paige offered to help instead of being outside with her father. This was appreciated; they could accomplish twice as much together as one person could do in the same amount of time. Patricia couldn't remember having so much fun while working. She hummed with Paige's radio as she picked beans.

Paige heard a rig pull up their gravel driveway. She peeked out her curtain and saw John Greenly. He pulled up in his beautiful Dodge pickup. Though the dusty road put a fine film of dust on its glossy paint, it was the prettiest truck Paige had ever seen. She couldn't believe he would drive it up here and get it all dirty.

When John knocked at the door, Paige went and opened it. "Well, Mr. Greenly, it's great to see you."

John smiled at her. "It is good to see you, Paige. I haven't seen you in a while."

"Yeah, I know," she said. "Papa has been pretty busy this last month, and with canning season here it's been pretty hard to get away. Come in and I'll go get my mom."

John took off his hat as he entered the house and followed Paige through. He was surprised at how well kept this simple little house was. The kitchen was tidy and small, no microwave or dishwasher, just the basics. On the range sat a pot of coffee simmering. They walked through the front room where on the walls were a few pictures of Paige and her father on horseback and one family picture taken several years ago. Then a picture of Abe's parents when he was a young man, John assumed. Surrounding that picture were two bridle bits Abe's father had made in Nevada by the Garcia Company. In the corner was a TV, which a person had to get up to change the channel. He smiled. He hadn't seen one of those in years. He was surprised by how little they had. Their furniture was old, but not rickety, and nicely taken care of. Everything was very neat and in order. As they approached the back door leading out to the garden, Paige called out, "Mom."

"I'm over here," Patricia answered as she stood up from her stooped position.

Her hair was pulled back in a French braid, and she had a baseball cap on her head. With her faded blue jeans and white t-shirt, she looked like Paige's older sister. She looked toward her daughter and saw John Greenly.

"Well, Mr. Greenly," she said. "What a nice surprise." She bent down and picked up her large pan of beans and walked toward them. "How is Samantha?"

"She's getting better every day. She goes to therapy every other day. They took her arm casts off last week. She's learning how to walk again—a pretty slow process. But we're working on it, one day at a time."

"I can't even imagine. It seems like yesterday, and yet so long ago at the same time." She paused. "I hope she heals fast." Patricia said as she walked toward them.

"Well," John said, kind of hesitantly, "like I said, one day at a time." He glanced at Paige as they walked in the kitchen.

Patricia set the beans down on the butcher block, and looked back at him. "I'm sorry, it probably seems like an eternity to you."

"Eternity is an understatement," he said with a laugh. He was in good humor and felt completely at ease with this family. "Yesterday she wanted me to get a glass of water, and out of habit I did it, until I remembered that she could have gotten it herself. So I drank it in front of her. Boy was she mad." He laughed again. "I think what she hates more than anything are those crutches. But she is far from helpless." He looked at his two listeners with a twinkle in his eyes. "I have to get out of the house and leave her alone so she doesn't have a maid twenty-four hours a day."

"In that case, if you have some time to kill, would you like to take a tour of the place? We would love to show you around." Patricia asked, liking this man's warm sense of humor. Then she continued. "Abe is out working a colt and I'm sure he would love a break."

"Sure, I would like a tour," John said.

Patricia grabbed a pitcher of iced tea out of the refrigerator as Paige grabbed some plastic glasses out of the cupboard. They headed to the barn.

"Thomas Pitt owns this place, doesn't he?" John asked, curious if the rumors were right.

"Yes he does," Patricia answered.

"How many men does he have out here? I remember when I was a kid and Ole Man Patton had this place, he always had three or four men helping him." He smiled at the memory. "During haying season he would hire a few of us kids to buck bales. We got three dollars a day."

"He only has us working for now. Abe is hoping he will hire a couple more guys before we get our first shipment of cattle the beginning of next month." Patricia stated this without showing her dislike for Thomas Pitt.

They walked to the barn. The breezeway was open, and a soft breeze was flowing through it. Some of the horses came from outside and nickered a soft hello with their heads over the stall doors.

Out of habit Paige said, "Hi kids," as she started the tour by opening the tack room door.

Inside were at least thirty bridles hanging on the wall. There were about ten saddles sitting on saddletrees, and the saddle blankets were hanging behind them on what looked to John like a long towel rack. In one corner was a circular rack where all the horse blankets and hoods hung, and in the other was a refrigerator that had the horses' vaccines and medicine. Then just inside the door were all the brushes and fly repellent on a shelf, ready for use and within arm's reach of the door. There was even a workbench set up with a light and tools so Abe could repair any tack that needed it along one wall. Everything was set up for convenience. John was impressed.

"Papa put this room together just the way he wanted it after the barn was built. He said that if he was going to ride five to seven head of horses a day, he wanted to set up his own tack room," Paige told John, proud of her father's work.

"Well your dad did a fine job of it. I have tack scattered from one end to the other in my tack room. Your father is a smart man, Paige." John stated with admiration.

Paige beamed as she opened the next sliding door which

was the grain room. All the horses nickered almost at once, hoping they might receive a treat for good behavior. Across the breezeway was the wash rack and then came the stalls. At the end of them were two large open stalls that had hay in them. "These can hold up to five tons of hay on each side, and the roof is elevated so that a bale wagon can come in and dump its load so we don't have to buck any bales," Paige said and then added, "Papa thought of this too."

As they started out the other side of the barn, they ended up in a large corral. To the left of them, Abe was working a colt in a round corral. It was the stud colt that came with the four fillies.

Abe had just started him, Paige figured, for the colt hadn't broken into a sweat yet. He was prancing around with his head high and his tail sticking straight out. Memories of Libby's first day in the round pen came flooding back to her. Everyone was quiet as Abe worked the animal. Paige went back to the barn and brought out two folding chairs. She tapped John on the shoulder to give him one.

He bent down to Paige and quietly asked, "What is he trying to do?"

"He is giving the colt confidence," Paige replied.

John watched the man in the round corral. He had a plastic sack tied to the end of a stick in one hand, and the colt was running from him. To the average man it looked as if the man inside the round corral was just chasing this colt and scaring him for no reason.

Abe would bring the sack up any time the horse turned his head away from Abe, then drop it when the horse looked his direction. If the colt turned his butt to him, he would gently shake the sack a couple of times directly behind him so that he learned to face his fear instead of trying to run. They watched for almost ten minutes, and John was feeling a little uncomfortable. He couldn't grasp the picture of what the flag and man were trying to accomplish. Making this colt go around and around in circles, to John, didn't seem like it would be giving confidence.

Then all of a sudden, the colt stopped and faced Abe. Abe stopped in the same instant as if he knew what the horse was going to do. The colt looked at Abe, and Abe looked at the ground. Abe wanted the colt to rest longer than he worked, but that had to be the colt's decision, not Abe's. Abe's shoulders were relaxed and his body posture was inviting and calm. There was no aggression or expectation, just a quiet man waiting for the horse to accept a new idea of language.

Abe talked in his quiet tones. Although the words meant nothing to the animal, Abe always told Paige it was the tones they understood, not the language. They understood body movement more than anything. "Kind of like unspoken words, they listen to your body language."

The colt's sides, flanks, and neck were now sweaty, and he was looking at Abe, curious and alert. The horse was looking for a reason to run, but Abe didn't give him any.

So he stood looking at this man, trying to understand the unspoken words between them.

Patricia and John were sitting in the chairs and Paige was on the ground between them.

John leaned over to Paige. "If he wants to catch him why doesn't he just rope him and snub him to a post?"

Paige looked up at the man. "Because he wants him to have confidence, not break him. It would destroy the trust he is trying to build in him."

A couple more times around the corral and he stopped and looked at Abe again. He bobbed his head up and down, smelled the ground, then rested again grinding his teeth and licking his lips. Each time he tried to make his escape, he tried with less and less effort. Every time the colt started to go in a circle, Abe would gently shake the sack. It finally clicked. When he heard the sack, he would stop and look at Abe. Abe stood quietly and interested. The colt bobbed his head, then started to take a few uncertain steps toward the man. A few minutes later and Abe was stroking the animal's neck with the sack.

John was speechless. He had never seen anything like this before. It took about thirty-five minutes to get to that point. There was more work to be done to increase the horse's confidence level, but Abe found a good place to stop, and seeing he had company, he decided they both could take a break. Abe turned his back to the colt and started walking to the gate, and the horse followed trustingly beside him. John was in shock. Thirty minutes ago, that horse couldn't be touched, and now he followed the man like he was his best friend. Abe turned back, stroked the colt's now almost dry neck and stepped outside the gate. Abe was covered in dust and dirt, but he didn't seem to mind. Patricia poured him a glass of iced tea and handed it to him as he approached.

"I think he's got it figured out. We'll let him think for a little while."

Patricia introduced the two men, and they shook hands and started talking about the colt.

"How in the world do you do that?" John asked in awe of witnessing such a feat.

"Oh, it is something my father taught me when I was a kid. I kind of grew up with it," Abe answered.

"Your dad taught you? I have never seen anything like it," John said still in awe.

"I always did all the ground work for him and he always rode them, a pretty nice assembly line. He would get the first five rides on them and he would let me finish them out," Abe answered. "Some nice memories we built back then."

John looked over at the colt and said, "We always roped our colts, snubbed them, then put a halter on and taught them that way. I had one hired man tie them to a wall and throw gunnysacks on them until all the fight was gone." John paused, "He told me that was the only way to break colts. Make them know who was boss right off the bat, that way they will always respect you out of fear, and do what you want them to, or suffer the consequences," John continued. "I didn't have the stomach for it. So now, I send my colts out to be trained so I don't have to watch what they do to them. They usually come back pretty nice horses. I guess I'm a horse rider and not a horse trainer."

Abe listened, "Well, John, there are a million ways to break a horse and I as one man can't tell the world which way is right. But I do know for as many miles as I have ridden, cattle I have roped, and as many predicaments I have been in, my horse has never headed home without me."

"Are they always that hard to get to follow you?" John asked eager to learn more.

"This one was easy, John. The hard ones are the ones that have already been messed with. They already have it in their minds what they do is right whether they hurt someone to get their way or not," Abe answered.

Abe liked John. He wasn't afraid to ask questions and listen to the philosophy of horse sense. Not that Abe knew it all, but just the fact that these were basic questions most people wouldn't ask for fear of embarrassing themselves. Not John though, he was eager to learn, and he wasn't a novice horseman from what Abe could tell. John had been around them enough to have common sense about the animals. He just didn't know how to think like them. Abe continued the conversation, "I like to build their confidence before I start to work them. A horse has it bred into him to run from his fears. As a trainer, I have to teach him to face and understand it. Changing a reactor into a thinker sometimes is not easy to do, but it can be done."

Now the whole session made sense to John. "So this made the colt look to you for security."

"Basically, yes," Abe said. "A man doesn't know for sure what actually goes on in a horse's mind. But it's proven that a man can work with the animal and get far greater results than if he wants to play cowboy and throw them down. In this session here," Abe continued, "he not only came to me for security, he also came to me with confidence. Actually, there is so much this colt has learned in the last thirty minutes, it's almost impossible to tell you because I won't know for sure until he tells me."

"A colt tells you what he's learned?" John laughed.

Abe knew he was starting to confuse John with too many details, so he laughed and said, "It gets pretty complicated, just know that it's true."

They were silent for a minute, then John spoke up, "You know, Abe, I do believe you, I don't know why, and it sounds pretty odd, but I do."

Abe smiled as he looked back at the colt standing at the corral gate looking at him.

"I wish the trainers that had Piper could see you work. Maybe they could learn something about confidence," John stated not to anyone in particular.

"You having problems with that Piper horse? Paige thought he was a pretty nice animal. She talked about him for weeks after the accident," Abe said, concerned.

"Ever since the day of the accident, he has been locked in his stall. He can't stand anyone at his side. He faces you head on with his head up and eyes wide. It looks like he sees right through you. Anytime anyone tries to saddle him, he just comes unglued. Once a person gets him saddled and puts any weight in the stirrup, he just about kills himself, or the person, to get away from them." John sighed sadly. "I just had a third trainer work with him the other day. Piper reared over backwards when he went to get on. They all said the same thing, that there is nothing that they could do for him. There are too many good horses out there to waste it on a bad one. They said the best thing for me to do is make him into dog food before he hurts someone and I end up with a lawsuit." He paused for a second. "They even demonstrated for me what that horse is capable of when he panics from the saddle. It's a sad thing to think of what that horse used to be and seeing what he is now."

Abe had an idea of what horses would go through to keep away from something that petrified them so badly. Sometimes they would darn near kill themselves to get away from fear. He first dealt with a similar incident when he was a kid of sixteen. A saddle went under a horse's belly. Even though the horse had been ridden about a dozen times and was fairly decent to handle, as soon as Abe stepped in the stirrup of that loose saddle, it slipped to the animal's side. The horse jumped away from the saddle and because it was attached to him, it slid further under his belly. He tried to kick it off, but in the attempt, his hind foot slipped in between his own belly and the back of the saddle. This made him fight with every ounce of strength, panic, and fury he had as he attempted to free his caught foot.

The back cinch of the saddle finally broke from the force of his terror. With every buck and jump, the saddle beat his belly. He started to run blindly, kicking at it with every stride, as it unmercifully pounded and beat on the tender underside of his belly. Abe watched helplessly and in horror as the horse ran through a fence, bucking and kicking it to splinters. By the time that horse stopped, the saddle was nothing more than scraps of leather, a couple of rivets and a hunk of rawhide and sheepskin. He stood shaking from fear, in a complete lather of sweat with a wild look in his eyes.

Abe remembered how his father walked up to the animal, cut the broken form of a saddle loose, and led him back to the barn. He never said a word to Abe. He watched his father put a wide leather band with rings on it, called a surcingle, around the sweaty horse's girth and take him out into the pasture. Abe followed.

The horse cut loose bucking as soon as his father tightened it, but only for a few minutes. Then he watched his father walk up, talk to the horse, and then tie two burlap sacks that he had folded into rectangles snugly around the front legs of the animal. They covered the leg from the knee down to the hoof, like an extra padding. Then he gently took a large soft cotton rope and tied it to one front foot and attached it to the surcingle. With soft, quiet words and honest hands, Abe's father, in about fifteen minutes, laid the animal down as gently as he could.

When it finally laid down, Abe's father looked at Abe and said, "Go get a towel, Son."

Abe never ran as fast in his life as he did that day. When he returned, his father was sitting on the horse's side, just behind the withers, with his feet sitting solidly on the ground. He was leaning over and quietly stroking the sweaty neck of the petrified animal. Abe saw a lot of worry in the horse's eyes as his father sat there, never taking his focus off the animal, and talking in low tones to it.

"Come here, Son. You can't undo what you have done out there."

Abe hesitantly walked up. "Now you sit right here and hold this rope just as I have done." Abe saw that the rope in his father's hand was the lead line attached to the horse's halter, and was run through a ring on the surcingle. "Now," his father continued, "if he goes to thrashing around, you hold his head just like that, so he can't beat it against the ground. I don't want him to hurt himself. And I want you both to sit here and think for a while."

Then he left the sixteen-year-old boy to sit and wait until

he returned. Abe sat there for a while with his towel in one hand and the rope in the other, looking at this horse who was laying on his side in the dirt. Without thinking, the boy started to rub the animal down. He leaned over the horse's neck as far as he could and gently started rubbing around his eyes, down his slick wet neck, his legs, his sides, and belly. The horse's muscles were as hard as rocks and his breathing rapid. He started talking to him as his father had done, feeling as if it was his entire fault for this horse's predicament.

"I am so sorry, Little Man." Abe said quietly and low. "I should have tightened the saddle more before trying to step into it. I just wasn't thinking."

Abe talked to the horse and rubbed him for about fifteen minutes. He noticed subtle changes in the horse beneath him. The animal's muscles were relaxing, and his eyes had a softer look in them. He continued talking. The horse's eyes closed and he laid straight out, taking a deep breath. He lay there as if he was taking a nap. About twenty more minutes went by, and Abe's shoulders and legs were burning from sitting there, but he continued to rub. Then just as easily and calmly as could be, the horse leaned up and brought his legs under him. He was covered in sweat on the down side of him. Abe took the towel and continued rubbing his neck and head. Then his father returned with a saddle in hand.

Abe's heart sank, "Dad, does he have to go through this?

Can't we just let him up?" Abe was not sure what his father was going to do. His heart was going out to this animal, and he wanted to defend him if he could.

His father squatted next to his son, put his large calloused hand on the horse's neck, and stroked him gently, looking into his boy's eyes. "Abe, this horse's trust has been broken. I know this doesn't make much sense now, but this gives him time to think for a spell. After what he's just been through with the saddle and fence, his mind has returned to a reactor. Now it is our job to put his mind back into a thinker."

Abe remembered looking down at the horse, his eyes were closed now and his breathing was easy. His muscles had turned soft as he had relaxed and become accustomed to the state he was in.

"We didn't hurt him, Son, we laid him down. We didn't throw him. We didn't whip, beat, or harm him in any way. He is just taking a time out." He paused to think of how this would make sense, "kind of like sending a kid to his room for a time out." Abe smiled then. His father had that done to him more than once.

His father smiled back and knew the boy understood now, then continued, "And if you have done your job right, I think he has already thought things through."

"What job, Dad? All I did was sit here like you told me to."

"You've done far more than that, Son, far more than

that." His father stood up and took a flag from the outside the corral and started flagging around the horse. "Stay where you are, Son, and remember hold his head."

Abe did as he was told and talked to that animal like he had never talked before. Fifteen minutes later, his father untied the horse's legs and stepped away.

"Stay with him, Son, and when he's ready to get up, let him. You'll know what to do after that."

Then he left and didn't come back. Abe sat there again, rubbed, and waited for what seemed an eternity. The horse's eyes were closed again and his breathing was easy, which meant he accepted everything that happened in the last hour and a half. Pretty soon the horse raised his head, and a few minutes later, he stood up all on his own.

Abe saw immediately what needed to be done, for the other side of the horse was completely wet and covered in mud. So with his already wet, muddy towel he set to drying the horse off. There was not a blemish on the animal from what his father had done. There were cuts and scrapes from the fence, but with a little salve and time there would be no scars. That horse followed Abe around with a sense of trust like no other he had ever felt. He stroked his neck and talked soothingly as he led him.

His father returned as Abe was walking the horse and checking him out. "Okay, Son, now saddle him again."

Abe was apprehensive, he had already ruined one of his father's saddles and almost ruined a horse. Now his father wanted him to do it all over again. But he did as he was told. The horse stood there and took the saddle without even flinching. He had one ear cocked back toward Abe and was listening to the boy's shaky words.

When Abe was done cinching him up, his father spoke one last time before he started mending the corral fence. "Do you understand? It's not the action that teaches the horse, it is the patience. He depended on you to take care of him when he was stuck, and you didn't let him down." He looked at the young man who carried his own name. "All I am saying, Son, is the confidence this horse lost, you gave back to him. You did a good job." Then he picked up his hammer and walked away to finish repairing the fence.

Abe was brought back out of his past when he heard John ask, "Would you consider yourself a horse whisperer?"

Abe thought for a moment, "Well I don't know for sure what that is, John…a whisperer. There ain't anything I could whisper to a horse that he'd understand." Abe took a drink of his tea and thought for a moment, "No, I don't think I am. I'm just a man who has spent a little time with horses."

"They talk of horse whisperers as people who can speak to horses," John said, trying to explain what he had asked.

Abe, a bit confused, replied, "Why would you speak to them, why not just listen?"

John thought for a moment, "Well I guess that's where I get a little confused. You say horses talk, others say people whisper…I just want horses I can trust."

Paige liked the sound of horse whisperer, it sounded mysterious and magical, yet didn't make any sense. What would you say to a horse that would make any sense to them? She thought of what she whispered to Libby, how she talked to her, and how Libby would cock an ear her way. But it was mainly for the sound, not the words. There was no meaning to Libby when she said, "I love you, Libby." It was more for just saying it and the emotion around it. What an odd thought, as she wrote the words "horse whisperer" in the dirt where she sat.

John paused for a moment to think of how to say the next few words, then took a deep breath and just blurted them out. "I'll tell you why I'm here," he began, "I was just wondering if Paige might come out and see Samantha sometime. She has locked herself in the house so to speak. She won't even come out to see Piper." He thought for a moment, "They used to be inseparable. Now she acts as if he doesn't exist. I guess it's best that way, if I have to do away with him. It just seems like she hasn't come to terms with the accident. I thought the horse might be able to help her in some silly way." He paused again, there was so much to say. He looked at the ground. "Well anyways, since I can't get her to go to the barn, and Piper being the way he is, I thought Paige would be the next best thing."

Abe was quiet for a moment, thinking about this man in front of him and how he would ask the same if it was his daughter. He was feeling some of the pain from this man, but he didn't know what to say or do. Should he answer for his daughter or let her answer for herself?

John now looked up. He felt embarrassed for trying to explain and putting his burdens on this family. It sounded better in his mind than it did coming out of his mouth.

"Look," John said, "I'm sorry for bothering you folks today. I guess it was a pretty silly idea. I know you're very busy. I guess I'll be going." He turned and started for his truck.

"Mr. Greenly," Paige called after him. "Wait!"

Paige grabbed his arm as he turned away. She wanted to do something, but she didn't know what. Even though she and Samantha were never really friends, Paige felt like she needed to see her and Piper. That poor horse, he was such a magnificent animal. She didn't want to see him go to slaughter. She'd seen it happen to some good horses, and she knew it had to be done in the case of a serious injury, such as broken leg, but not to a healthy young horse that wasn't hurt.

She finally blurted out, "I'll come to visit Samantha if you allow my father to work with Piper."

It had come out differently than she wanted it to. It sounded like a stipulation instead of a friendly gesture.

John turned back and looked at Paige's young face. He saw care and concern in her eyes. "Thanks, Paige, but that's okay. There isn't anything anyone can do for Piper. I had the best trainers I know work on him."

Patricia spoke up for the first time since the two men met. "That isn't exactly true. I think you should let Abe at least look at him, Mr. Greenly. I've seen him do some pretty miraculous things with some pretty rank horses." She knew Abe signed a contract with Thomas Pitt that no outside horses were allowed on the place. But if Abe went to the Greenly's place, what would it hurt to look at him?

Johns face lightened, "Do you think you could do something for Piper?"

Abe looked over at his wife then Paige. He was surprised at them. "Well, Thomas doesn't want me to take on any outside horses," Abe said, a little dumbstruck.

Patricia glanced at her husband. "Abe, Thomas said you couldn't work any horses on this place. He didn't say anything about you going to the horse." She was smiling.

Abe was put on the spot. He looked at his daughter, then back at John, then over to his wife. Their faces were lightened with hope and confidence in him.

"Tell you what I'll do," Abe started. "I'll go and look at this horse my daughter likes so well and mess with him while Paige visits Samantha for a spell. If I feel like there's something I can do for him I'll let you know at that time." He looked seriously over at John then Paige and said, "But I can't make any promises. A horse has his own mind, and if I can't work with it, then I can't help him. Okay?"

John, Paige, and Patricia beamed and agreed almost at once.

"How about you come over for dinner tonight?" John said. "You could look at him and see what you think, Abe. Then Samantha," he paused, "well, Paige, I will just turn you two loose and see what happens."

Abe smiled. He hadn't done anything for his daughter in a long time, and the way she beamed at him, he knew there was no way he could turn her down. Just looking at Piper couldn't be all bad, so he had agreed.

John looked grateful, "How about five tonight?"

Abe looked at Patricia and said, "That'll be fine. We could do chores a little early and call it a day."

Paige was excited, "So if I am going to ride Libby today, I had better do it now. See you, Mr. Greenly." She took off to Libby's stall. She wanted to go out to her little fort today. She had a few hours to draw a picture that etched itself in her head. It just had to be put on paper. She remembered seeing her father on the ridge the day he came out to find her a few weeks ago. It seemed to be burning a hole in her mind and she had to get it out. Out there, she could draw without being disturbed, and she could put her heart and soul in the drawing until it was done. So she jumped on Libby's awaiting back, rode past, and told them she would be back in a while. She headed at a high lope across the hill five miles away to her little corner of the world.

John admired the girl who rode away, "Boy she is some crackerjack, isn't she?" He looked at Abe and smiled, "Give her another couple years and you'll have boys crawling all over this place, Abe."

"Oh man, I don't even want to think about it." Abe chuckled.

"It seems like they're growing up too fast, and I wouldn't be surprised if you have boys already knocking on your door. Samantha is a beautiful girl," Patricia said.

John smiled, "She takes after her mother. I give her all the credit in that department. Well, I suppose I should be getting back. I'll see you around five o'clock this evening then?" He hesitated, "I want to thank you for all you've done."

Abe draped his arm around Patricia's shoulder, thankful he had his wife. "Yep, we'll be there. I think you would have done the same for us if it had happened the other way around."

John looked silently at them for a moment. Would he have?

22

Abe finished working the colt, then spent the rest of the morning working on the cattle chute that was going to be able to handle large numbers of cattle and semi-trucks. He had never built a chute for a big rig like that, so he had gone down and measured the chute at the sale barn in Baker City. He wanted to be sure and do it right the first time. He had hoped Thomas Pitt would buy him a tractor and auger, but for now his little hand post-hole digger was getting a daily workout. His body was lean and solid, his muscles were tight and sore, but he pressed on. He had three weeks to do a month's worth of work.

He didn't get in the house to eat lunch until about one o'clock. He went in, took off his dirty, sweaty shirt and put it in the hamper. He washed himself then changed into a clean shirt for lunch. It was a good morning, and they had accomplished a lot. Paige was still gone, and he and Patricia were sitting on the little deck in the shade, talking of John Greenly and Samantha. Abe saw a little sports car coming up the driveway; it had to be Thomas Pitt.

Abe looked at his watch, it was one thirty, "I wonder what he's doing out here in the heat of the day?" Abe said, rather curious.

"Maybe he's here to pay you your bonus on those fillies you've been riding," Patricia said, hopefully.

"Maybe," Abe replied. "You know, he hasn't called at all

this month. I guess we'll find out what he's been up to."

Abe put down his coffee, got up from the table, and put on his old crumpled Stetson hat as the car screeched to a halt. Dust and rocks went everywhere. Patricia got up and went into the house. She had nothing to say to this man.

Thomas Pitt was a brisk, heavyset man. He had a temper and a very narrow imagination. He had in his mind what he wanted and how he was going to get it and always had to have the last word. He was taught early in life not to let anyone get in his way. When he hired someone, they were to do what he said when he said. That's why he paid them. He was also a man who could make a penny scream when it came to spending on nonmaterial things such as wages.

Thomas saw a clean man walking toward the car and said, "Well, Abe, you look all fresh and happy today."

"I just got done eating lunch, have you eaten yet?" Abe answered.

"Yes, I ate about an hour ago." His voice sounded a little irritated. "I thought since I hadn't heard from you, I would come out and check on your progress with the corrals and colts. I've changed that shipment of cattle to a week earlier, so that gives you two weeks to get things into order around here." He was out of his BMW car and shuffling toward the barns, his baldhead reflecting the sun.

"Well," Abe started, "I have four holding pens done, and I have about another three days' work on the loading chute, then it ought to be done. So the alley into the chute and the other four pens on the other side need to be completed, but that's at least another month's work for me." Abe said. "There isn't any way I can have them done in two weeks by myself, Mr. Pitt."

"Not with you sitting at the house, there isn't." Thomas stated flatly. "Christ, you haven't even gotten your shirt dirty today."

They had made it to the barn by this time and were standing in the shade of it. Abe was quiet, his face was set as he let his employer have his say.

"How about those fillies, Abe have you even ridden them yet today?"

"No I haven't, but…"

"Jesus," Thomas cut him off. "You told me how hard you're working, and I pull up to check on you and you're in the house."

Abe stopped him right there. "Hold it, Thomas, I've ridden those colts every day for three weeks straight. They are as trustworthy as they come. I've been working from sunup until sundown every day for you, and you don't even notice what I have accomplished." His tone was flat and solid as he stood face to face with Thomas Pitt.

"What are you saying, Abe? Is this job not good enough for you? I gave you a roof over your head. I pay your electric bill, and I even pay you a salary for your work. All I ask in return is for you to build a couple of corrals on schedule and break a couple of colts. Hell, I don't even ask for money for boarding your kid's horse."

Abe was quiet, for a minute. "Her name is Paige."

"What?"

"My daughter's name is Paige," Abe repeated it slowly and deliberately. "I would appreciate you calling my family members by their names. After six years you should at least know their names."

"Well of course, Abe. I knew that…Paige. And your wife's is…" Thomas hesitated.

"Don't bother, just don't even bother." Abe stated in disgust.

Thomas changed the subject. "Well let me see what you have done out here." He walked out the back of the barn.

He saw the stud colt in the round pen. He lifted his head and nickered to Abe as the men approached.

"That horse kind of likes you," Thomas stated.

"Yeah, he's coming along," Abe said, not impressed with the animal right then.

"I kind of expected you to have at least four weeks on those fillies, Abe. I gave you an extra two weeks. I promised the people I sold them to thirty days of riding." He had anger in his voice.

"Thomas, have I ever given you a bad horse?" Abe asked. His patience was wearing pretty thin. "These fillies are solid and good horses. I can have them ready next week if you want to ship them out."

"They're supposed to be here tomorrow. If they are as good as you say then we don't need to tell them they only have three weeks on them."

Abe looked at the ground and shook his head.

Thomas watched him. "What, Abe? You don't have the stomach for business? Well let me tell you, this is a dog-eat-dog world, maybe you should get a reality check, you know," Thomas looked directly at Abe. "I used to kind of pat myself on the back for helping you out when you needed it the most six years ago. If you remember, Abe, you were about to lose your apartment and everything you had, which wasn't a lot. Now I look at what I gave you, and I feel like you're taking advantage of me. I could have left you out on the street, but instead I took you in and gave you a place to stay."

Abe didn't raise his head, "All I'm saying, Thomas, is I need some time off with my family. I just need a day or two. Paige is growing up so fast I hardly recognize her, and Patricia and I haven't had a day together for so long I can't remember. I missed my daughter's horse show, her being in the hospital, even her interviews. When she needed me most I wasn't there."

"What are you saying, Abe? Do you want to quit?" Thomas felt as if he had the upper hand on this man and he was taking all the strength Abe had. "Did you not hear what I just said? After all I have done for you and you can't even seem to ride four colts a day for four weeks straight. And these corrals, I could have had them done in half the time it took you."

Abe's posture started to straighten. He knew he couldn't

quit this job but he wasn't going to cower down to Thomas Pitt. "Look, Thomas, all I'm asking is for a day off, or maybe a little help. Is that too much to ask? My family works just as hard as I do and I just want to spend some time with them." Abe's voice was solid and direct. He had controlled his anger the best he could.

"Tell you what, Abe, if you want a day off, how about you take Sunday off." Thomas paused, "After the chores are done."

Abe looked him squarely in the eyes. Quiet fury had taken over his body, and he'd had enough. He continued to watch the short, bald weasel before him shift uncomfortably.

Thomas couldn't look him in his eyes. "That's my offer, take it or leave it," Thomas stumbled.

He started out of the barn, and Abe followed. "Thomas, one more question before you leave," Abe's voice was strong and direct. "What about the bonus you promised me for riding those fillies?"

Thomas said nothing until he made it to his car and waddled into the seat. Then he glanced at Abe and back down the road. "Well, since you didn't fulfill your part of the agreement, what do you think, Abe?" Thomas lingered for a minute. "But I won't let you go empty-handed," he paused for a moment as he started the convertible. "I will give you that little horse in the corral." Then he drove away.

Abe stood silently for a minute, and then he turned back toward the barn. Anger and a sense of confusion boiled within him. He walked to the haystack and back to the tack room. His head was spinning. He needed tires for his truck. He needed time to think. He put everything he had into this place and yet it wasn't his and would never be. Everything here he designed with Patricia's help—the barn, the layout of the corrals, the round pen. No two people worked as closely as when they worked on the barn design—Patricia's eye for detail, his ideas of where the gates should be hung, the stalls, the tack room with the repair bench and leather tools from his dad. He remembered how excited Patricia was when she had Harrison's draw up the blue prints and how they complimented her work. This barn was a part of him and her and Paige. Yet it wasn't theirs, and it never would be. It belonged to a greedy little man who had found a desperate family and knew how to work them to his advantage. Abe now understood that he worked for a man he could never satisfy. He also knew that all of this could be taken away in an instant. His family would be homeless with two words if he didn't keep this job. He paced back and forth in the alleyway of the barn, his mind racing with all that was said.

"How will I ever be able to get my own place? What am I going to do with a damn horse?" He asked out loud. He choked back tears, trying to release the anxiety he was holding for so long. "Shit! You asshole, Pitt!" he hollered. He walked up to the barn wall and kicked it, then kicked it again and again. Tears were running down his face. He finally gave into them, leaned against the wall, sank to his haunches, and cried.

"What the hell am I going to do? There has got to be more than this in life. I want to do something nice for my family," he sobbed "God, where did I go wrong? How can I get us out of this hole?"

Abe began to regain control of his emotions and his pride. He stood again drying his eyes on his shirtsleeve and thinking in total concentration on his family's future. Then he walked out of the barn.

"Thomas Pitt, you will not win. I will not let you walk on us any longer." He stood erect, his shoulders back and his head high as he headed for the house.

23

Paige stood in Libby's stall, tears streaming down her face. She had heard the whole conversation. How she hated Thomas Pitt. She had seen her father cry for the first time in her life. He was a human just as she was. He was made of flesh, blood, and bone. He had feelings and emotions just as she did. How come it took so long for her to see it? He was always the strong one when things were down around there. He was always there to pick up the pieces and put them back on course. Now she had seen her father hit the bottom for the first time in her life. She took a deep breath and felt an odd sense of determination come over her.

She dried her tears and walked out of the barn. She went out the back way so she would look like she had just come out of the meadow. She thought of something, and her determination showed as she went to the house. It was going to change her life forever.

As Paige entered the house, she allowed the screen door to slam so that her parents could hear her enter. She started to her room, as she had some planning to do. She heard laughter in the kitchen on her way through.

"Hey, Sis, I have Sunday off. How would you like to go for a picnic?" Abe said in a festive voice.

She looked at her father then her mother, who was almost glowing with happiness. She didn't have a clue as to what had happened outside not ten minutes before.

Paige decided to play along although she didn't understand his happiness. "Really, Papa? That sounds great. Are we still going to the Greenly's tonight?"

"Yep, I'm going to do chores early, and we're going to go out for the evening," he said. His eyes were shining with mischief.

"I'll go out and help you," Paige stated as if he couldn't do it himself.

"Nonsense, you stay in here and get ready to go. I'll have the chores done in an hour or so." He smiled at his two women. "Then maybe the bathroom will be empty and there'll be enough hot water for me to shower and shave." He chided them both, "I'm just glad there aren't any more women in the house, a man wouldn't have a chance to get cleaned up."

Paige was filled with mixed emotions. What was all that emotion in the barn not fifteen minutes ago? How could he smile when he had just cried? What was he going to do about Thomas Pitt? Yet, her mom was so excited about going to town.

She wanted to sit down and cry, and yet she had an indescribable feeling of calm within her. She almost felt numb as she watched her father grab his hat and go out to do chores.

Patricia called again, "Paige? Did you hear me?"

"I'm sorry, Mom. What did you say?"

"Go get your shirt and I'll iron it for you." Patricia looked at her oddly. "Are you okay, Sis? You look a little pale."

"I'm fine, Mom, just a little nervous about going to the Greenly's I guess." Paige smiled at her mom then quickly retreated to her room. She returned with a white blouse that she seldom wore, gave it to her mother, and then jumped in the shower.

She stood in the shower soaking in the hot water, her mind swimming with emotion and determination. The water sounded like a constant drum inside her head as she just stood there allowing it to run down her face. She was going to do it, she had decided. It needed to be done. With the decision made, she felt a wave of calm come over her as well as fear and excitement. It put her into a good mood as she stepped from the bathroom.

Patricia walked by her bringing in some fresh clean towels off the clothesline. "I thought you drowned in there. I was on my way to call 911."

Paige looked at her mother and smiled. She could see Patricia had vibrancy and passion for all she had. Paige asked her, "Mom..." she paused, then continued, "do we have a good life?"

Patricia looked at her daughter as she brushed on past her once again, "We have it better than some, not as good as others. But most important we do the best we can with what we have."

Patricia put her hand under her daughter's chin and raised it up. She looked into her deep beautiful eyes and said, "I am proud of who I am and who I have for a family." She brushed Paige's wet hair back behind her shoulder and then said, "Now it's my turn in the bathroom. I got to get a shower before your dad gets in here and takes my hot water." She smiled again as Paige stepped out of the doorway.

Paige slipped on her newest jeans and her white blouse her mom just ironed. She started brushing out her blonde hair, and as she looked into the mirror, she paused and stared into it, "I'm proud of my family too." At that moment she realized for life to change she had to change her life. She took a deep breath and began braiding her hair.

By the time Abe came back in from chores, both of his girls were dressed in their Sunday best. Patricia looked radiant in a white floral summer dress with her hair pulled back from her eyes and laid smoothly down the middle of her back. And his beautiful daughter had her hair braided and was wearing fresh, clean clothes. He couldn't be more proud.

As Abe jumped into the shower, Patricia brought in the new pair of Wrangler jeans she bought him for Christmas almost a year ago. When he got out of the shower, Abe saw the jeans and smiled. He pulled off the tags and slipped into them, and the crisp feel was good. He started humming, then singing: "The yellow rose of Texas, I'm coming home to see. Nobody else has held her, her heart belongs to me. We have traveled down some dusty roads and slept out in the rain. She's my yellow rose of Texas and I coming home again."

He didn't know all the words, but it didn't seem to matter. Paige hadn't heard him sing in so long it sounded odd.

Patricia finished pressing his shirt, and as she handed it to him, he grabbed her around the waist and swung her around. He did a couple of two-step moves and brought her down into a dip. Patricia was laughing, still holding on to his shirt. He kissed her and said, "Would you marry me again if I asked you?"

Patricia looked him squarely in the eyes and said, "You know I would."

"That's all I need to know," he said as he brought her back up to standing. He took his shirt, gave her another kiss, and said, "Thanks for the special delivery."

Patricia grabbed a loaf of her homemade bread and wrapped it in a towel on her way to the door.

Abe grabbed his newer straw hat, slipped it on his head, and opened the back door, "Ladies, your chariot awaits." He tipped his hat as they passed by him.

His handsome tan and chiseled features were highlighted under his white cowboy hat and white shirt. His grin was as broad and happy as Paige had ever seen. She giggled as she went by. She had never seen her father in such a happy mood.

Patricia smiled at him, "Now I know why I don't let you go to town looking like that every day. There would be women knocking down the doors for you."

"Me? Look at you. If I'm not careful I might lose you to some lawyer or doctor of some type."

"Not a chance, Cowboy, I like the rugged type." She grinned at him as she passed by.

He opened the old Ford's green dented door for his girls. It creaked in complaint and then Abe slammed it hard to get it shut.

"This Old Green Mare ain't what she used to be," Abe said as he walked to the other side of the pickup. He climbed in, pushed in the clutch with his left foot, turned the key, and just like magic she came to life. He released the clutch and the Old Green Mare started out of the driveway kicking up dirt and dust as they left. He ground the gears as he tried to find second but nobody really noticed because they were laughing about a joke Abe was telling.

It was a good feeling to leave the house with the family and just have a good time for no apparent reason—just going to be going. They drove through the sagebrush hills of open space, dirt, and alkali soil.

Abe started to sing again, an old Hank Williams song:

"Hey, hey, good lookin', whatcha you got cookin'?

How's about cookin' somethin' up with me?

Hey, sweet baby, don't you think maybe

We could find us a brand new recipe?

Got a hot-rod Ford and a two dollar bill,

I know a spot right over the hill.

There's soda pop, and the dancin's free,

183

So if you wanna have fun come along with me.

Say hey, good lookin', whatcha got cookin'?

How's about cookin' somethin' up with me?"

There was a freshness in the atmosphere as they traveled along.

24

As they pulled up to the Greenlys' Ranch, an odd silence fell among the family. Before them was a white rail fence that led all the way up to a large two story white Victorian style house with a deck all the way around the base of it. The drive was paved, and on both sides of it was alfalfa thick and rich, almost ready to be swathed for hay.

To the north of the house was a magnificent barn that was painted red with white trim. It had stalls all along the east side with horses standing quietly in the paddocks. There were broodmares in a large pasture farther behind the barn. There looked to be maybe twenty to thirty of them standing lazily in the shade of a grove of trees. They were standing head to hip, swishing the flies off of each other's faces and not concerned with anything going on around them.

Abe took a deep breath and let it slowly out. He turned his old Ford up the paved drive. If he hadn't talked to this man earlier and gotten an impression of him, he didn't know if he would be driving up to this huge house right now. He wished he could provide a place such as this for his family. His heart sank as they got closer.

Paige felt like she had waited for this all her life. If she had a place like this, she would never leave. As they drove closer, she saw the yearling horses in a lower pasture next to the alfalfa fields close to the barn. There were two bay colts bickering back and forth. They looked identical with sharp little heads and nice long necks that fell perfectly into the front shoulders. Their short manes tossed precariously back and forth as they played. They had nice solid short backs drawn up into a rounded hip that ran smoothly down their hind legs and into the hocks. There was no choppiness to these colts, Paige noticed. It was as if they were all made of circular motions bound together with hide. She could actually envision drawing these two colts with her pencil in hand. One colt was nipping the nose of the other as he tried to sleep. His eyes half-droopy, he laid his ears back and nipped back at the intruder but didn't want to go after him. He just bobbed his nose at him.

Paige smiled then looked back toward the house. All of a sudden, she got a pang in her stomach.

Abe felt a gentle hand on his leg. He looked over to see his wife looking at him.

"I don't know if I want you to come up here," Patricia said in a teasing voice.

"Why's that?" he replied kind of shocked because she was reading his mind.

"I can hear you now," she came back at him, trying her best to mock what he would say. "This is the place I've always wanted!" Then she continued, "And then you'll beg and plead me to buy it for you and threaten to leave me if I don't give in. You'll want to use our life savings as a down payment and go into debt for the rest of our lives." She smiled at him.

"Isn't this what you want?" he asked.

"Right now I have all I need right here in this truck," she said as she put her hand around his neck and gave him a kiss on the cheek. Then she leaned over and did the same to Paige. She sighed as they pulled to a stop at the front of the house.

Abe looked at his small family sitting in his truck. Then he looked out at the large white house he just parked in front of. *Who is richer,* he wondered as he opened his door.

Paige was silent as they talked. She wondered how much of it was true. How could her father be so happy when Thomas Pitt had just insulted him to the point of nothing more than dirt on the ground? She had sat there and watched him cry for the first time in her life, and now he was acting as if everything was alright, like he had not one worry in the world.

She glanced out the pickup as her father stepped out. John Greenly was standing on the porch with Samantha. She had braces on each wrist and was holding herself with crutches, a look of humiliation on her face. She had a walking cast up to the calf of her left leg. She was dressed in a pair of cutoff sweats and a tank top.

Paige glanced at the well-groomed lawn and trimmed evergreens that were neatly placed along the porch. Above, hanging in between the pillars were hanging plants. A wide sidewalk ran from the driveway to the house with three steps in the middle of the lengthy path. There was an archway of latticework with vines growing over the top. It had rich pink roses throughout the latticework. Paige suddenly felt dirty and uncomfortable even being there.

Abe and Patricia also felt a little uncomfortable, but they heard John's anxious voice.

"Come in. Come in."

Samantha rolled her eyes, her face hot with embarrassment. She couldn't believe they were actually there. What did they think of her being so clumsy and foolish on that day?

She couldn't think of anything she could say to any one of the family, especially Paige. Well, maybe she wouldn't have to say anything. She knew Paige didn't like her anyway, so maybe she would just stay in the house as her father showed them around the place. Paige would surely like to see the barn and the horses. As far as Samantha was concerned, she could just stay in the house. She'd seen it all before, and there was nothing to be impressed about. *It's a barn and a bunch of dumb horses. If you've seen one, you've seen them all.*

Abe got out of the truck, went to the passenger side, and opened the door for Paige and Patricia. It again clunked and squawked as he opened it. Paige felt her face redden.

Abe commented quietly. "We'll have to get some oil for that, don't you think, Paige?"

Paige glanced at him and rolled her eyes. His eyes were twinkling with excitement and anticipation.

"Well you're the one who said you wanted to come over

and have me look at Piper, so here we are, darlin'." He winked at her.

She got out of the truck and her mother followed. Abe clicked the door behind them and Paige took a breath.

She thought about what her father might be able to do for Piper. If she had only known what their place looked like she would never have offered. *I'm doing this for Piper*, she thought. *I'm doing this for the horse*. It eased a little of the tension. She heard footsteps coming down the walkway.

John was walking out to meet them. He walked with confidence and happiness and held out his hand to Abe.

"I'm so glad you guys could make it. It's good to see you this evening." His voice was chipper and fresh. He had an energy about him that made Paige feel comfortable, as if she were at her own home.

"May I say, Patricia, you and your daughter look lovely this evening."

"I think they do too." Abe said as Patricia took his arm.

Patricia smiled and looked at the ground.

Paige couldn't fathom looking lovely. She was just trying to take everything in. John stepped off to the side so that Abe and his family could walk down the walkway where Samantha was waiting. *Here we go,* Paige thought, her heart beating in her throat. She then took a deep breath and walked forward with purpose, stepping up on the porch.

"Hey, Samantha," she said, her voice a little shaky. "How are you?"

Samantha glanced at her for an instant and said. "Well

I've been better." She then gave it a second thought. *This is the girl who saved my life.* She continued, "But I'm getting stronger all the time. They said my arm braces will be off in another week or so. I can't wait. This thing is itching like crazy."

"What about your leg?" Paige asked feeling more relaxed now that the ice was broken.

"Well they aren't sure about that. They filled my leg full of pins and screws, and it was broken right at the anklebone. But at least I still have a foot."

Paige smiled, "Yeah, I couldn't imagine being without a foot."

John interrupted the two girls. "You girls go on in the house. I want to show your folks around. We'll be back in a while."

Paige wanted to go with them. She wanted to see the horses and the barns and everything. Samantha wanted her to go too. That way she wouldn't have to make conversation with her.

"You can go if you want to," Samantha said. "You don't have to stay here with me."

"No, that's okay. It's all grownup stuff anyway."

There was an odd silence between them, Samantha said, "Well, you want to see my room?"

"Sure," Paige answered, trying to get her nerves under control.

They both walked through the grand entryway of the

house. Paige was silenced as they entered. Above her head was a huge chandelier. To the left was a grand staircase with an oak railing. The landing had a large oak scroll at the beginning of the staircase.

Samantha hobbled up next to her. "We have to go up the stairs. I slept down here for a while when I couldn't get around too well, but now Dad makes me sleep upstairs. I'm getting better at it, but it's just silly. We have a spare room downstairs and it doesn't make much sense why he won't let me move my stuff down here."

She stood at the base of the stairs then hoisted herself up the first step. Then putting her crutches on the next step, she again hoisted herself up another step. Paige looked at how far she had to go.

Samantha said as if reading her mind. "Twenty-two steps, twenty more to go. When I get my own house, I'll never have a staircase. Just in case I ever break another part of my body. This is a pain in the butt."

Paige laughed, "Yeah, it looks like it. I can't believe you actually climb these things with your crutches."

Paige climbed another five steps then waited for Samantha. "You know we don't have to climb these things. It's not like I really have to see your room."

"No, that's okay, it gives us something to do. Dad will be gone for about a half-hour or so. I know dinner won't be ready for at least another hour."

Paige looked over the banister. She could see the front

room, and there was a huge bay window where she could see clear across the open fields, across the valley, and all the way to the Blue Mountains. Down below her, she could see a leather sofa and love seat, a large oak coffee table with a large doily sitting squarely, and upon that was a bouquet of flowers. The matching end tables had white doilies on them as well. Then beautiful bronze horse heads arched, with manes flowing and mouths agape. She wondered for a moment why people liked to see a gaping mouth on a horse. Then her attention was turned to the windows that had bright floral patterned curtains hanging from them, draped down and tied back with golden tassels.

The walls were covered with richly painted art and a few photos. Paige stared a little too long, then Samantha's voice interrupted her thought.

"My mother decorated this house, and Dad keeps it exactly the same. He doesn't alter anything. He even orders in new flowers every week just as Mom did. That's her hanging above the fireplace."

Paige glanced over to the right and there stood a huge fireplace framed by river rock with a large oak mantel above it. Above that was a large painting of Samantha's mother, her long golden blonde hair swept around and draped over her right shoulder. Her eyes a rich green, and her smile the same as Samantha's.

"She is beautiful, Samantha," Paige stated looking from the picture to her. "She looks just like you."

"That's what Dad says too." Samantha said, putting her crutches on the next step and hopping up. "Five more to go," she stated. "I don't think I look much like her. Sure, I have her green eyes and blonde hair, but that's about it. I don't think anyone will be as pretty as she was."

They made it all the way up to the top. As they walked down the hallway, they could still see over the entire front room. Then Samantha opened the door to her room. She hobbled over to her bed and plunked down on it.

"Ahhhhh," she said, "home sweet home."

Paige stood in the doorway a minute. There before her was a canopy bed. It had a light flower pattern on white background with lace ruffles all around the top of it. Everything matched her comforter and the ruffles around the base of the bed. She had four pillows stacked together at the head of the bed. *Why does she need so many pillows?* There was a white ottoman in one corner and a huge pink beanbag in the other. She had a bookshelf full of books. Paige tried to act nonchalantly, went over, and sat on the edge of Samantha's bed, running her hand over the comforter's flowers.

Paige thought of the handmade quilt on her bed with no headboard, her one pillow, her rope rug that sparsely covered the floor in front of her dresser, and the few pictures of horses on the wall.

Samantha was quiet for a minute. Then she took a breath and stated, "Paige, I don't think I ever thanked you for doing what you did. Dad said you pulled the saddle off." She paused, her mind was racing for things she wanted to say. She was mad at her dad when he told her that Paige and the Casons were coming over tonight. She couldn't believe that he wanted them here. Yet now that Paige was right in front of her, Samantha realized that Paige was the only one who really knew what was going on that day. She felt that Paige was someone she could talk to. She took another breath, thought for a second, then started at the beginning.

"When I woke up in the hospital, Dad just held my hand and cried. I looked at my arms in casts and at my leg. I had tubes running out of me from all over. I didn't know what happened, if I was in a car accident or what. I didn't have a clue until he told me."

"What? You didn't remember the horse show?" Paige asked a little surprised.

"Things were pretty hazy at first. I don't remember a lot of stuff, but they said I got knocked around a lot and that helmet I had on was the only thing that saved my life." Samantha paused again. "I remember the horse show alright. I also remember you and your pretty mare and me trying to pick a fight." Her face turned red. "I can't believe I did that to you."

Samantha looked away and was watching herself run her forefinger around her thumbnail. "I remember Piper acting really odd that day, fidgety or something. Anyway, I remember the balloon and getting really mad at Piper. He wouldn't hold still. I was kind of showing off, with all the kids laughing, then the balloon popped. The rest was like slow motion. I guess Piper had had enough." Samantha stopped for a moment.

As Paige looked at her, she saw Samantha's face distort and her lip start to quiver. Samantha took a breath as if to force herself to say what was on her mind. A tear rolled down her face. "I had Piper standing next to the arena fence and I felt him flinch when the balloon popped. And as I reached down, I slapped his head at the same time. I knew Piper was going to run as it popped. So I thought I could step onto the fence. It was only a foot away. I reached for it and I remember feeling the top rung of the panel on my fingers. Then I felt a jerk on my foot as Piper took off. Then I felt like I was falling. That's all I remember until I woke up in the hospital three days later."

Tears were running down both cheeks now. Samantha was just letting go of some of the guilt. She took a breath and sat quietly.

Paige sat silently, listening and reliving all that had happened, her feelings and emotions of that day stirring within her. Then she began.

"When that day started for me, it was the biggest day in my life, or so I thought at the time, actually taking Libby into a show. I don't know if I was ready for what was there, but I did it anyway. Libby was being really obnoxious. Her attitude and everything I had worked for seemed gone. I couldn't get her attention no matter what I tried. Then after you came over…" Paige paused. "Then it all clicked. All of the sudden everything changed. I knew I had to take control and finish what I started no matter what others thought of me." Paige stopped there, and then continued. "After the show I was getting ready to load Libby and was talking with your Dad." Paige left out why, a knot all of the sudden tied into her stomach. She paused again to get past the idea. "All of the sudden your dad and I heard a loud pop and the next thing we knew you were being dragged by Piper. There was no time to think, Samantha. I just untied Libby, jumped on her back, and headed for the gate. When it was all done I felt really dizzy. I couldn't get my bearings, and my eyes wouldn't focus. It was really odd. The next thing I knew I was in the hospital too."

Samantha looked at Paige, "Have you ridden since then?"

"Sure, every day," Paige replied.

"Did it affect Libby at all?"

"Not really. She was a little high headed for a day or two after that, but she worked it out."

"I guess Piper isn't doing so well," Samantha replied looking down at her walking cast. "Just…if I would have done something differently—not been so mad, or not try to make everyone watch me, or something, Piper would be okay now."

"Piper is going to be okay, Samantha," Paige said reassuringly.

Samantha looked at Paige with anger in her eyes. "No, he's not! I was on the porch the other day when the horse trainer was here. He said if it were him he'd just put Piper down because he'll never get over it."

Tears welled up in her eyes again. Then she blinked them back. Paige didn't know for sure what to say. Should she say that her father was looking at him now or leave it alone? John didn't think that Samantha knew.

"If I ever face Piper again, I would like to tell him I'm sorry, but I can't even bring myself to go down to the barn. I can't look in his eyes and say I'm sorry but I have to kill you. I just can't do that."

Tears started running down her face, and this time she let them fall again. She didn't care if Paige saw them. They had been hidden for over a month now and had built up in her mind into a guilty conscience. She felt that she had no one to talk to or anyone who might understand until now.

Paige knew that if something like that had happened to Libby, she couldn't face her either. She didn't know for sure what to say.

Samantha continued. Now that she had started and someone was listening, there was so much on her mind. "Dad wants me to go out and see him. He thinks it will be good for me. But it isn't going to do any good. I just don't know how I can face Piper. What words could I use, Paige, to make him understand?"

Paige wanted to say something to get her out of this state

of mind, but she just couldn't think of anything. Then Samantha leaned up from where she was. She grabbed her crutches and hobbled over to the ottoman. She grabbed a tissue, dried her eyes, and blew her nose.

"Sorry," she said as she threw the used tissue in the garbage pail by the head of the bed. "At times it seems that I don't have anyone to talk too."

"What about all your friends from school?"

"Yeah, right," she scoffed. "Things have changed. I don't even know if I have friends anymore. Some friends came out to see me about two weeks ago and stayed for about a half hour. Then one called her mom to come and get her. I guess I'm not someone people want to look at and be around with these casts and crutches."

She looked out the window and down below she could see the mares grazing lazily in the pasture, their tails swishing back and forth.

Paige got up and went to the window too. "You know, Samantha, if you wanted to go see Piper tonight, I'd go with you."

The aroma of dinner wafted up into her room. It smelled of roast beef and potatoes. It lingered in Paige's mind for a moment. Her stomach growled, and her mouth started to water. They heard the back door open, and the voices of both fathers echoed in the empty house. Samantha turned from the window and looked at Paige for a minute.

"I don't know if I'm ready," she said as she looked at the plush taupe carpet, raking her crutch softly back and forth.

"He's going to hate me as soon as he sees me."

"You never know, Samantha, until you try."

Samantha looked at Paige for a moment, then quietly headed for the stairs. Paige followed.

As they came to the bottom of the stairs, Samantha, without saying a word, opened the front door and walked out onto the porch. She turned abruptly to Paige, putting her finger to her lips, as Paige closed the door behind her.

"Let's go for a walk," Samantha said quietly after the door clicked shut. "I want to take one look at him just to see if he is okay."

"Don't you want your dad to go with you?"

"No. He'll want to make a big deal out of it. He'll put more into it than me just wanting to see Piper. All I want to do is just see him for a minute just to see if he hates me or not."

Samantha's courage and curiosity got the better of her as she spoke of Piper. Paige listening to her and being beside her without judgment or anger made her think that maybe Piper might feel the same way and forgive her for the stupid act she committed almost two months ago.

"I know I'll be able to tell how he feels about me. He gets a look in his eye when he is mad." Samantha took a deep breath. "We shouldn't be gone for more than a couple of minutes. Dad will think we're still upstairs. He won't need to know."

Paige looked hesitantly at Samantha. Then a thought

crossed her mind. Mr. Greenly did want her to get Samantha outside. "Well what are we waiting for? Let's do it then."

They cautiously crept off the porch and around the house to the barn. Samantha hobbled along silently, determination etched in her face. A soft breeze played with her hair, crossing her face and pushing it into her eyes, but she didn't take time to brush it away. She didn't stop until they got to the barn door. Samantha looked back at the house, her breathing a little unsteady, and she transferred her gaze to the inside of the barn. She looked at Paige a long moment, then without saying a word, walked into the breezeway and hobbled her way down to the far end of the barn.

Samantha could smell the fresh hay, the sweet smell of horses and leather, and the damp earth that was under her feet. She could hear rhythmic chewing of hay, the stomping of the hooves, and the swish of tails as the horses tried in vain to rid themselves of the few pesky flies that forever attempted to land on them. She approached the stall door and peered inside. There was Piper in the warm light of the barn. He looked at her from his feed bunk and immediately quit chewing. He pricked his ears toward her, putting his nose to the bars and breathing in. Her familiar sight and scent flickered in his eyes.

Samantha held her breath. Silence seemed to fill the barn, a reunion of tension and of love filled the space between them. A tear streamed down Samantha's face. Then ever so slowly, she raised her hand through the bars to touch his velvety soft nose. She felt reunited with an old friend. Yet, they had both changed.

Then, as if to lighten the mood a little, Piper blew his nose through the bars, all over both girls. Green flecks of soggy hay flew everywhere. Both girls squealed and started to laugh. Piper buried his nose back into his feed bunk as if he had done his job well and went back to eating.

Samantha laughed as she wobbled on her crutches trying to get away from the green shower. "You haven't changed at all, have you?" she chided him as he lifted his head again from his feed bunk, stems protruding from his mouth. "I came here to apologize to you and this is what I get. Well, see if you get sympathy from me again," she joked, her eyes shining with delight. "See, Paige, you feel sorry for a guy and this is what you get for it."

Paige laughed. She didn't care that Piper had covered her white blouse in green. She had envisioned this horse as whipped, deprived, and totally uncontrollable. He seemed just fine to her.

Samantha looked at Paige with a certain calm and determination. "Paige, I don't want him to die. Do you think your dad can help him?"

It surprised Paige that Samantha knew her father was here to look at Piper and that he worked with horses.

"Do you think I would be able to ride Piper again?" Samantha's voice faltered.

These questions were asked with such intensity, and Samantha's eyes never looked away from Piper. Whether for fear of the horse dying or for fear of being vulnerable to another person, maybe even looking for belief in hope and the future, Paige didn't know. But she also realized this girl was like her in so many ways.

Paige wanted to say yes, that her father could do anything with horses, but she thought better of it. "I don't know, Samantha, he does some pretty amazing things with horses, but you would have to ask him."

"Well let's go do it then." Turning abruptly on her crutches, she hobbled back to the house, the strides with her crutches long and deliberate. Samantha's attitude had totally changed since their arrival in the barn. Her head was up and her actions were sure. She was the Samantha that Paige knew, yet a Samantha that had changed forever. They entered through the back door of the house with a thump of the crutches and a bang of the kitchen door. They strode into the kitchen where Patricia, Abe, and John were sitting at the breakfast bar, drinking iced tea the maid had just poured.

Samantha entered and without a second thought said, "Mr. Cason, I want to ride Piper again, can you make him better?"

Abe looked at both girls a moment, stunned. He saw green flecks freckled across the girls' faces and blouses and the determination gleaming in Samantha's eyes.

John interrupted, quite stunned himself, "Samantha, where have you been? Have you been down to the barn?"

"Yes, Daddy, I have. Paige and I went out there, and Piper is fine. He blew snot on us both." Samantha was direct, focusing on Piper and keeping the attention off of her.

"I know that you're thinking of putting Piper down or sending him to slaughter or whatever." The thought made her eyes tear up but she blinked them back as she continued. "I've seen him rear over backwards and throw himself down when the trainers tried to saddle him. I sat up there in my room and watched and I cried. But he's not bad. Please, Daddy, don't kill him because of me." Tears were running down Samantha's cheeks.

John listened to his daughter, his heart ripping in two because of her pleas. "We will see what we can do, Baby."

Abe swallowed hard as he looked at Samantha, "I can't guarantee anything with Piper, but I sure can give it a try for you."

John was shocked and pleased, yet nervous of what the outcome would be. His heart was in his throat. He had three other trainers work with this horse and the outcome was not good. Would it just be false hope? Yet, his daughter hadn't been out in weeks. She seemed so wrapped up in her own pain she hadn't given anyone else's a thought. Now here she stood before him, eyes lit up, color back in her face, and posture tall and straight. Did he allow her to live the dream of Piper being okay, or should he bring her back to a possibly bleak reality?

Abe was quiet. This was a matter between father and child, and he was not part of it. He thought of Piper, when John took him to the barn with Patricia. Piper was a quiet horse for the most part, a smart little head and a keen eye. When John opened the stall door, Piper backed himself into a corner and stood, head high and his eyes wild. Abe entered the stall just beyond the doorframe and saw Piper stand so still he could hardly see him breathe. His ears were cocked to the side and his head was straight and high. Abe backed out of the stall and closed the door. Piper stood still for about five minutes after the door was closed before feeling safe enough to step up and reach his nose out to grab a few sprigs of hay. Abe would like to see him out of the stall and move him around a little to see what the horse was really thinking, but that was not going to happen this evening. Piper already had spoken volumes about what he thought was expected of him.

"Well, Samantha," John said with a sigh, weighing his options as he spoke. "I think we could have Abe work with him and give Piper one more try. But I want it understood, young lady, there are no promises." His voice was stern but his eyes were hopeful. "Abe, if you think you have some time, we sure would appreciate you working with him."

Abe looked at Patricia, then Paige, and last he looked at Samantha, and gave her a long look before he turned back to John.

25

It was after dark when the Cason family got in the truck with its doors clunking shut with a slam. It was a long quiet ride home. The closer Abe drove toward home the quieter he got. Reality was once again sinking in.

Thomas' words kept sneaking in. "What are you going to do, Abe, quit? After all I've done for your family. When you had nothing I gave you a roof over your head and a place to call home."

Home, Abe thought, home what did that mean? He was thinking of the work he had done the last six years—the barn, the corrals, the horses. All his work and nothing of what he did would be his own. He felt a sense of pride about the work but he was also thinking he was disposable. He could be fired tomorrow and someone else would come in and take his place. And he would have nothing to show for it. He had the memories, the pride, but what did that give him in return? What was home? A little, run down shack at the end of a dirt road.

Patricia could see the tension on Abe's face in the reflection of the dash lights. She casually put her hand on his leg and gave it a soft squeeze, trying to let him know that he was not alone. He still had his family. They were right beside him now. He didn't have to do this alone. They would be there in whatever he was going to do.

Wait a minute, she thought, *what is this thinking? What is he*

205

going to do? That all of a sudden didn't make any sense to her. Why was she waiting and depending on him to make all the decisions for this family. She started to look at her life and what she had to offer this family.

Abe responded to the squeeze with a glance at her and a strained smile.

"We're going to be alright," she said looking at him. "We've been through tougher times than these."

"I know," he replied. "I know," He repeated with a sigh then went quiet again.

Paige was quiet. From being in the barn earlier and hearing Thomas to feeling nervous about seeing Samantha to looking at Piper and reliving all the chaos of that day, she felt drained and exhausted. She laid her head on her mom's shoulder and closed her eyes. Sleep was already there waiting.

After they got home, Paige went straight to bed, Abe sat with his elbows on the kitchen table, his head cradled in his hands. He ran one of his hands through his hat-worn hair, then leaned back in his chair.

Patricia came and sat across from him. "What's going on, babe?" She asked rather bluntly. She wanted Abe to be honest with her and not try to candy coat his mood.

"Well," he said with a sigh, "I've been doing a lot of thinking. I feel like we are at a crossroad and I don't know which road to take." He sighed again and ran his hand through his hair. His eyes were tired. Through his mid-summer tan, his face looked stressed. "Thomas is not happy with the work I'm doing. And I'm not happy with the workload he has put on me," he continued. "For the bonus on the fillies I have been riding," he paused, "he gave me that little stud colt." He shook his head. "He ain't gonna be worth much, babe, he's too damn little. If he had a little size to him or something maybe, but he sure doesn't look like he'll be able to cover the country like the others can." He stopped again trying to find something good to say about his "bonus" then said, "That little guy showed some promise today when I played with him. He is quick, smooth, and smart, but damn, babe, he's real little."

"Do you think his size really matters? He's a sharp, catchy looking little guy," she agreed.

"If I kept him until the annual Hermiston Horse Sale in January we might get something for him. But we can't wait that long because we won't have any tires on the truck to get him there." He got up, walked across the kitchen, got a glass of water, and took a large swallow. He propped his hip against the counter and crossed his ankles. "That ain't all of it." He put his glass down and crossed his arms. "Thomas has a shipment of three hundred bred cows coming in two weeks." He shook his head.

"I just don't get it."

"When I left with you and Paige this evening I had the intention of asking John for a job. But, as I was around the ranch and spent time with him, something made me stop from asking." He paused, thinking. "Patricia," he stuttered, "I don't want to work for somebody else anymore. After Thomas got done with me today, telling me all the things I haven't done." He paused again shaking his head. "This is just crazy," he continued, relieved to get it out in the open, yet embarrassed to have let it all get to him. "I'm sick and tired of not having enough, not doing enough or not being enough." Tears welled in his eyes, and he blinked them back. He looked at Patricia to see if he was being understood, or was overreacting.

"I just don't have the answers any more, Patricia. I just don't know where to go from here."

She nodded, looking him in the eyes. She walked across the kitchen and took his hand. "Abe, you don't have to have all the answers. Why don't you let me help out?"

"What can you do, Patricia? I have dug a pretty deep hole and I don't know how to fill it right now."

Patricia kissed him on the cheek. "We've been through some pretty tough times and we've pulled through, so just give it some time, Abe. Give it a little more time." She stepped back, giving him room.

He grabbed his glass again and took another swallow of water, wishing it was whiskey. His heart wasn't in it. He had pretty much reached the end of his rope. "I can work here for the next five years and we will still have the same as what we do now. This is a dead end job, babe. There is nothing here for us." He slammed the glass on the counter, a little harder than he intended to. He paced around the table, getting angry at his own weaknesses and venting them toward his wife.

Paige woke up from the commotion in the kitchen and stood inside her bedroom doorway listening to what was being said. Everything that happened this evening was far behind. Now, the reality of what her father was really feeling surfaced and was biting into her heart. She had spent the entire summer riding Libby, playing around, and living life as a free child as her parents struggled to keep things together. How could she have been so naïve, so stupid, and so fussy about what another kid thought?

A shadow moved in the hallway as her father walked across the kitchen. She moved away from her bedroom doorway and crawled back in bed. She had heard enough. She pulled the covers up over her shoulders, under her chin, and held them close. Tears fell silently from the corners of her eyes as the conversation gradually ebbed away into a mumble of words. Her exhausted body fell back to sleep.

Patricia let Abe have his say, let him get it all out. She was not about to argue. She had a calmness about her that kept the family together. Now it was time to step up. She had a plan.

"Abe," she said, "can you give me a month? Just one more month." She wasn't asking.

Back when Thomas wanted a barn, Abe told Patricia, and she picked up paper and pencil and sketched out Abe's measurements and design. She took it to an engineer friend, David Harrison, who complimented her exuberantly for her work and helped her create the blueprint for the contractors.

When Patricia was in high school, she loved to draw and work with colors and had taken several art classes. She was a natural with shape and dimensions, and math was a breeze for her. Although when she met Abe, she put all that stuff behind her because she had just been playing and how could anyone make a living drawing sketches or coloring?

Patricia was good in math and with angles and seemed a natural at design, so she had played with different floor plans and measurements that she created on quiet afternoons or in the evening when she couldn't sleep. She designed landscapes, house floor plans, barn floor plans and designed the outsides of structures and corral layouts. She always tucked them away, where they were never seen or noticed by anyone. Some of them had laid silent for years.

That morning before John came out, she saw an ad for David Harrison, the engineer who looked at her plans. She thought for moment about her designs then shrugged it off because she did not have a degree of any sort. She was just playing anyway...right?

Patricia decided not to mention this to Abe. She would gather up her collection and drop by to see David and see what he had to say. It had been a few years since she had seen him, but they had known each other since high school. It wouldn't take long to get reacquainted, she was sure.

"Abe, it is a quarter after eleven, why don't we call it a day?"

Abe looked at her. "Yeah, it's been a long one," he replied. "Let's do." He took her hand, pulled her close to him, and held her. He breathed in the scent of her hair, wrapped his arms around her lean frame, and sighed. Then he brushed his lips against her neck and kissed her gently below her ear.

Patricia felt a shiver go up her spine and fell into his embrace. No strength was needed tonight. She tilted her head and found his lips with hers.

26

Patricia had a restless night. She had visions of David looking at her work and laughing at her. Waking with a start, she would lie awake and think of the possibilities of what could happen. David might not even remember her. The thoughts tortured her mind. *I have only a high school diploma,* she thought to herself as she lay awake, *what if this just blows up in my face.* Then she would drift off to sleep again, tossing and turning, trying to get comfortable, trying to rest. Now her day had begun. Her morning chores melted away one by one and her errands in town had come.

She pulled in front of Harrison's Engineering and left the pickup idling as she tried to gather her thoughts. She looked at her portfolio sitting silently beside her. Its battered leather folder was worn at the corners and some of the thread from the seams was worn a little thin. She looked in the rearview mirror and straightened her windblown hair from the window being down, then opened the door with the familiar creak and pop of the hinges.

As she entered the building, a receptionist politely greeted her. Patricia thought she might just leave her portfolio with her and ask that David look at them when he had time, but on second thought, she walked up to the desk.

"Is David in today?" she asked politely, glancing at the office door nervously.

"Do you have an appointment with Mr. Harrison?" the

receptionist questioned as she glanced up from her typing.

"No," Patricia replied, "I just have a couple of questions for him and thought he might be able to help me out."

"Well he's with a client right now. Can I have him call you when he gets done?" The receptionist replied, looking a little bit too busy to be bothered with someone who didn't have an appointment.

"Well I'm in town today and would really like to speak with him when he has time," Patricia commented feeling a little downhearted at the anticipated meeting, and a little silly for not creating an appointment.

"He has an opening at three this afternoon." The receptionist replied, her manicured hands typing as she talked.

Patricia didn't want an appointment, all she wanted was to talk to David for a few minutes and see what he thought of her building plans. "I only need to see him for a few minutes," she said more urgently.

"Well three o'clock is the best I can do for you, ma'am." She stopped her typing and looked up at Patricia. "Would you like me to schedule you in? He'll be out for the next couple of days on some projects. He won't be back in the office until next week."

"I guess that will have to do," Patricia replied, losing her nervousness and replacing it with disappointment. She glanced at the clock, 11:30 a.m. She didn't know what she was going to do for three and a half hours.

As the receptionist started to ask for her name, the phone rang. The receptionist picked up the phone before Patricia could even begin to say her name. Patricia felt like maybe she should just go ahead and leave. Maybe this was just a bad idea even coming here. She could call and make an appointment some other time since he was busier than what she thought he would be. She turned to start out the door when the office door opened.

"Doug, I am really glad you stopped by today and I'll keep my eyes open for a layout plan for you. That property you bought is a real nice piece and I'm sure it will make a good home site."

"Dave, I sure appreciate your help on this. I was going to fly someone down here from Portland, but I was told to come here first."

"Glad you did, Doug. Glad you did." Dave said as he held out his hand and Doug shook it firmly then walked out the door.

The receptionist was still on the phone. Dave glanced in the lobby at Patricia as he turned to go back in his office. He stopped and looked back.

"Patricia?" he exclaimed.

Patricia shifted uneasily, looking from the receptionist then back at Dave. "Hey, David."

"What a pleasant surprise. What brings you in here?"

"Well, uh, I had a couple of questions and I thought you might be able to answer them for me if you had a minute."

"Sure! Sure come on in!" he said enthusiastically.

"I don't want to bother you," she replied politely as she looked at the receptionist just finishing up with her phone call.

"I have a few minutes, come on in. It's been a long time."

Patricia shifted her portfolio and walked into the office.

Now what? She thought to herself as she sat down in the chair that Dave offered her across from his desk.

"What's going on, Patricia?"

"Well Dave, remember those plans I brought into you when Abe was having the barn built a few years ago?"

"Yeah, on that place Thomas Pitt bought on the west side?"

"Yep, that's the one." Patricia paused.

"You did a really nice job on those, Patricia. How is that barn working out for you guys?"

"Actually, real nice," she stated. "Abe sure likes the way it's set up."

"Well it sure looked good on paper. I think you did a really nice job on that plan." Dave looked at her intently.

Patricia noticed his dark brown eyes and closely shaved face. His white shirt was freshly pressed and his sleeves were rolled a quarter of the way up his arms. He propped his elbows on the desk.

"Well actually, Dave, that's why I'm here. I was wondering if you would take a look at some things I've drawn up and see if there is anything here I might be able to sell."

He looked down at her portfolio. "What do you mean?" he asked as he watched her fumble with the papers.

"Well, I was thinking…if maybe there was a market for selling plans for different ranches or something." She stumbled a little as she didn't know for sure what she was asking, but continued on. "You seemed so impressed with the plans that I had drawn up for the barn I wondered if maybe someone else might like to have a barn like ours or something like that." She paused not knowing if she was making any sense. She handed him her opened portfolio.

"Well, that's something I normally don't do." He took the open leather folder and glanced down at a sketch of the outside of a log home with big bay windows, a nice deck, and the landscaping in the front. She used colored pencils to add a trace of a color scheme to it. It was a nice touch. He said nothing.

She fidgeted a little, wanting to explain as the silence deepened.

He turned the page. A picture of a barn came into view, the corrals were next, then floor plans and structures. He turned more pages, not saying a word.

The silence was almost more than she could bear, and she heard the clock ticking each second as it passed in the background. He turned another page, then another, then closed the folder and looked at her. "What are you thinking, Patricia?" he said in a flat tone.

Patricia knew her few minutes were almost up and she

didn't have time to beat around the bush. She leaned forward in her chair and sighed deeply, "Well, I was thinking I might be able to sell some of these or help someone plan the layout of a place they want to build. Or something like that…" her voice trailed off but confidence still held her steady.

He was quiet again, and he looked at her long and hard. She met his gaze with a determined will. He noticed her deep blue eyes were shining with confidence or excitement. Whatever it was, he could sense she was serious.

"So, are you looking to sell these plans or are you wanting to draw custom plans?"

"Either way." Patricia stated seriously, "if someone has an idea, I think I can put it together for them and help them with the layout for what they want."

"Well, Patricia," he paused, "I think you are exactly what I am needing." He said it with relief. "I have a client who just bought some property here and wants to build. He is flying out later today. Do you want to meet with him?"

"Today?"

"Well if you show him what you have here at least he can think about it for a little bit before he gets back to Portland."

She took a breath, then blew it out her mouth. "I'd say let's do it!" she said with nervous enthusiasm.

"Let me give him a call really quickly and see if we can catch him on his cell," David replied with a grin as he opened a manila folder sitting on his desk and started dialing the phone.

He was silent for a moment as the phone started to ring. Then he said, "Hey, Doug, this is David and I think this might be your lucky day. I have someone I want you to meet who might be able to help you create your plans."

Patricia watched him nod, "Yes." He nodded again as if Doug was in front of him. "Well, she's right here at my office, so if you wanted to see her work…" he paused again.

He took his sticky pad out and wrote one word on it as he listened.

"Lunch?"

She looked at him questioningly.

He pointed to the phone and then to himself.

She nodded.

"Sure. Sure, Doug." He jotted down more notes. "Yes, she has them right here. We will be right down. Okay." David hung up the phone and looked across at Patricia. We are going to meet him at Barley Browns for lunch. He just got seated, so he'll wait to order.

Patricia was not in any position to buy lunch, hers, or any others. So she said rather panicky, "Uh, I have already eaten lunch but I can sure meet with him."

David had a half grin on his face. "Don't worry. I'm buying. We'll take my car, then you can drop back by here to pick up your rig if we need to go over any further details."

Patricia stood up, "Do you have a restroom I can use before we leave? I would like to freshen up a bit."

"Sure, down the hall and to the right, first door. I'll go pull my car out front."

Patricia stepped in the bathroom and looked in the mirror. Things were happening a little too fast. She leaned her trembling hands on the sink and stared for a moment. *Could this be so easy?* She thought to herself. *One minute I am asking if these drawings could be sold then the next I'm going to meet a man who might buy them or my ideas. What am I supposed to charge? Oh crap! What am I going to charge?* She said to herself.

She turned on the cold water, cupped her hands under it, splashed some water on her face, patted it dry with a paper towel, fixed her hair, and grabbed her portfolio. *Here we go,* she thought as she unlocked the bathroom door and walked past the receptionist. Patricia looked at her with a smile and said, "Have a good day," as she walked out the door to the awaiting car.

They were four blocks from Main Street where Barley Browns Restaurant and Brewery was. David was full of all kinds of information for Patricia. "Just let him do most of the talking and be honest with him. If you think you can do the job, tell him. If you think it won't work, Patricia, let him know why."

Before Patricia knew it, David had pulled in the front of the restaurant, parked, and was out the door. As she was grabbing her stuff, David opened the door for her and escorted her into the building. The scent of food filled her nose and her stomach growled in anticipation. She told herself, *I have groceries in the truck. I can wait until I get home. I am not that hungry.*

The waiter walked up and said, "Hi, David, I believe you're sitting with Mr. Walters. He's waiting right over here."

"Thanks, that'll be great." David beckoned Patricia before him and they walked to where Doug was seated and glancing at a menu.

"Hey, David," Doug said enthusiastically. "You don't waste anytime do you? When someone puts you on a job, you go right to it. And who is this pretty lady?"

"Doug, this is Patricia Cason. She has some drawings she would like to show you. I think she might be able to help you design your new property."

"Really? Well, have a seat and let's order some lunch then we can talk drawings and plans."

Patricia was nervous as she looked at the prices in the menu. She stammered a little as she ordered a glass of water and a dinner salad with ranch dressing.

David looked at her small frame and sensed her nervousness. Then he said to the waiter, "Get her a breaded bowl of clam chowder too. I think I will have the same with iced tea."

They sat and made light talk. Patricia brought out her drawings, and Doug looked intently at them, focusing on the details from the barn to the houses to the corral layouts. David chimed in every now and again as they talked about working out the detail of each drawing and what kind of material it would take to make it reach code. Patricia was a little lost but held her own when questions came her way on the position of the house and barns.

"No, no." she heard herself say, "the house should be positioned north because the wind blows east during the winter and in the Elkhorn Mountains, your garage would drift in if you put it there."

Then the conversation came to the barn. Patricia again found herself mentioning a few bits of information, such as her experiences through so many winters there in Eastern Oregon. Doug seemed to be impressed and stopped to listen to her and her ideas.

When lunch was finished, Doug reached over and shook David's hand. "Patricia," he said, "I think I would like to see what you come up with for plans of my new place. I would like to have you come out and see it. I'll be back next week with my wife."

"I'm looking forward to it, Doug." Patricia stated as she scooted her chair back from the table and started to stand. It was time for her to go.

Both men followed suit. She was ready for the challenge. David walked up to the cashier to pay the check as Doug asked for Patricia's business card.

"I don't have a card," Patricia stated. "I'll give you our number and you can call when you get in next week. I'll meet you."

"Boy, you guys are out west, aren't you?" Doug chided with a grin as they walked to the door.

The trip home seemed a blur. Patricia's mind was racing with anticipation and possibilities. As she drove by Flagstaff, on the old highway, she casually waved as she recognized John Greenly's red Dodge and horse trailer as he drove by her. She subconsciously turned her blinker on another half mile down the highway and turned down the old dirt washboard road. Patricia was surprised when she realized she was sitting in front of their house. She took a deep breath. She sat there a moment, and thought of how fast things moved today, yet she had taken it all in stride. Now, her mind ran back to Abe. Usually they discussed everything before a decision was made. But she hadn't expected things to move so fast. She thought she would meet with David, show her drawings, he would say, "Those are nice, but…" But he didn't.

Now she was not going to jump the gun. She would wait until next week to tell Abe, when she met up with Doug and his wife to make sure they were seriously going to hire her to custom design their house and layout of the corrals and barns with the outbuildings. She stopped at the library to pick up a couple of books about starting a home business and finances. She thought she could glance through them in the evening when she couldn't sleep.

She got out of the pickup, noticing sawdust in the driveway. She walked in the house to start dinner.

27

The morning after dinner at the Greenly's brought an early chill in the air that told fall was coming in fast.

When Paige awoke in the morning, she was quiet and reserved, keeping her thoughts to herself. Her normal, bubbly personality during morning chores was withdrawn and somber into a new reality. How could she have been so blind as to how much financial trouble her parents were in? She had not even noticed. She realized for the first time ever that her parents were actually human. Seeing emotion and hearing the troubles they faced every day, how had she not seen them until now? It seemed like so much had happened from yesterday morning with John's visit, then the owner of this ranch hollering at her father like he did, and then seeing her father lose his control. She realized how all they had could be taken away in an instant if her father lost a job that he didn't like.

She could help. She knew she could, but she also knew that her parents would not let her. Her life had changed, and there was no going back to the child she was yesterday.

During the morning chores, she haltered Libby and took her out to the big corral. Libby was full of spunk and ready to play in the brisk morning air. She trotted next to Paige, shook her haltered head, and even jumped up in the air about six inches to get Paige's attention. Paige tried not to notice. She didn't want to look at Libby, so she just kept walking, forcing one foot in front of the other. Libby followed suit, walking side by side pausing at the gate as Paige opened it and led her through. As Paige reached up to unbuckle Libby's halter to turn her out, Libby dropped her head and pressed it close to Paige, as if she understood. A tear ran down Paige's cheek and another one followed. She held Libby's head in her hands then lay her head on top of Libby's. Libby closed her eyes and stood there. Paige lifted her head, ruffled the forelock between her ears, and walked away, not looking back.

After her mom left for town and her father was out building corrals, Paige picked up the phone book and looked up the number. Her fingers were numb as she waited for the rotary phone to finish each number. A tear ran down her cheek as the phone rang in her ear. Then she heard a man's voice answer on the other end.

"Good morning, Mr. Greenly, this is Paige." She paused, "Yes, I had a great time last night. Well, the reason I'm calling…" she paused again, she kept her voice steady as another tear ran down her cheek. "I was wondering…are you still interested in buying my mare?" She couldn't say Libby's name.

She was convincing and firm. She explained how she was saving money for college and she would not dicker in the price. She kept her parents out of the conversation with him. When she hung up the phone, the deal was done. She was numb, yet she knew this was the right thing to do. She had lived a little girl's dream, now it was time for reality. She trudged into the bedroom and reached in her top drawer and pulled out Liberty Bell's Quarter Horse papers. She didn't need to look at them, she had them memorized. She turned them over and read the transfer side. As tears welled up in her eyes, she signed the transfer. There was nothing to do now but wait.

It was one-thirty when Paige heard the cherry red Dodge diesel pull up, towing a four-horse trailer. He was here.

She went to catch Libby for the last time. She kept the conversation with John light and professional. She had seen horses come and go on the place, and as long as she thought of it as just another horse, she should be fine. Libby walked behind Paige this day. She sensed something had changed and didn't walk at her side as usual. She sensed Paige wasn't looking for a new adventure with her. As they approached the back of the trailer, Libby raised her head and cocked an ear toward the awaiting man.

"Are you sure this is what you want, Paige?" Mr. Greenly asked, his voice concerned, yet business like. He held out a check.

"Yep. I have a lot going on and I know she will be going to a good home." She glanced at John, then to the distant mountains over his shoulder. *He's a good man*, she told herself, *this is right*. She didn't look at the mare. She held out the lead line and took the check.

John reached out and took the lead. Libby didn't move. Paige stepped away, and Libby started to follow her, but the rope held snug in John's hand. Libby stopped. Confused, she reached out and touched the man's hand with her nose, sniffed the unfamiliar scent, then looked toward Paige. John touched Libby's neck and then stroked her face.

Paige opened the trailer door and John paused before he led her in. He looked at the stressed young face of this girl. The fresh sawdust on the trailer floor spilled out as Libby stepped inside. The hollow thud of her hooves hitting the trailer floor was like the hollow beat of Paige's heart. *Stand tall*, she told herself. *Do what you need to do.*

"You know where she's at, Paige." John said as he snapped the tie on her halter and secured the slant bar. He walked out of the trailer and secured the door.

Paige held out the papers in her hand. She had seen her father do this so many times. But she never knew until now how final it was. "Yeah, I know," she stated flatly, her voice becoming quiet.

John took the papers, sensing it was time to go. He reached out to shake Paige's hand. He put a hand on her shoulder and patted her lightly before walking toward the pickup and starting the diesel engine up.

Libby shifted in the trailer and put her nose to the barred window. As the trailer started to pull away, Paige heard a familiar soft nicker.

"Libby," Paige muttered as the tears began to flow. She stumbled to the porch of the house, her legs heavy and weak. She made it to the old wicker chair and released herself to pure exhaustion. Paige dropped the enveloped check to the floor, cradled her head, and sobbed like a girl with a broken heart.

Libby was gone.

John didn't look in the rearview mirror as he pulled out. He already knew the transaction with this horse was out of pure determination. He sensed something had happened and that Paige was not willing to talk about it. The first time he saw Libby, he knew he wanted her. When Paige called this morning, he was surprised about the request, and he couldn't say no. If she wanted to sell the horse, he wasn't going to turn it down.

From the first time he met Paige, he knew her to be honest and up front. When she wanted something, she worked to get it and went at it with gusto. He remembered the first time he met her at the horse show and how she looked at him when he put his hand on Libby's withers. How he mentioned who broke her and most of all he remembered the fire in her eyes when she replied that she had started her.

He remembered how she jumped on that mare's back without hesitation and surged forward to save Samantha and stop Piper. The two seemed to be inseparable, reading each other's minds without flaw, without question, just motion, pure beautiful motion. Now with a pit in his stomach and a slightly heavy heart, he owned the horse that he saw clear across the fairgrounds three months earlier. He owned her, but the sense of pride and the ideas of having her seemed bittersweet.

28

No words could express the emptiness in Paige for the next few weeks. She tried to play it lightly, that it was not a big deal that Libby was gone. She made the decision, she made the call, and she knew she had to grow up. She consumed herself in art and words. When she wrote, she wrote with a fierce will, keeping her mind busy with words on a page. When she drew pictures, they had the detail of a professional. Every ounce of her being brought alive a whispering strand of hair among hundreds in the wind, a bead of sweat on the brow, or a ripple of water as it was touched by a velvet soft nose to drink. When she went to the barn, an emptiness, deep and hollow, seemed to engulf her entire being—as empty as the stall that once belonged to her beloved Libby.

Abe was quiet when he found out Libby was gone. He looked at his daughter and a deep feeling edged to the surface, a sorrow as he remembered the loss of his first horse. He asked, "Are you sure this is what you want, Paige?"

She looked at him with tears brimming, yet she would not let them fall. "Yes, sir," she said with all the strength she could muster. "It is time, Papa."

"You know that it's permanent and there is no turning back?"

"I know," she said quietly.

Paige was unwavering and laid the check on the table. She was insistent and persistent that she didn't have time for Libby, and they could use the money to get caught up on some bills and tires for the truck.

29

Who would have guessed the turn of events that would happen in the next couple of weeks?

Patricia didn't keep her design ideas to herself for very long. Abe, not fully understanding the design world, was confused yet committed to supporting his wife, with measurements and ideas.

Doug and his wife wrote a check to Patricia for her design of the ranch as soon as Dave approved the prints. The check was a welcome sight with five digits gracing the paper. Two other clients wanted to have her design custom barns for them. Patricia was looking forward to the challenge of creating.

Paige took down the last pictures off her wall and put them in a box. She glanced at the framed article with Libby. She read the title, *Poor Girl Saves Wealthy Man's Daughter*. She slipped it in the box along with her silver platter. She thought of the day that Craig Curry came and helped her hang her awards. Now, she felt like she understood his pain. She blinked back a tear.

She was packed. Grabbing the box, she started down the hallway. The house sounded hollow as her boots struck the hard wood floor. This would be the last time she would be in this old house they called home. It felt bittersweet. She put the box in the back of the truck. She crawled into the cab and shut the door. It had been a month since she sold

Libby, and the emptiness had not lifted from her heart. But at least she wouldn't be walking into the barn every morning expecting to hear Libby's soft nickers or anticipating her head to come out of her empty stall and hoping it all had been a dream.

The early November winds were blowing the leaves of the old weeping willow, billowing around the back door and trying to get access into the empty kitchen. To Abe, there was a finality about shutting the door and stepping off the porch one last time. He secured the tarp over the loaded truck and the single horse trailer that was loaded to the hilt. They were ready to go for the last time. From here on out it was up to Thomas to pull together a plan to make this ranch work. Nothing here belonged to Abe and it was not up to him to maintain it any longer. The horses stood in the corrals eating hay, the new cattle shipped in were turned out in the fields, and a friend of Thomas' was supposed to come and check on everything until a new ranch hand could be found.

Abe thought for a moment when he made the call to Thomas and told him that he was giving his two weeks' notice. Thomas laughed through the phone. "What do you mean, Abe? You can't be serious."

"Thomas, I have never been more serious in my life as I am right now. I will be out of here in two weeks." It felt so good to say those words.

Now, here he stood looking at the barn that was built, the

horses he had tended, the fields he had worked, the hay he put up, and the corrals and fences he had built. They were staying, all that was going with him was his horse gear, the belongings in the house, and the little stud horse Thomas had given him for a "bonus" that he playfully nicknamed Shorty.

"Well," he said as he climbed into the driver seat and slapped his hands on the steering wheel. "Are you ready?" He looked at Paige. She looked pale. He hadn't noticed that before. He paused a moment. "Paige, Are you alright?"

"Sure, Papa, I'm alright." She looked at his denim jacket instead of his eyes. Then she looked at the dashboard of the truck. Her heart ached and she didn't know how she was going to fill it.

Nothing was as it used to be. What would the future hold for her? She felt alone and confused. She felt like no one could understand the uncertainty in her heart.

Abe notice her eyes looked hollow. And he also knew that she wasn't looking at him, just giving him the answer that he wanted to hear.

"When we get settled, I want to go to John Greenly's and see about Piper. I haven't seen John since we went out to his place. I gave my word that I would see what I could do for him."

Paige didn't answer. She stared out the window at the cold empty house before her.

"Paige, I want you to go with me." He waited. "I want

some help with him."

Tears filled her eyes, and she swallowed hard. "I can't," she answered. "I can't go back there, I have a lot of stuff going on." She looked out the window to the empty lands she once called home. Her horse was gone, her home was gone, and there was an ache so deep within her heart, she felt she was going to die. She could not go there and see Libby being owned by another person. She just didn't have the strength.

He looked at his brokenhearted daughter a moment then started the truck and pulled out of the drive one last time. Paige looked in the rear view mirror, watching her old life get smaller. Abe looked straight ahead, looking toward the future.

Patricia had stayed at their new place as Paige and Abe had gone for their last load at Pitt's place. She wanted to start unpacking the first bunch of boxes they hauled in. A little ranch house and fifteen acres in Haines were nestled at the base of the Elkhorn Mountains. They put it on a lease option to buy. It hadn't been lived in for about five years. The old man who had owned it was in a nursing home and left it to his kids after he passed. The two kids, who had families of their own, now moved on—one to Colorado and the other to North Carolina—and they couldn't be bothered with trying to keep up with the place. It had run down shabby corrals, an old barn, and a couple of outbuildings. They figured if someone wanted it the way it was, it would save money, time, and travel to just get rid of it. So when the Cason's offer came up for a lease option, they agreed readily and had the papers drawn up.

And here she was unloading boxes and putting things together for a new life they had been working so hard for. Sure, there was a lot to do but at least it was theirs and they had the strength to make it work.

Already, Abe had torn down a couple of the old corrals and recycled the wood to repair the main corrals and build a round pen. Then he put up a couple of paddocks outside the barn. There was a nice little pasture for Shorty where Abe quietly prayed that he might get some exercise and maybe get a little leg under him. People who saw him wanted to bring their mares to him for breeding because of his size and speed. With his bloodline, he could produce some really nice cutting horse prospects.

Abe was enthusiastic at the prospect of working his own place. He already had four colts that he contracted to start riding, and the way it was going, his horse training reputation was greater than he anticipated. This is where he felt he belonged.

He called John Greenly the following morning, and as the phone rang, he thought of what he might say about Paige. But when John answered, he thought better of it. "Hey, John, this is Abe Cason."

"Hey, Abe, good to hear from you, what have you been up to?"

"Well, a lot has been going on this last month and I thought I would give you a call and check how you're coming with your horse Piper."

"Well to be honest, Abe, I haven't done anything with him. I know you mentioned you might be able to work with him, but I hadn't heard from you in quite a while."

"John, I know I haven't gotten a hold of you, but I thought you would like to know we moved to Haines. We have a little bit of property out here and I'm starting to work some colts. Piper is one I want to get started on because I promised Samantha I would. That is, if you're still interested in me working with him."

"If you think you have the time, you're welcome to him. I know that Samantha was pretty excited to think that something could be done with him. When would you want him?"

"Well, I would like Paige to come out to your place and look at him with me. I think it would do her good to get out and work with horses again."

John was quiet for a moment, "How is Paige?"

"She's alright, been pretty busy moving, and tearing down a few corrals. But she's doing good."

"I'm glad to hear that, Abe. Libby is turned out with the broodmares and seems to have settled in pretty good. I told Paige to come out anytime but…" John paused. "I guess I wouldn't expect her to."

"I'm glad to hear that she's settled in. She's a real nice

mare, John, I'm sure she'll throw you some nice colts."

"Well, Abe, if you want to come out this afternoon I'll be home, and I'm sure Samantha would like to see you and Paige if she chooses to come out. Will one o'clock work for you?"

"See you at one then." Abe hung up the phone.

After lunch, Abe mentioned to Paige that he was going out to John's and wanted to know if she wanted to tag along.

Paige was quiet for a moment, then looked at her father. "Yeah, I could go. I haven't see Samantha since we had dinner at their place." Yet, she also wondered if she could see Libby, and if Libby would even remember her. After her father mentioned it the day before, Paige knew she needed to move on and face whatever was waiting there for her. She had to let go. She also wanted to see Samantha again. It felt like forever and she really seemed to have hit it off with her when they were at dinner. She went and got her coat.

The ride out to Greenly's was quiet. Abe rode in silence as Paige contemplated what it would be like to see Libby without owning her. She was anxious and the short trip seemed to take an hour, yet it only took fifteen minutes.

As they pulled into the long driveway, Paige could see some broodmares up by the barn in the front pasture. As Abe started down the driveway, a golden mare with a blazed faced raised her head and watched, then started walking, then started at a full lope toward the fence and the Ford rattling up the driveway as it always had.

Libby remembered! She ran down the fence pacing the green truck. Paige's hand was on the window. "Well looks like someone remembers you," Abe said with a smile.

They pulled up to the house and Paige got out of the truck. John started walking down toward them. Libby slid to a stop at the corner of the pasture next to the truck and circled around, loping and bucking and nickering all the while.

Paige looked at her father, "Can I go see her?"

John overheard her words and said. "I think you better or she will come through the fence to see you."

Paige grinned and ran to the fence and crawled over, Libby trotted up to her and put her nose to Paige's hand.

"Hey, little lady, look at you! You're getting a little fat out here aren't you?" Paige brought her arms around and Libby laid her head in them. Paige's heart filled, and a tear tumbled down her face as she laid her head on top of Libby's.

John and Abe were both silent and just watched for a moment. Then John cleared his throat and said, "When you're done here, Paige, you can come up to the barn."

Paige had forgotten she had an audience. She lifted her head and smiled. "I guess she remembers me."

"Someone might think so. She doesn't do that with anyone around here. Actually she prefers not being caught."

"Really?" Abe asked as he looked at the two across the fence.

"Well, I guess it depends on who is doing the catching." John grinned.

"I'll be up in a minute, if you don't mind. I just want to visit with her for a second."

"Come up when you're ready, Paige."

Paige stroked her neck and rubbed Libby's face. It felt so good to touch her and breathe in her scent again. Paige decided to walk through the hay field that the horses were in to get to the barn. Libby followed beside her. As she went through the gate, Libby was anxious to follow and let out a low nicker as Paige walked into the barn.

John and Abe were already at Piper's stall. As they stood on the outside like Paige and Samantha had done, Piper was quiet and curious. But as soon as Abe opened the stall door and started to walk in with him, Piper's head came up and he started tensing up. As Abe started to bring his hand to Piper's neck in front of the shoulder, Piper backed up into the corner, hitting the wall hard. Abe backed away, releasing some of the tension he was putting on him. Piper stood there with his muscles rock solid, his head up, his ears like antennas searching for a signal, and his eyes half wild.

Paige was surprised. He didn't act like that the night Samantha and she came out here. But when Abe backed out and closed the stall door, Piper stood frozen in the corner. His head was up, one eye on the wall the other on the door, his ears twitching, listening to his fate in a language he did not understand.

"Well, John, he's a little tight, but I would really like to get him out of that stall and see what he does in the open."

"We were afraid to get him into anything bigger than this stall. If nobody can get next to him in there, how will they get close enough out in a corral?" John asked.

"Let me worry about that, John. We need to get him in a place where he feels like he can go somewhere. This is a little too cramped for him and me to have a conversation."

"Tell me what you need, Abe."

"Right now I think a round corral would work. I'll probably need my buggy whip and a couple of plastic sacks out of the truck, Paige."

"You need what?" John asked, his eyes filled with concern.

"Trust me, John," Abe stated. "Just trust me."

"I'll run and grab them," Paige piped in. Her eyes were bright, the color was back in her face, and she was alert and eager.

She ran to the gate she had come through, and Libby stood eagerly waiting. As she closed it, Libby trotted after her, excited to be a part of something. She shook her head and kicked up her heels, trotting beside her as if to say, "I could get you there faster if you would just jump on."

Paige jumped the fence, reached in the back of the truck, and pulled out what looked to be a broken down stock whip or maybe a makeshift bullwhip. It was a thin twine with a handle about a foot and a half long. She opened the pickup door, reached behind the seat, and grabbed a couple of empty plastic grocery bags. She tucked them into her coat pocket, then was back across the fence in less than a minute.

Libby was anxious to be a part of the excitement. She kicked up her heels and loped around Paige wanting ever so much for the girl to jump on like old times so they could race around the pasture.

Paige got to the gate, huffing, and looked at her best friend. She put her hand out, and Libby touched it, then dropped her head.

"I'll be back," Paige said as she caught her breath. She wanted to be rested before she walked back into the barn.

John was helping Abe with a couple of panels to get Piper down to the round corral. Abe said any corral could do, but the round pen gave the horse forward motion without any corners to get caught up in. Since John had a round pen, it would work best.

One of the ranch hands, Toby, came out to help. They got things set up and Abe opened the gate to the round pen and looked back at the alley they had just created for Piper. He would have complete run of the barn all the way down to the round pen. "As easy as it gets," Abe said with a satisfied sigh.

John called to Toby, "Go and run Piper down here would you, Toby."

The sandy haired kid started to jog down to the stall where Piper was when Abe stopped him. "That's okay,

Toby, I'll get him."

The kid stopped and looked at John, then back at Abe.

John, said, "That's alright, Toby, he'll get him." John figured it best to just shut up and watch. "Why don't you hang around and watch this with me, maybe we can learn a little."

They followed Abe down to the stall. Paige handed him the whip which she dubbed "the wand" and a plastic sack, which he tucked into his back pocket. He opened the stall door, stepped across the alley, propped himself against the corner panel, and waited. Paige came and did the same.

Piper stood against the back wall of his stall. He didn't move, his ears flickered back and forth, and his muscles were tight.

"What do you think, Sis?"

"Well, Papa, I think I needed this. Thanks for bringing me today."

"It is a good day, huh?"

John was confused. "Abe, do you want Toby to run that horse out for you?"

"No, but I could use a cup of coffee."

Even more confused, "Well we could close the stall and get some coffee up at the house." He didn't understand what Abe was wanting to do.

"Well actually, I think I'll stay right here...I think I found me a cozy little spot and I'll wait right here."

John was a little bewildered. He shrugged his shoulders

and brought his hands away from his sides a little frustrated. "Is there anything you want us to do?"

"Nope, it's all up to Piper right now. We don't have to do anything but wait."

Silence filled the barn, minutes ticked by, just dragging every second of the clock. John looked at what he could do to get the horse down the alley and in the round pen so Abe could start working him.

"Well when you're ready to start working him, Abe, let me know and we can get this show on the road."

Piper still hadn't moved from the back wall of the stall, he had one eye on the open door and the other locked on the security of the wall. The muscles in his shoulders were shaking.

Abe wanted to release John from his anxiety. "John, if you want to do something, then a cup of coffee would be great."

"Well, at least it's something" as he started to walk out the barn. Libby nickered and trotted back up to the gate.

Toby sauntered up to Paige. "What's he doing?" he asked in a whisper.

Paige looked at him and grinned. "I could tell you, but then I'd have to kill you. No actually it's an ancient tradition, known only to a few horsemen."

"Really?"

Paige silently nodded her head, as if she could not reveal her secret.

"What's it called?" Toby asked as he propped his foot on the bottom rail and settled in for a lesson on ancient traditions.

"It's called…" Paige paused and put her hand up to tell him in a whisper. He leaned his ear next to her mouth. "Patience," she whispered and grinned at him again.

He looked sheepish and raised his eyebrows with a grin. "Really, I haven't heard of it. What do you do?"

"Well you strike a pose and stand there for as long as it takes."

"As long as it takes for what?" Toby asked, confused as John was at this crossroad. "What are we waiting for?"

John came back in the barn with a thermos of coffee and two cups.

"Yeah, I wanted to know that too."

Abe held out his hand to the cup that John offered, then waited as John filled it. Abe took a sip.

"John, what do you see when you look in that stall?"

"Well I see a horse standing in the corner that needs someone to work him." He sent out a little sarcasm as to the reason they came here.

"Do you want to know what I see?" Abe offered as he took another sip of coffee.

"I would like to know that. You've been here thirty minutes and that horse hasn't moved."

"That's right. That horse is trying to say something and he has no words for you to understand. This is like you

243

getting in a car accident in a different country, where they speak no English. A person comes in and pokes and prods on you to get you well, but they are not helping you. They are hurting you and you try to tell them. But each time someone comes in, it's a new person who speaks a different language. They poke and prod on you again, so you try to argue or maybe even fight back and still you can't get them to understand. So the communication barrier gets farther apart and there is no rapport. They come and work on you and then lock you up in a cell where it's quiet and safe. So every time that door opens, you get poked and prodded with no way to communicate or understand because of the language barrier. Now John…look at Piper and tell me what you see."

"I guess he looks scared," John answered, "now that you explain it that way, Abe. I guess I would be too."

Piper's muscles were shaking and sweat had started running down behind his shoulders and behind his ears. The horse hadn't moved. Every ounce of his being was absolutely terrified of the open stall door and what might come in.

"It was never his intention to hurt Samantha, John, and after the accident Piper was put in a stall until Samantha was released from the hospital. After soaking on the accident for that length of time, he lost his courage and didn't know how to find it. The people you had come out here to work on him were working him as if he had done something wrong. It is not in his nature, John. It just is not in his nature," Abe repeated. "Right now I'm waiting on him to come to terms with the door being open and me being on the outside of it. Today, this is what I want."

So as time passed, Toby was the most inquisitive. "What is he afraid of, Abe?"

"He's afraid of doing the wrong thing. He doesn't know what's right, so he chooses to do nothing at all. He just thinks he should be doing something and doesn't know what it might be. That's what makes him sweat. As soon as he chooses to do something different and doesn't get into trouble for it, he'll start relaxing a little. All I'm asking of him right now is to just be himself. And that is almost more than he can take.

"As far as I can tell, the people who came to work with him, came to work *on* him. It looks like they wanted results. He just needs someone to help him find his courage again."

John listened and waited. Over an hour passed and Piper was still in his stall and had not moved, although his sweat had dried. "Abe, I didn't realize it would take this long. The other trainers would have done something by now. And I really wanted to watch you work him, but I have got to be in town by three thirty to pick up Samantha."

"That's fine," Abe said unwavering in his method. "I'll be here when you get back." Abe talked in normal tones, no whispering or trying to hide that he was there and not going anywhere. Every now and again, he would move to another spot in the alley where Piper could still view him. There was no being sneaky or quiet in this waiting game. He wanted to be honest with this horse and let him know that he was safe.

Abe squatted in the middle of the alley with his back to the horse. He sat there for a bit, then asked, "Hey, Toby, you have a stool or chair that I could use?"

"Sure," Toby said as he went to the tack room and came out with a light barstool.

When he returned, Abe said "Take your time, Son, take your time."

Piper moved his head to watch Toby walk out and put the stool down in front of Abe.

"What are you going to do with the stool?" Toby asked, very curious after all this time and wanting to keep interested.

"I'm going to sit on it," Abe replied. "My knees aren't as young as they used to be."

"Oh," Toby replied sheepishly.

"Toby," Abe said, wanting the boy to get a little more than a smart comment. "Do you notice anything different about this horse?"

Toby looked at him, "No, not really." Piper was still standing in the same place as he had been for the last hour.

"Are you sure there's nothing different?"

"Well," Toby said, being a little sarcastic, "he has moved his head."

"Yes he has, and here pretty quick he'll be moving his feet."

He took a seat on the stool and sighed, "Paige, would you run to the truck and grab some of that halter twine out?"

"Sure, Papa, I'll be right back."

Toby trotted up next to her, hungry for some action. "I'll go with you."

"Alright," Paige said happy to have the company.

"Boy your dad is unlike any man I've ever been around. When is he going to work that horse?"

"He is working him."

"No I mean really work him. Like running him around in the round corral like everyone else does." He said it half sarcastically. He wanted to get to the part of horse training that he was familiar with, where he could recognize some of the work.

"That round corral," Paige made a woooo, ghostly gesture, "is just a tool. It's just the beginning of forward motion, turning, and learning the language. He's working his mind more than his body because his body is fine. It's his mind that needs a workout."

"Well, I think if a horse has issues, keep him busy and he'll work it out for himself. For instance running him down the alley and to the round pen, getting him in motion and keeping him there for a while, he'll figure it out."

"Sure, and then you'll have to do it the next day and the next day and whenever he's feeling fresh, you'll take him to the round pen to get the "work" done. That's what my father is working on right now. He doesn't need work, he needs confidence."

"I don't even know what's wrong with that horse. He looks fine to me. What's all the fuss about?"

They walked out to the truck, and Paige pulled out a roll of cord from the toolbox.

"What are you going to do with that?" Toby asked as they headed back up to the barn.

"Papa is going to make a halter while Piper is figuring out what he needs to."

"I would love to learn how to make a halter."

"Well, let's see if he'll show you."

As they returned to the barn, Piper had ventured two steps forward to get a drink. He jutted his nose as far as it would go, dipped his chin into the water tank, and took three swallows.

Paige walked in with the roll and Toby followed. Piper backed up to his familiar corner. Toby noticed the horse was back where he was at the beginning.

"I'm sorry, Mr. Cason, I didn't mean for you to lose ground with him."

"Oh I didn't lose any ground. He just went to his comfort spot. He'll be back."

Paige, spoke up. "Toby wants to learn how to make halter."

"Sure." Abe said as he purposefully turned his shoulders

away from the horse and started unraveling some of the rope. He measured the rope as a seamstress would material. He took out his pocketknife and with one swift cut sliced the cord. He did two more for Paige and Toby then he bent the cord exactly in half and started measuring out where the first knot would go. Paige and Toby did the same.

As they started working on the halters, Paige said, "Papa, can you explain how you are 'working' a horse when the horse is not being worked."

Toby looked at her with consternation.

Abe looked at Paige, then over to Toby. "Well, sometimes we get in a hurry to do things when a person might learn a lot more by stopping and watching. Just like Piper, he's learning to trust himself again. He lost that when the accident happened with Samantha. He knew he really messed up. The last thing he ever wanted to do was to hurt that girl, but circumstances played out differently. Then bringing him home and putting him in his stall, he felt safe. Then someone came out to work on him, without understanding where his mind was. Piper couldn't figure out what was right because the rules kept changing. The only comfort he got was when he stood in the stall."

"Oh, so more or less whenever people come around him, he thinks he's doing something wrong, so he's basically hiding in his stall."

"Yep," Abe replied. "When he decides to venture forth out into the big world again, we'll be waiting. But first, he has to play the, 'What If' game. And that's what he's been thinking about all afternoon."

Abe heard Piper shuffle in his stall and knew it was time to move again. "Hey, Toby, why don't you get a couple more stools for you and Paige? It'll be a little easier to make these things sitting down." He finished another knot.

"Sure," Toby said as he trotted to the tack room.

Abe heard Piper back into his corner.

As Toby came back, Paige asked her father, "What do you mean the 'What If' game?" This whole day had been pretty much a mystery to her, and she was as intrigued as Toby.

Abe mimicked what Piper might be thinking.

"What if I moved my head while those people were in here?" Abe stated as if he was Piper.

"What if I moved a foot?"

Nothing.

"What if I stepped to the water?"

Nothing.

"What if I looked out the open stall door?"

Nothing.

"What if I poked my nose out the open stall door?"

Nothing.

"What if I poked my head out the open stall door?"

Nothing.

"What if I put a foot out the open stall door?"

Nothing.

About that time behind them Piper had his head out the stall door with one front foot striking the ground.

"Sometimes it's not about making things happen." Abe winked at Paige. "It's about allowing things to happen. Today Piper was allowed to be curious and look for his old self, still with us in the same place he is, but without our influence. He is looking for the horse he used to be before that accident."

Abe kept tying knots and measuring, undoing and retying, as the kids watched and mimicked his moves. He kept talking in normal tones. Every now and again, he would stand, pick up his stool, and move it someplace else in the alley, closer to the stall door for a little while, then farther away from the stall door.

Toby couldn't understand this action and finally asked, "Are your knees still bothering you, Mr. Cason? Why do we keep moving?"

Abe chuckled, "No, I just want Piper to know that we're mobile. We are not stuck in one place and we are people he can learn to trust."

With that, like a breath of wind, Piper walked out of his stall. Smelling the ground with what sounded like rollers in his nose.

"He's out!" Toby whispered in a semi-panicked voice. "What do we do now?"

Abe continued tying knots and measuring the symmetry of his halter.

"Mr. Cason," Toby whispered again a little louder as Piper continued exploring the ground away from his stall. "He is all the way out now. What are we supposed to do?"

Paige looked at her father and then at Toby, she was feeling a little anxious too. What were they supposed to do? Had her father not heard him?

"Well," Abe said, as he finished another knot on his halter. Both of the kids had stopped making theirs. "I think you guys should finish with your halters. He'll be here in a few minutes."

Both of them looked at Abe questioningly. "Keep doing what we've been doing. Work on your halters," Abe repeated. "That's what we're doing. Piper will be here in a little while."

Just as he stated it, Piper started walking toward them. Toby's eyes got big.

"Toby, keep making your halter," Abe stated again, "don't worry about Piper, he'll be fine."

As Piper came closer to them, curious about what they were doing, Abe said. "Let's move. We're going to give him lots of room. So grab your chairs and come with me."

Without question, both kids picked up their stools and moved with Abe about twenty feet away. Then sat back down and started back on the halters.

Piper stopped and looked back at his stall door, thinking he could go back in, but instead he stayed where he was and watched the people move away from him. He thought about them for a while then started toward them once again. As he did, the people got up and moved away from him again. Curiosity was getting the better of him. What did they have that they didn't want him to see? He started after them again and when he was almost to them, Abe got up and moved again. The kids followed with a giggle, mimicking his movements. Within minutes, Piper followed, more curious than ever. The next time they moved, Piper more curious than ever, followed in suit just as if they were leading him.

Abe set down the stool and had a seat. Piper stood behind him, and Abe turned his shoulder away from him. Piper took another step toward Abe and touched his nose to Abe's shoulder. Abe acted like he didn't notice, and Piper took another step toward him. Now he was standing so close that he didn't have to stretch his neck to be near Abe. Abe continued his rope tying. Piper nibbled on his shirtsleeve then followed his arm all the way down to his hand and took a deep breath in. Abe stopped what he was doing and moved his hand enough to touch Piper's nose. Piper did not withdraw. He stood and waited. Abe brought his hand up and stroked his nose and then his face. Piper sighed and licked his lips. He was tired of being alone and was happy to have some company.

Abe looked at Paige and Toby. "Are you guys going to finish your halters? We don't have all night you know."

Paige and Toby both picked their mouths up from the

ground and had forgotten what to do next.

Abe stated, "Now measure out your next knot on the right cheek." he held up his finished halter to show how his was done. Piper watched, then moved his nose toward Paige, smelling her shoulder and watching her hands. Paige faltered and Abe counseled her hands to keep moving and watch what she was doing. "Piper will take care of himself," he said nonchalantly.

Piper nuzzled the barstool she was sitting on, then walked across the alley to the other stalls. He then came back toward Toby, whose hands were shaking as he fumbled with another knot. This didn't bother Piper. He kept investigating and exploring a world he used to know and wanted to know again.

"Keep focused, Toby, tie that knot right there. Yep, that's it," Abe said guiding the boy's hands to the work before him. "One more right there, now work your knot down, that's it. And there you have it," Abe stated as they both held up their finished halters. Neither one looked quite like Abe's, but they were halters, in a sense, and they were done.

Piper got bored, then walked off to explore the rest of the barn. As he did, Abe said to Toby and Paige, "Grab the pitch forks and some sawdust and clean out his stall. Give him a reason to want to go back in."

Piper watched as they pitched sawdust and horse manure in a wheelbarrow. He nibbled the handles, smelled the clean sawdust, and came to reinvestigate as they worked. When the stall was cleaned and lined with fresh sawdust, Toby went to get some hay to put in the feeder. As he returned, Piper followed him into the stall and started munching his feed easily, not worried in the least that someone was in the stall with him.

John and Samantha were leaning against the temporary panel fence as Abe closed the stall door. John said, "I'll be damned. I wouldn't have believed it if I hadn't seen it with my own eyes, Abe."

Abe had no idea how long they had been standing there, and it surprised him. "This is just the beginning, John, just the beginning," He repeated. "We're not done yet, but we have a real good start."

Samantha just stood there. Her crutches propped next to the fence. She couldn't say a word.

The next day Samantha and Paige both went out to watch Abe with Piper. Abe had brought his plastic grocery sack, tucked it in his hip pocket, and left it hanging out so it could be seen. Abe brought out his stool and moved it across the alley, then went and opened the stall door one more time. Piper hesitated as Abe stood in the stall doorway. Then Abe turned his back on him, and Piper moved cautiously after him, watching him go to his stool and sit. Abe took out his plastic sack and started playing with it. Piper watched as Abe played. Abe rubbed it up and down his arms, wrapped it around his neck and so on. Then when Abe knew he had Piper's full attention, he turned his back on him and played with the sack by himself. Piper couldn't stand the curiosity. He had to see what Abe was doing. So with cautious and deliberate steps, Piper walked up, his eyes wide and curious, yet brave and deliberate. He presented himself directly in front of Abe.

Abe reached out his empty hand and Piper greeted it by dropping his head so Abe could pet it. Then he brought his nose toward the plastic sack, and using his whiskers and the velvet hairs of his nose, he nibbled at the plastic. Abe brought the sack up and tickled Piper's nose with it, then rubbed his cheek, then gradually rubbed and scratched his neck. Then he got up from his stool and walked away. Piper followed.

Abe reached for his new halter and slipped it on Piper. He took his sack and again played with it. Piper cocked an ear to him as Abe brought it back to his neck and started rubbing him down. Every now and again, he would shake it out and bring it back to Piper's body. When he moved to his back, Piper raised his head and cocked back both ears, his eyes worried. But he held fast as Abe flicked from his back to his shoulder then to his neck again. Then he ran the sack from his neck, down his back to his hip then back to his neck. Abe repeated this several times until he saw a change in Piper's posture, then he stopped for a moment. Then the process started all over again. Moving to the other side, he did the same thing.

Samantha asked, "What is he doing with that sack?"

Paige grinned, "He's sacking him out."

"I guess that's obvious, but I'd never seen it done that way before," Samantha replied. "I've seen it done with cloth, but never a plastic sack."

"Well, it seems to work pretty good on building confidence in areas that are pretty touchy, such as floating balloons and sack lunches. You know, that kind of stuff."

Abe took his stock whip, or as Paige liked to call it, the wand, and tied the sack to it as they walked to the round corral. "Let's go move him around a little bit."

The girls followed.

He played with him in the round pen and got him moving steadily and confidently with the sack on the end of the wand. He was able to stop him, back him up, and rub him all over with it. Piper seemed to enjoy the crackling noise and accepted Abe's cues.

He took Piper back out of the round corral and closed the gate. He brought him back into the alley and sat back down on his barstool. He brought up his sack again and rubbed Piper down around his head and neck and his sides. Abe then took off the halter and continued rubbing. Piper loved the sack around his head and dropped to be rubbed around his eyes and behind his ears.

He told Paige and Samantha that he wanted them to come in too. Samantha stood on the outside of the fence. "I don't think I should, Mr. Cason," she stammered at him, "with these crutches and everything."

"Nonsense," he replied. "If Piper is willing to forgive himself for what happened, you must forgive yourself too."

Tears welled up in her eyes as she looked at Piper. "I've seen what he did with the other trainers. I can't do it. I just can't do that to him. What if I scare him and he goes back the way he was?"

"Well if you don't get your butt in here and find out, we'll never know, now will we?" He looked at her, his blue eyes bright and inviting. "You can do this, Samantha. If not, what's the alternative? It's up to you, now." He looked back at the halter in his hand and tightened one of the knots.

Paige opened the gate and Samantha entered, hobbling along on her crutches with tears streaming down her face. They came to the stool where Abe sat. Abe stood and had Samantha sit on it.

"It is a safe place, Samantha, let him see you." Piper noticed the girls and instantly started over toward them. "He doesn't want to be alone anymore. Allow him to come visit and explore."

Piper first came to Paige and investigated her hands. Paige reached up so that he could allow his head to be touched willingly. She rubbed his cheek then ran her hand down his neck. Then he saw the crutches and Samantha sitting on the stool. He took a deep breath and let the air out. He wanted to investigate.

Samantha's body started to shake, then Abe's voice came in, "Samantha, he's asking permission to come see you the only way he knows how. What'll you say to him? You don't have to speak, it's unspoken language. Say it with your heart, no excuses, no lies, he'll respond."

Samantha took a deep breath and let it out. She reached out a shaky hand, her vision blurred by the constant tears streaming down her face. "I'm sorry," she whispered inaudibly. "I am so, so sorry. Forgive me."

Piper walked to Samantha slowly yet with courage. He breathed in and dropped his head to be touched. He pressed himself tenderly for her to hold his head, and he closed his eyes.

Samantha was quiet. She was holding Piper's head and rubbing his neck.

Abe said, "Samantha, I want you to get your crutches and I want you to walk away from him."

Samantha didn't move she just sat there holding his head.

"Samantha," Abe said, a little more forcefully. "I want you to release him and get your crutches. I want you to walk away from him."

Samantha snapped her head up as if out of a trance. "But I don't want to."

"Do it, Samantha, trust me. Just walk away from him," Abe said calmly and steadily.

Samantha took her crutches and started to hobble away from Piper toward Abe. Piper followed.

"That is what we wanted," Abe said. "That is what we wanted."

For the next week, Samantha couldn't wait until Paige came out and would wait anxiously for her arrival. They would go to the barn, get Piper, lead him around the barn, and turn him out in the corral. They would rub and brush his coat to a glistening shine. He enjoyed every minute, finding the courage and confidence he had before the accident. Samantha was also getting better and stronger every day.

One afternoon Abe and Paige pulled up in the truck and took Piper out to the round pen. John and Samantha walked to the corral. This was the day everyone was waiting for. He sent Piper around the corral a couple of times then asked Piper to approach him. Piper did this without question. Abe slipped a halter on him, then walking to his side, he slipped on bareback. Piper's head came up, his ears twitched back and forth and moved out with grace and confidence. There was no prepping for the moment. It was just a horse and a man in a single moment, becoming one.

They all stood outside the round corral and watched Abe move him around the round pen a couple of times. Then he asked Paige to open the corral gate. Paige complied without hesitation. Samantha was shocked as he walked Piper out and kicked him up into a lope, across the paddock into an open field. Piper was eager, willing, and accepting.

Abe brought him back to the round pen and slipped off his back. He said, "Paige take him for a ride. See what you think."

Paige looked at Samantha, "Do you mind?"

Samantha looked at her, surprised, "No, not at all, go ahead."

Paige walked up to him and took his lead. He cocked back an ear as she swung onto his back and moved him out. He seemed to be as pleased to carry her, as she was to be riding him.

She walked him around the paddock, did a couple of figure eights, nudged him up into a canter. He was flawless in his willingness to please her.

When Paige returned, Abe looked at Samantha. "Alright, now it is your turn," he said as he opened the gate to let her in.

"I can't ride him! I still have crutches and I can't get on bareback," she said resisting the offer with excuses.

"Sure you can, Samantha," Paige said as she brought him to a stop and slipped off his back. "Come on, I'll give you a leg up."

John looked uncomfortable, "Abe, are you sure this is going to be okay?"

"It will be if Samantha wants it to be. It's all up to her now. Piper has done his work, now it's time for Samantha to do hers," he said as he waited by the unlocked gate. "Come on, Samantha, you can do it, I know you can."

Samantha walked through the gate. Abe talked her through it. "Now I want you to walk him around a bit. Move him in a figure eight, that's it." Piper followed her willingly. Abe felt that this was a war for Samantha only. Piper had accepted her and her crutches. "Paige is going to hold him and I will help lift you on. All I want you to do, Samantha, is to take a deep breath and let it out. Let it all out."

She took a deep breath.

"Give Paige one of your crutches and put all your weight on your good leg. That's it. And up you go." Abe lifted her up and she swung her bad leg over Piper's back. Piper cocked an ear back, then began to move forward. Samantha caught her breath and gripped with her legs.

Paige held him confidently. "Relax. Just relax," she said in soft tones, as much to Piper as to Samantha.

Abe had a hand on her thigh, and said, "Samantha, I want you to breathe. Close your eyes and breathe. That's it. Feel his breath underneath you. Can you feel his breathing?"

She closed her eyes and sat there a moment, unable to feel anything but fear. She tried to focus. *Breathe*, she told herself. *Feel him breathe*. Then all of a sudden, she could feel his soft relaxed breath moving under his rib cage. Expanding and relaxing. "Yes, I do!"

"Breathe with him. Can you do that?" Abe said.

As she mimicked her breathing to his, a calmness came over her. Her tension melted away, and as she opened her eyes, Abe had her move him forward. Piper was willing, eager, and kind.

They moved around the round pen easily and slowly as

Samantha found herself and began going with the motion of Piper's body.

"That's it, Samantha, find yourself with him. That's it."

She found herself breathing deeper and relaxing more with every stride, her body swaying and molding to his movements. Within minutes, she forgot about her leg, her injuries, and time. She was one with Piper, in the moment and free.

She stopped him, leaned forward on Piper's back, and wrapped her arms around his neck. He was the horse she remembered. He was going to be fine. They were all going to be fine.

John stood there silently through the whole thing, not knowing if he should believe what he saw or if it was all a hoax and would wear off in a couple of days. But as he watched, he was beginning to understand, maybe a little, the language that had been foreign and unnoticed to him before Abe and the Cason family came into his life. There was no battle nor ego. There were no whips or unsightly gimmicks—just a horse, a man, and an understanding between the two. And his daughter had her horse back. Who could put a value on that?

He heard Abe say, "Let's get him saddled. It's time." Abe had brought his own saddle and got it from the truck. Piper cocked his ear to it and then smelled it. Then with a touch of the blanket, accepted it like the old saddle horse he had been. Abe stepped up on him and took him through his paces. Piper was happy, willing, and confident. "Here, Paige, take him for a spin would you?"

Paige again looked at Samantha for her approval then walked up, stepped on, and rode him around the paddock and out into the pasture.

While she was gone, Abe walked over to Samantha. "I'm not going to put you on him with a saddle until you have that cast off, alright? I think it would be better to wait."

John nodded in agreement. "I agree, Abe, that's way too much stuff to get caught up on."

"Alright," Samantha said, a little disappointed.

Paige came back with a grin on her face. "He's fantastic, Samantha. I can't wait to see you ride him."

"Not today," Samantha said. "Dad wants me to wait until I get my cast off in a couple of weeks."

Paige stepped off Piper and walked him over to Samantha. "He's a really nice horse, Samantha. You'll be back in the saddle in no time."

"I can't wait."

They walked him to the truck to unsaddle.

On the way back to the truck, John finally asked, "How did you know what to do, Abe?"

"I just listened to what Piper had to say," Abe replied. "When I opened the stall door that first day and he backed away like he did, it told me that he was half scared to death to be with me. He didn't do that because he didn't want to be caught. There was far more fear in his actions than that.

So I began from there. And I just let him tell me his story as he could and I just listened. He did the rest."

John shook his head. "I am so glad you know what you are doing."

"Well, most of the time, we are so busy 'doing,' we forget to just be. Sometimes it's just being that can make the biggest changes. As for Piper, the other trainers probably wanted to fix him for Samantha, when Piper needed to fix himself and reestablish his own confidence. That was what we did here. That's all we did here. Piper did the work, we just set up the opportunity for him."

John nodded. "So what you're saying is that every time someone came to work on him, he was losing his confidence."

"In a sense, yes," Abe answered.

"So we need to keep his confidence up? How do we do that?" John was taking all this in as if he had to have the answer for everything now so Piper would not go back to being scared.

"John," Abe stopped in mid stride and looked at him. "Don't treat him as a victim. Keep him focused on the future and what he's going to be doing, not where he's been." He paused, then said, "He'll do that willingly, it's the people who want to hold on to the past and relive it."

"Yeah, but what if he starts going back the way he was, getting all scared again?"

"He won't, as long as you keep looking for tomorrow,"

Abe persisted. "The longer we live in the past, the longer he will live in the past. So when you decide to move forward, he'll be happy to. He's ready. Are you?"

"Yeah but…" John repeated, then stopped. "Ohhh," he sighed nodding his head. "Boy, that's easier said than done."

"You get used to it, and Piper will help remind you from time to time." Abe grinned.

They finished walking back to Abe's truck in silence. When Abe opened the door to get in, he said, "Come on, Sis."

Paige and Samantha had wandered over with Piper to the corner of the pasture so Paige could get one more peek at Libby before they left.

"She's happy here," Paige stated, but she noted that she was still a little bit of an outcast. The pasture full of bred broodmares, heavy with foal was not her idea of fun. She was always off by herself, looking for things to do and there was only one person she wanted to do them with. As soon as she heard the familiar pop of the pickup door as Abe opened it, she lifted her head and nickered and started trotting across the pasture.

"Yeah, she does seem to be pretty happy. But she really loves to see you coming," Samantha said as she rubbed Piper's head.

Paige crawled on the fence and waited for her. "Just a minute, Papa." She whistled for Libby to hurry and Libby kicked herself up into a lope and was at Paige's side in seconds.

Paige gave her a few scratches then started for the truck. "Sorry, little lady, I don't have a lot of time today."

Libby hung her head over the fence, nosed Piper, and watched them walk away.

"Do you think they remember what happened?" Samantha asked as they turned back toward the truck leading Piper.

"I guess they might, but I don't think it's that important to them. I don't think they keep reliving it like we might. I think they like to get on with life."

Libby nickered softly, and Paige looked back.

John watched the girls. "Boy that horse loves that girl."

"They sure made quite a pair," Abe replied as he started the truck.

Paige crawled in the passenger side and waved at John, "See you later."

John walked over to his daughter and Piper, "Yep, we'll see you later. Thanks for helping us out."

"Any time, John, just give us a call when Samantha has that cast off. We'll have her in the saddle," Abe replied as he put the Ford in gear and pulled away.

John and Samantha turned back toward the barn, Samantha still leading Piper.

30

Paige's birthday was coming up too fast for Patricia. How could her daughter be another year older when it seemed as if she just was just learning to walk a few years ago? And now here she was turning seventeen. Patricia wanted to throw a little party and celebrate. She had to celebrate because if not, she would want to cry. One more year and she would be gone. How can that be? She's a child, no, a girl, no, she's becoming a young woman. Patricia was just going to have to face the facts. *There will be a day when Paige will be on her own, but for now, she is turning seventeen and I'll celebrate*, she thought. She picked up the phone and made a few phone calls.

The Cason's new place was transforming nicely. Abe finished up a couple of the broken down corrals and repaired the barn roof. As word got around of what Abe had done with Piper, the phone started to ring for Abe to work other troubled horses.

Patricia had found a niche in art and design and had begun taking computer classes to bring herself up to speed. She had two more clients that she was designing for, and she couldn't be happier.

The house was coming along nicely and she had plans to create a garden area for next spring's planting.

Paige bought an old '76 short box green Chevy pickup with some of her money from Libby. She was going over to the Greenly's often, and she got to see Libby almost every day. Libby would come loping up to the gate to see her. She would nicker and buck around as if asking her to come and play. Paige tried not to notice, but when she thought no one was looking, she would lean on the fence and whistle to her to come and visit. She longed to jump astride her back and run like the wind. In her mind she knew those days would never be again.

John had plans to breed her in the spring. So for now, Libby was just a free spirit out in the pasture, although she cared nothing for the horses that were pastured with her. When she saw her old friend walking toward the barn, she would race to the fence to greet her with the enthusiasm of a puppy wanting to play, not understanding why Paige wouldn't jump on like old times.

On Paige's birthday, Samantha and Paige planned to go out for pizza and a movie. There was a real blockbuster lined up for the weekend and they had to get the tickets early. Paige was going to drive and Samantha was going to buy the popcorn. Patricia had other plans and had to have the girls negotiate that she got the afternoon before the pizza and movie. It was agreed, they would leave after her mom put on the party.

About ten o'clock Patricia asked Paige if she could make a run to town and pick up a few things she had forgotten for the party. "We need soda and ice cream, honey. There's a list on the counter."

"Sure, Mom, I can do that." Paige answered. Any time she could drive into town without adults was like icing on the cake, and she got to lick the spoon! "Is there anything else you need while I'm there, Mom?" Paige asked as she grabbed an apple and her keys.

"Nope, I don't think so, Paige. But be sure to hurry back, okay? There's money on the table for gas."

"Okay, Mom, thanks." She picked up the list and money. "I'll hurry." And out the door she went.

It was a great day, the sun shining and the fall leaves turning a golden rustic brown. She never felt so free. She drove into town and picked up the groceries, then stopped and put ten dollars of gas in her tank before heading home. As she pulled in the drive, she noticed people had already shown up for her party. Paige shut off her truck, got out, and grabbed one of the bags out of the back. A strange, yet familiar, voice spoke from behind her.

"Hey, need any help with that?"

Paige jumped, dropping one of the two liters of soda. It exploded on the ground. "Oh crap!" she said as she felt it happen. A second bottle landed and burst into a fizzy ocean of sticky mud. Then she turned to see Craig Curry at her side.

"Man, I'm really sorry, Paige. I didn't mean to scare you. I just wanted to surprise you." His rich hazel eyes met hers.

"Well, I guess you did that for sure, Craig. When did you get here?"

"Flew in from JFK to Boise last night and Dad picked me up from there. Got home about midnight." Craig took a deep breath. "Man, it's great to be back for a while."

"How long are you gonna stay?" Paige asked as she finished picking up the plastic grocery sack and stood back up, looking at Craig for the first time since he had dinner with them just after the accident. Then she remembered what he said to her before he left and the kiss. She felt her face flush.

"I'm going to stay a couple of weeks, then head back," he said with no emotion.

Craig reached in the back of her truck and grabbed another sack. Then they headed toward the house. The four liters of soda on the ground were forgotten.

"What's it like in New York?"

"It's another world compared to this one. I've never seen my mom so happy," he said avoiding any emotion toward the subject.

"What do you do there?" Paige persisted. Thinking her life would be so much more boring after listening to life in New York.

"Well there is a lot to do there," Craig said, "but I would rather talk about horses and stuff here. I have two weeks and I don't want to waste it on a place I have to go back to."

Paige dropped the subject as they walked into the house.

She set her sack on the counter and began putting the groceries away as they talked. It was easy to talk with Craig. He was light hearted and charismatic.

"Samantha said you sold your horse to her dad," he said, not knowing if it was a sore subject.

"Yeah, I don't know if that was the smartest thing I've ever done, but at the time it was the only thing I thought I could do." Paige paused, thinking, then continued. "She does have a great home. She should be happy there."

"Samantha said that you come up and see her every now and again, when your dad works Piper. She can't believe that Piper is the same horse after all that he's been through. And she's riding again, with the help of you and your dad…"

"That was pretty amazing, I had never seen Papa work a horse like that, but it was incredible to see how everything pulled together. I thought Piper was never going to leave that corner of the stall. Papa just kept waiting and pretty soon, here he came. I wished you could have seen it Craig, just like magic." Paige was happy to be talking of something else besides Libby. "Toby got to watch. There for a while they were all wondering if my dad had gone off his rocker for waiting so long, but you know the old saying 'Good things happen for those who wait.' I think they think it might be true." She smiled.

"I couldn't believe it," Craig chimed in. "When I went out to the Greenlys' and Samantha took me out to see Piper. The stories she said she had seen with the other guys who worked him, it's amazing that he's still alive and someone didn't take him out and shoot him."

"That was an option that John was thinking about when

he came and asked Papa to come out and take a look at him," Paige replied. "But John really doesn't have the heart for that kind of lifestyle. If he did, I would have never sold Libby to him. He always seemed to be a very kind man."

"I know that he has always been good to our family," Craig said matter-of-factly. "Even when things fell apart between my parents, he always seemed to have a door open for us. I think it's kind of cool."

"Every time we go up there and Libby comes running, John kind of gets a kick out of it. He says that if I don't go and say hi, she might just come through the fence to me. So that gives me an excuse to at least go and pet her for a moment."

"I bet that's hard," Craig replied, "to see her and not be able to do what you want with her. Samantha says that no one can catch her when they go out there. I think it's kind of funny because, you never seem to have any trouble getting a rope on her."

Paige kind of grinned. "Papa always told me that when he sells a horse, he never wants to see it again. That way the tie is broken and the history is behind him. The horse can go on being a horse with a solid background living for the future. I kind of feel bad for Libby and myself because neither one of us wants the past to be the past, we want it to be the future." Paige grew silent for a moment. "I just didn't realize how hard it was to let go, especially when I see her so often. I used to like her being so excited about seeing me at the Greenlys'. But now, it just seems sad I'm not letting her move on. Next spring Libby will be bred and become a broodmare. That's got to be a good life, right? She's safe and will never be hungry." She paused again. "It's got to be a good life. I'll be graduating next year, and I wouldn't be able to keep her. When we lived out on Pitt place and I knew my parents wouldn't be able to keep her, it seemed like the right thing to do." Paige propped herself next to the counter and stared at the floor. "Now that we moved and things are looking up for us, I second guess myself for selling her."

"Most broodmares love being moms, I would assume. Libby'll get the hang of it, I'm sure," Craig said, listening to the hurt in Paige's voice and looking to get off the subject. "So what does your dad have going on now that he has his own place? I heard that he has quite a few horses lined up for the next couple of months."

"Yeah, he gets his first colt next week, he's pretty excited. There's a lot that he wants to get done, corrals repaired and barns fixed up so he can attach a couple paddocks. He plans to house the horses here while he rides them. Then he'll bring the owner out so they can ride with him for a day or so to get the feel of riding, before he sends them home."

They had the groceries put away and headed out the back door where Samantha was sitting at the picnic table with Patricia. They looked like they were in deep conversation. As the screen door slammed shut behind Paige and Craig, they looked back at her and burst into song—John, Craig, Samantha, Abe, and Patricia—all singing Happy Birthday a little out of tune, but the sound warmed Paige's heart.

She laughed, "If you guys want to go on the road with that show, you might want to start practicing in a choir."

They laughed. Samantha handed out the knife to cut the cake. "Made it myself, with crutches and all," she said with pride bubbling in her voice. "I got a new airbrush for my art and tried it out on cake decorating.

The cake was a horse head shape that Samantha decorated to look like Libby, very meticulous on the detail with fine airbrush strokes. "Samantha, this is incredible, it almost looks like a photograph."

"I know," Samantha beamed. "I was so proud of it I almost couldn't wait to show you. I went out the other day to take a couple pictures of Libby, and she came right to me and posed. That was the first time she has approached anyone since we bought her. Usually she just walks away. Oh my God, I have to tell you!" Her voice was as excited as a child at Christmas, "I went out this morning on my crutches and caught her, put the halter on her and everything! I even led her out of the pasture! I'm so excited, I never thought I could do it Paige, but I did!"

Paige smiled weakly, but there was a pang in her heart. She knew now that it was coming to an end with Libby, and she was moving on. She looked down at the cake. She didn't want to cut it. She didn't want to eat it. She had lost the excitement of turning seventeen.

Patricia came up with a camera and took a picture of the cake. "Pose with it girls," she said enthusiastically.

Paige shifted her thoughts and got back into the celebration. She leaned next to Samantha and they held the cake together. They cocked their heads so they touched and they both grinned.

"Work it, girls…work it!" Patricia said as she continued to click pictures as the girls made goofy faces.

Paige took the knife and with one more look at the horse she once owned, her Libby, she made the cut, then another. She started putting pieces of her on plates as Samantha dished up the ice cream, a nice small party to close her past and begin a new year.

Patricia brought out a present wrapped in happy birthday decorated, deep blue paper with balloons floating. She set it in front of Paige, "Happy Birthday, Honey."

Paige looked at the package for a moment, then carefully, popped off the tape and unfolded the wrapping. Her heart was still a little hollow.

"Come on, Paige, rip it open!" Samantha called. "Don't be so careful!"

Paige looked at her and grinned, yet took her time. As she unwrapped, she noticed it was a boot box, and her eyes teared up, a pair of new cowboy boots. She never had a new pair of boots. Here they were without a scratch mark or a crease in the toe. She looked at her mom. "They are beautiful," she said quietly. "So beautiful, Mom."

She slipped off her old tennis shoes and pulled the first boot out to put it on. She started to slip it on her foot, but it didn't fit. Sheepishly she looked at Craig as her face got red. "Oops, wrong foot." She grinned. Grabbing the other boot, it slid on like a glove. "Mom, they are perfect, so perfect!" She breathed out. She stood up and began walking around with them.

As they sat around the table, Craig looked over at Abe, "Would you need any help these next couple of weeks? I could help you get those corrals set up, maybe help you with a colt or something."

"Now that's an offer I just about can't turn down," Abe replied. "What are you looking to do, Craig? I could sure use some help building a fence if you're up for it. And there are a couple of stalls in the barn I want to fix up too. I got my first horse today, and I'm running out of time."

"I thought you were getting your colt next week," Paige said.

"They were leaving town and wanted to deliver it early, so it got here this morning," Abe replied, looking back at Craig.

"Sure, I could help out a little. I am pretty handy with a saw and hammer. What do you have in mind for the barn?"

"If you want to take a walk out there I can show you and see what you think you can do."

"Sure," Craig said as he got up from the table with Abe.

"You want to come too, John? Let the girls have some girl time?" Abe asked.

"Don't mind if I do." He excused himself from the table, and they started walking toward the barn.

Patricia and Paige started stacking the dishes and getting the ice cream back into the freezer. Paige kept repeating the words from Samantha in her head. Paige felt a sting of jealousy grab her and knew now that there would be a day where she would see Samantha riding Libby if they decided not to make her a broodmare. She knew now why her father never wanted to see a horse after he sold it. It was almost more than she could bear.

She had gotten an armload of dishes into the house and put in the sink and was gathering another load when she heard her father call to her.

"Hey, Paige, you have a minute? I think you ought to hear Craig's idea for the barn."

"Sure, Papa, let me get these into the house and I'll be right there."

She had some plastic cups and napkins in her hands, but Patricia cut her off. "Here, I got them, Paige, go and see what master plans those guys are conjuring up. I'm sure whatever it is, they'll need a woman's touch. And go look at your dad's new project, I know he wants you to see it."

Paige looked at her for a moment. She had never heard her mother consider her a woman. "Thanks, Mom." She didn't know if she wanted to see another horse right now. She smiled, handed her armload to her mother, and kissed her on the cheek. "I'll be right back," she stated as she jogged out toward the barn with her new boots, happy to get out of dishes and be summoned to the barn.

Abe waited for her at the entrance. He put his arm around her shoulder. "Did you have a good birthday, Sis?"

"I did." Paige paused, then half-heartedly said, "It's odd how fast things change." The afternoon sun had a golden glow of late afternoon and made their shadows long. They turned into the barn as the smell of fresh hay filled her senses and made her heavy heart lighten a little. "A lot of things have happened these last couple of months, Papa."

"Yeah, I know," Abe replied. "We really don't feel like we have much control over our lives, but we just make the best of it, the best we know how."

John and Craig were looking in the back corner stall.

She heard Craig saying, "If we replaced that beam there and put in a couple of four by sixes right there, that would add a lot of stability and bring the loft up level."

John added, "Then frame in a door right there and he could have a paddock without too much cost."

"Yeah," Craig replied, "I could do that. We have enough timber out here to make it work. We could have it done in a couple days."

Paige noticed the new horse standing in front of them. Then she took a second look and with astonishment, Libby nickered at her and bobbed her head in anticipation. Paige looked at her father, then at John, then back at Libby standing there with a small bow between her ears.

"Libby?" Paige said.

John slipped an arm around her shoulder and said, "I don't think she's ready to be a broodmare yet. She has a lot of things she wants to do first." He paused, "Happy Birthday, Paige."

Paige blinked back the blur of tears as she started to open the stall door. She couldn't see the latch, and she fumbled with her fingers, not taking her eyes off of Libby, not wanting to blink, and yet not being able to see either. She touched Libby's face, then looked back at the people standing around beaming at her. Patricia came in with Samantha hobbling behind her, one crutch under her arm, a huge grin covering both of their faces.

"For Real?" Paige asked in disbelief. "Is she really home?"

"She is home for good," Abe stated.

She opened the gate and ran her hand down Libby's neck as if in disbelief. Libby brushed her head against Paige.

"Hey, little lady" Paige whispered, a weakness overtaking her. She wrapped her arms around Libby's golden neck and sobbed. "You're home. You're home. You're really home."

The End

PAIGE'S STORY CONTINUES
FINDING HOME

Written by
A. K. Moss

Abigail used her crutches to get outside, feeling penned up and irritated. She just couldn't figure it out. Paige was supposed to be pushing her to exercise, but she wasn't. Abigail was supposed to be walking and strengthening her legs, working on getting the mobility back, but Paige never pushed her. Why not? She was sick of sitting in the house, and the walls felt like they were closing in on her. But she sure wasn't going into town and talking to the counselor either. She didn't want to see anyone, especially the case worker. She couldn't stand him.

Paige can go by herself. She is the one who wanted me to live here, she thought to herself. Abigail felt restless, she needed to do something and decided to go for a walk. She wanted to go down to the spring. It was a nice walk, and it was fairly flat. Blue followed her to the gate. Abby looked at the closed gate then back at the dog.

"No, you stay here," Abby said sternly. Blue looked at her then stared at the gate. "I said, you stay here," she repeated.

Blue dropped her head and whined, then she trotted to the corner of the yard and looked in the direction of the spring. She barked.

Abby got out of the gate and latched before Blue came back. "You are going to stay here. I don't want you to get all wet and yucky at the spring." Her voice was softer.

Blue looked helpless as she put her paws on the gate and looked at Abigail again. She barked twice.

"I will be back in a few minutes." For the first time since Abigail had been at Paige's house, she reached through the fence and stroked Blue's head for a moment. Blue looked at her with intense eyes and whined.

Abigail turned, maneuvered her crutches, and began to make her way down to the spring. It was a clear, beautiful day and a breeze teased and wrestled with her auburn hair. She focused on her crutches and where she needed to put her feet. She made it through the pasture gate and closed it behind her. There was a small clump of trees to her left, and the grass was long and dry so she had to make sure she stayed on the path.

She let her mind wander to what life would be like if things were different. But they weren't. The wind still blew, the grass still waved, and the spring water still rolled through the curves and crevices that lined the banks, drawn by a force of silent whispers—a force so strong yet subtle. Abigail saw a small twig in the water and watched it flow with the current. It got tangled in some tall grass for a moment then continued on its journey. It tumbled over rocks and flowed around the bend. All of a sudden she had a thought. Life was like this spring, forever moving forward, not stopping for anything. Yet it had turns and twists and things it ran into but always kept flowing. If you get hung up, you have to figure out how to get loose.

A cry came from the spring outlet where the water seeped from the depths of the ground to reach sunlight and air. Then silence, just the breeze playing with the tall grass. *Was that a puppy or a kitten?* she wondered. Or maybe it was just her imagination running wild in the silence. Nope, there it was again. It sounded like an animal that was hurt. Abby bit her lower lip in concentration, then lifting her crutches, she placed them carefully on the narrow path that lay before her. She hobbled toward the sound around the bend. What she saw made her stop stone cold.

There lying in the boggy mud of the spring, was a baby colt, its little blazed head about two feet from solid ground. His little head left imprints in the mud where he had been banging it with the effort of trying to get out. His nose was sticking out in hopes of reaching solid ground. His little nostrils flared with anxiety and effort. His eyes almost closed. Half of his little body was hidden by mud, his sides heaving from exhaustion.

Out of the corner of her eye Abigail saw a movement, something golden. A cougar moved stealthily through the grass, silent and focused and circling the baby. She had seen pictures of them but never a real one. Abigail moved forward to see if she saw correctly, and a grouse flew out from the tall grass next to where she had put her crutch. Abby jumped, startled by the beat of wings. Her crippled leg ached from the pressure, and she froze. Not more than thirty feet from her, the cat cocked an ear toward her direction and brought her to reality.

What should she do? Her heart was in her throat. The cougar hissed, but then the sound of purring resonated the still air.

The baby lifted its exhausted head and squealed with effort. One front leg lifted out of the mud and bent at the knee. Holding it out of the hole, it rested a moment, then tried to get the second front leg up. It banged its little head in the mud again. Abigail heard the suction of mud attempt to hold its grip. The young cat paced back and forth in front of the baby. Again he struggled and moved a couple more inches. The mud was losing its grip. The cat walked by the baby's head, reached out its paw, and tested the mud, then reached toward the nose of the baby as if playing with a new toy. It touched the colt's nose gently with the pad of its large paw.

The baby screamed again, hoping in vein that its mama would come and save it. It tried to turn its body, to attempt again to get out of the reach of the cat. The mud finally released its other front leg, and its sharp little hooves reached more solid ground. He lurched forward but his hind legs were still mired in the muddy tomb of the spring.

FINDING HOME

The cat hissed again. He seem to know that the baby was almost out as he watched patiently. The colt struggled again, his sides heaving, giving another lurch forward. His hind end moved a little. As if that was a signal for the cougar, the cat crouched down behind the colt's neck, stock still. The only thing that moved was the tip of his tail twitching back and forth. He had played this waiting game before. The colt turned a little more and had his shoulders completely out of the mud. The cat was ready to make a spring at him. Just as it went to leap at the colt's neck...

FINDING HOME

Made in the USA
Monee, IL
12 August 2023